In Search of the Grail

Svetislav Basara

IN SEARCH OF
THE GRAIL

THE CYCLIST CONSPIRACY, PART TWO

Translated from the Serbian by Randall A. Major

DALKEY ARCHIVE PRESS

Originally published in Serbian by Akvarijus as *Na gralovom tragu* in 1990.

Copyright © 1990 by Svetislav Basara
Translation copyright © 2017 by Randall A. Major
First Dalkey Archive edition, 2017.

Library of Congress Cataloging-in-Publication Data
Names: Basara, Svetislav, 1953- author. | Major, Randall A., translator.
Title: In search of the grail / Svetislav Basara; translated by Randall A. Major.
Other titles: Na Gralovom Tragu. English
Description: First Dalkey Archive edition. | Victoria, TX : Dalkey Archive Press,
2017. | Series: The cyclist conspiracy ; part two | "Originally published in Serbian
by Akvarijus as Na Gralovom Tragu in 1990."
Identifiers: LCCN 2017005017 | ISBN 9781943150199 (pbk. : acid-free paper)
Subjects: LCSH: Civilization, Modern--20th century--Fiction. | Conspira-
cy--Fiction. | Alternative histories (Fiction)
Classification: LCC PG1419.12.A79 N3413 2017 | DDC 891.8/2354--dc23
LC record available at https://lccn.loc.gov/2017005017

This translation has been published with the financial support of the Republic
of Serbia Ministry of Culture and Information.

www.dalkeyarchive.com
Victoria, TX / McLean, IL / Dublin

Dalkey Archive Press publications are, in part, made possible through the
support of the University of Houston-Victoria and its programs in creative
writing, publishing, and translation.

Printed on permanent/durable acid-free paper

And ye shall be betrayed both by parents, and brethren, and kinsfolk, and friends; and some of you shall they cause to be put to death. And ye shall be hated of all men for my name's sake.

The Gospel according to Luke 21:16–17

God does not like outer works, which are enclosed by time and place, which are narrow and which can inhibit and repress a man, which begin and become exhausted from time and use.

Meister Eckhart, *The Book of Divine Comfort*

Foreword

The novel we are placing in the reader's hands, at the moment when the author is writing out the lines of this foreword (and thereby with that hackneyed act testifying to the fact that he repudiates any connection to modernism and the postmodern), still does not have a name. The course of its future is completely unpredictable and random, just as life is. It is only known that it will be the offspring of *The Cyclist Conspiracy*. But at one point, the unpredictability of this novel was at a great advantage over the unpredictability of life, since the latter is a counterfeit meant to hide its one certainty—death—from the eyes of our trepidation. For, writing a book or, even better, appearing as the compiler and editor of others' writings, the author is always motivated by the hope that he will stumble upon a conglomeration of words, a sentence, which will enlighten him and liberate him from the shackles of this determined world and carry him into the heavens.

This, of course, happens quite rarely. The names of the fortunate remain unknown, since they surpass the history of literature, the branch of General History, from which it is ultimately difficult to escape, "to rise from the sea," as Joyce once wrote. In spite of the fact that the possibilities of literary enlightenment are negligible, the novel is always also more human and real than the "reality" with which we are **presented** in schools, textbooks and the media, through the myopia of paraliterary scholarship, philosophy and ideology, and as we perceive it through the even more bleary lenses of our senses as being consistent, tangible, and logical. Only in a novel can one meet the dead; only there is it possible to rectify injustice; only through the novel is it possible to expose errors and falsifications to the light of day; only in obscure sentences can one learn the fate of little girls who, overnight, disappeared without a trace, and about whom nothing more was ever heard.

In the end, the writer (or composer) at one moment can encounter himself (honest writers are always more on **this** side of the text), awed by the appearance of his doppelganger who suddenly arises from the material and, protected by the immunity of the literary protagonist, begins to reveal the dark side of the moon of his subconscious.

Therefore, it is wiser not to see this novel as an object of this world. It is more like one of those Borgesian objects, a *hrönir*, coming about through the action of pure longing; an object that is seemingly no different than everyday ones, but which begins to pale and disappear as soon as it has completed its task.

As already mentioned, this book differs from others also in the fact that, in addition to the classical horizontal (x) axis it also has a vertical (y) one; besides the left and right side, it also has the dimensions of forward and backward. So the novel creates a coordinate system and a cross; it is no longer a means of passing the time, but a crucifixion, both of the writer and the reader. Henceforth, all who take this book into their hands are given notice that they are doing so at their own risk.

And so it is, the novel will soon begin. It will happen one night when the operatives of the Secret Police break into my apartment searching for documents about the secret organization of the Evangelical Bicyclists of the Rose Cross. Instead of compromising material, they will find a pile of heterogeneous manuscripts, press clippings, letters, and photocopies. Thinking that this is a compact manuscript, they will put that material on microfilm and unconsciously determine the structure and composition of the fragments. The conclusive and multi-faceted relations between them are the product of their paranoid connecting of facts. Thus, the agency searching for fictitious crimes of individuals will accidentally find the true crimes of everyone, as if they are students of the maxim of that ancient magus (later also cited by Freud): flectere si nequeo superos, acheronta movebo.[1]

---

1 If I cannot bend the will of Heaven, I shall move Hell.

In Search of the Grail

INITIATION

TO THE REPUBLIC SECRETARY'S OFFICE OF THE SECRET SERVICE

No. 234/89

In accordance with directive number 123/89, and after a broad-sweeping investigation of those suspected of membership in the subversive organization "Evangelical Bicyclists of the Rose Cross," the following has been established:

1. Milovan Đilas, Dragoljub Protić, Žarko Basara, Radiša Kovačević, Jovan Kaljević, Milisav Savić, Gojko Tešić, Amfilohije Radović, Nikola Miloševic, Dobrica Ćosić, and Predrag Marković are the secret leadership of the illegal organization known as the "Evangelical Bicyclists." All of the abovementioned were placed under direct surveillance (mail censorship, wiretapping, tracking of movements).

2. Over all other persons mentioned in the **List**, all investigation has been suspended because it has been confirmed beyond all doubt that they have no connection to the illegal organization and that they were inserted into the **List** in order to create confusion and to turn the investigation in the wrong direction.

3. However, there is justifiable doubt that, in the **List**, not all the members are included of the Southeast Group, and that among them there are a significant number of artists, journalists, academics, authors, upper echelon officers, scientists, diplomats, and athletes, which is quite in keeping with the strategy of the organization. We are facing an exceptionally clever set of tactics; the war being led by the "Evangelical Bicyclists" is not like any we have faced before. This is an all-out media war. Consistent with their doctrine in which enforced mystique serves rather

pragmatic political goals, they are attempting to infiltrate all spheres of society and thus execute a quiet *coup d'état* and reestablish the theocratic Eastern Roman Empire. Since a large part of our territory used to belong to former Byzantium, increased alert is called for.

4. Likewise, it is necessary to strengthen the surveillance of all bicyclist clubs, "green" organizations, etc., especially because recently a propaganda pamphlet also appeared in the form of a novel (just one more means of mimicry), *The Cyclist Conspiracy*, which perniciously indoctrinated some of its readership.

5. Related to that, a search was done of the writer (or editor) of *The Cyclist Conspiracy*, S. Basara.

During the search, it was established that the apartment where said S. Basara lives, with the exception of one room, is completely empty. Further, except for a bed, a bookshelf, a chest of drawers and a desk, there is nothing in that room either. The walls are decorated with painted copies of Christ, the Virgin Mary, Saint Nicholas and the Archangel Michael, a graphic by Slobodan Milivojević and a framed picture of Stalin.

The desk drawer was not locked and we surveyed its contents without difficulty. We microfilmed all the manuscripts and composed a list of objects found (Addendum 1).

6. We were highly surprised by a letter to S. Basara from a certain M. Dimitrijević from Lausanne, in which he **warns Basara that the search will be carried out**, which indicates that the "Evangelical Bicyclists" have an infiltrator among the ranks of our agency.

7. Upon completing our assignment, the manuscripts, photographs, and things from the drawer were returned to their original state, and we left the apartment unnoticed.

Embossed Stamp
Signature

The Constitution of the Novel
In Search of the Grail

Article 1

In the novel *In Search of the Grail*, God exists. Regardless of that, the novel can also be read by atheists, idolators, and the undecided.

Article 2

The banner of the novel holds a blue field with a double-headed white Byzantine eagle. The coat of arms is a blue shield with a white double-headed eagle, holding a sword in its left claw and a cross in its right.

Article 3

The novel, like the Earth's crust, has several semantic layers. The surface of the paper is only a membrane which divides the **original** text from the soul of the reader. But, like in a mirror (which it is, in a sense), those semantic layers are found not in the text, but within the readers themselves.

Article 4

The novel has no connection whatsoever to the Masonic order known as Postmodernism.

Article 5

The publisher of the novel is Dalkey Archive, in a print run of 5,000.

Article 6

The novel is 222 pages long.

THE AFTERLIFE POLEMICS OF CHARLES THE HIDEOUS AND GROSSMAN

Grossman! Wake up, you lazy bastard. At your service, Sire. Your wish is my command. Forget the courtesies, you idiot. I always said: call me by title only when my subjects are present, the masses enchanted by vain titles—your excellence, majesty, etc. What's the point of calling me "sire" now when my subjects, almost every last one, is several floors beneath us, in hell, where the two of us will also end up, unless a miracle occurs. In the meantime, while you were nodding off, **down there** a book came out which I myself came up with, exerting superhuman effort to smuggle my meditations from this **nothing** and **nowhere** into Malkuth. Forgive me, Sire, could you please explain the meaning of the word "Malkuth" to me. Malkuth, in Hebrew, means kingdom, "the presence of the divine in the world," the lowest sphere of creation. Anyway, Grossman, the book came out. After a hundred years, we arose from total anonymity; the novel was relatively well received and let that be a consolation to your vanity. Your shameless adventures are entertaining our beloved audience. Could you please, at least in vague terms, describe the appearance of that book by which we were in some way resurrected, to the dismay of the Pope and his entourage? It won't be easy, Grossman, but I shall try; keep in mind that typesetting has advanced since Gutenberg's time, you haven't got a clue even about books from that period because you were burned at the stake in time, before printing techniques were invented, and thus the world was saved from one misery— the one where you write and publish a bunch of rancid garbage. I don't believe you would miss the chance to do so. I can just see the title: Maiordomus Grossman, DISPUTATIO DE TRINI-TATE, LIPSCIEAE, 1548, or something like that, if only you had lived that long. Thank God, you didn't, so now listen, memorize well the book's description. Its format is 12.5 x 21 centimeters. Hardback, black, with the embossed letters, if I'm not mistaken: SVETISLAV BASARA FAMA O BICIKLISTIMA on the front, and in gold letters: BASARA FAMA O BICI-KLISTIMA on the spine. Don't ask me what the spine is. On the outside, the dust jacket is yellowish in color, gradually turning gray, then black toward the bottom. svetislav basara, yes, just like that, enlarged lower case, printed in black, with lines above and below, and beneath that fama o biciklistima in red. In slightly smaller letters under the title it says: savremena proza, prosveta, globus, mladost. Below that, two angels hover in the emptiness holding the coat of arms of the Evangelical Bicyclists. However, there is one strange thing here, unnoticed at first glance. Above the shield, covered and overshadowed by the bright red title, if one looks closely an angel's bodiless head appears, in the upper left corner just next to the initial S of the author's name there are the tips of four feathers. This practically forces the person holding the book to turn it over, the back cover facing up, and then the whole scene becomes clearer. In a masterful solution by the artistic director, a headless angel is situated in the most unexpected of places, that is to say in the no-man's-land of the east and west of the book, and thus the whole scene can be described like this: a beheaded angel in panic reaches out toward the angel who is holding the right side of the shield, looking at his suffering companion with boundless worry. The melodrama of the scene is somewhat diluted by an excerpt from the book's reviewer on the far northeast of the cover. In the light of medieval symbolism, which is more proximate both to me and you, the right side of the book is Byzantine, and the left is Roman (the side of devil worshippers, thieves, anarchists and bandits of all shades); this is confirmed by the internal geography of the novel as well: the book open, the letters facing the reader, on the left side it contains texts of warning and prophesy, and on the right it holds tracts on the downfall, devastation, and the end of the world. Forgive me, sire, but some things here are unclear. You just said that the right side is Byzantine, and the left Roman. That's what I said, you idiot, but why not hear me out? The inversion is only illusory; in the beginning, books were read from right to left so that God's word could enter the world from the higher spheres. This didn't sit well with some people so the custom was introduced that words were read from left to right just to increase the amount of disorder. That's how AMOR became ROMA. Remarkable, Sire! But that's not all, Grossman. Now, let's talk a little about the Cabala. According to the Cabala, what is Rome? The first letter of its infamous name, ר, Resh, indicates, according to Suarez, ". . . the cosmic habitation of all existence (which) finds its roots in the overpowering organic movement of the universe"—meaning, that which will be called the "id" in Freud's day. The second letter מ, Mem, is ". . . the cosmic realization of fertility in the intelligent or non-material part of man, and in the body itself." And the third letter א, Aleph, expresses ". . . ultimate power, cosmic energy, the all-imbuing, the timeless, the unimaginable." What do you see? What can you conclude from that? Not much, actually, Sire. Of course you don't see anything. Not even the fact that, through pernicious inversion, the idol worshippers rerouted the primary course of the cosmic forces by giving primacy to the dark compulsions, instincts, and materials that suppress God's emanation. An ancient conspiracy, that one, Grossman. Anyway, let's forget about the Cabala. Where was it that we stopped? Oh, yes, I left the most interesting part of the description for the end. As you know, or rather, you can't possibly know . . . It is customary that when you open a book you encounter the grinning face of the author in a photograph . . . I apologize for interrupting, Sire, but you said photograph. What is that? Didn't you learn Greek at Uppsala, you damned plagiarist of doctoral dissertations? I did, Sire. Then, translate. "Recording of light." Excellent, Grossman. Recording of light. That's a filthy and modern bit of trickery that the masses think is entertaining and I don't know what all else. It consists of a *camera obscura*, you know what that is, we had them even back in our time. I do, Sire. Right, you see, in the opening of that camera, a lens is placed which projects a diminished world onto the background, a world just like the one that is, upside down, standing on its head. Here, they place a film. Film, Sire? Oh, yeah, I forgot that you don't speak English. Pelicula. Now, I understand. You're lying, but never mind, let's go on. The film is covered with a substance that is unusually sensitive to light, so that which is light and white in nature becomes black on it, burned out, and that which is black becomes transparent. On the film, people appear to be black devils, like those in Gottfried's drawings, which basically they are. Now, the magic gets more complicated. The film is placed on paper that is also covered with light-sensitive chemicals, it is exposed, and what do we get? Wherever the film was black, on the paper it's white and vice versa. We now have a faithful rendition of a person or an object. But why do they do that? So that their faces will outlive their deaths, Grossman. To convince themselves that they exist. In this case, the picture of our author is not as clear as it could be. Sharp contrasts, half his face in the dark, the other half fuzzy. Nothing very interesting. At first. Then, suddenly, a form on the shelf above the table catches your attention. By removing the nuances and emphasizing the shadows on the scattered objects, from the entire mess a marvelous figure of a fish emerges from the darkness, a figure that even has fins and speckles, appearing from that authorial-editorial-typographical chaos, symbolizing the oath of silence we have all broken, and hiding in its name (ICHTHYS), the way, the truth, and the life, the initials of our Savior: IESOUS CHRISTOS THEOU YIOS SOTER.

Is that a good omen, Sire? Good, Grossman. But we still have plenty of work to do. What sort of work, your Majesty? Don't call me your Majesty, you mindless twit, because I'm not even a trifle, but the most common nothing, just a little less nothing than you are. Our job is history, if you've forgotten, fake doctor. I won't allow those counterfeiters, the princes of the netherworld and their hacks, to conjecture about the past unhindered, staring at their piles of papers like a Gypsy woman at her crystal ball. Should the past be left at the mercy of dilettantes? No, or my name isn't Charles the Hideous, and as long as I'm dead I won't give them a single inch of my vanished property. But now, slip back into your lethargic sleep until I call you, until a new set of orders comes. Yes, Sire. I'm already falling asl . . . Good. Grossman has been turned off. The following pages are private. I don't trust him. Sometime near half a year that my majordomo was sleeping through, I decided to go to hell and visit Margot. I descended into Hades, like Dante, and next thing you know— I'm standing in front of my ex-wife. At first glance, she wasn't suffering much. "So, how's it going, o, unfaithful wife?" I asked her. And she was like, "It's really awful for me here and I can't even begin to describe to you even the least bit of my suffering." Again, I felt sorry for her. "If only," I said, "you hadn't bowed to the temptations of the Devil, you wouldn't be complaining now in the depths of inferno." Then Margot hissed, "Out of your sick jealousy, you judged me, innocent though I am, to be demented, and you had the baron executed because you envied him for being handsome." I thought about it for a while, recalling the theological disputes, those of my majordomo and the rest, and then I fell into a mild depression. Is there no end to the lies? Even post-mortem, why does she so anxiously hold onto her self-delusion, patiently withstanding indescribable torture for it—the lack of mirrors, smells and balsam, the absence of suitors and babbling courtiers—for, what other kind of suffering could she take when she is a woman, and women have no souls. Non habet. "But maybe they do, maybe Grossman was right at least about that," I thought dejectedly. And then I shuddered and the nonsense passed. Women and the soul! Yuck. Vade retro, Satanas!

There you have it, those intangible and practically torn away webs of connection to worldly things seem to be holding me captive in this limbo where, supposedly, I go on in the afterlife company of Grossman. I just can't get over Margot. Come on, Charles, you must make your confession, you can hide nothing, God knows everything. Even more than you. Muster some courage. Don't blame anything except your own lust and nonsense, perhaps vice versa, which, at that county fair drove you to stop repeating your Hesychast prayer of the heart and to stare into the blue eyes of your wife-to-be, Margot. I admit it, Lord, I forgot about you. The witch completely caught me up in her spell. For days I didn't leave the bedroom, justice and the rest was handed out by a mechanical copy of me made by Ferrarius. Copulating, I poured myself into that empty bellows; she took all the parts of my soul, filling herself up, enticing me and forcing me. She almost became ontologically grounded, to the detriment of others' souls, causing knuckleheads of Grossman's caliber to repeat, parrot-like: habeat animam. Oh, how fatuously happy I was? Pater familias! I was proud of her pregnancy. Of the heir to my barroom throne. Just before she gave birth, I threw a huge party in expectation of the joyful news. Idiot. I can say that now; Grossman is sleeping and my authority won't be damaged. A thorough idiot. At some point in the evening, the midwife came, with the slackers and court leaches, to reap the rewards of their good news. "It's a boy, your Majesty." "The spitting image." "A man's man." "Hung like a donkey." And there was plenty for me to see. Beelzebub composed a bit of grandiose malice for me. I immediately recognized my ostensible son according to the description of Radbertus of Odensis, from the book "On the Multitude of the Devil's Tyrant-Sons

who are Born to Introduce Chaos and on the Signs by which
Ye Shall Know Them." Degenerate. Not even two or three years
passed, and the bastard was running about the court on his
crooked legs, blabbing about injustice, about slave labor and,
way ahead of time, about higher values. When was he born? In
the general confusion, no one remembered the date. He hung
around another two or three years before he kicked off, on his
own initiative, realizing that his hour had not come, that there
were other princes to come, that people still believe in God and
that lowlifes had no chance. "The dark, dark Middle Ages," my
ostensible son kept whining to the hour of his death, and he
wouldn't have lived much longer, because if he hadn't died after
all that bitching, I surely would have beaten him in the back
of his head with a hammer or had him drawn and quartered. I
wanted to throw him to the court dogs, but in the end they buried him in an unmarked grave. How did he die? No one could
remember that either. But still, as Radbertus wrote, the relief
from my troubles was only temporary. I knew that he would be
born again, that he would arrive from bumfuck nowhere, from
the whorehouse, from the worst of all dungeons, and usurp
the throne to rule over my Rascia, that I had fairly paid off
with savings earned through trials. Again he would shout about
injustice, slave labor and, this time in the fullness of time, about
higher values. Neither the date of his birth nor the date of his
death would be known. And he would, like the prototype that
Margot aborted, be buried in an unmarked grave. Let history
be damned, and blessed be the lazy who heed not earthly goods,
the snake's lair of future nasty fellows.

And what all happened during this time as Grossman has
been hibernating, as I let him snooze away so as not to bring him
into temptation? Nothing. Multiplying, perfecting, leading to
the paroxysm of all seven mortal, seventy-seven venial, and seven
hundred and seventy-seven less serious sins. As that thrill-seeker,
Hegel, would say: people never learned anything from history.

And so let them forgive me; I wouldn't give a red cent for all the volumes of studious historians, and from this very spot, suitable for such activity, I am supervising their nonsense. I make my proclamations **beneath** the page and destroy their **scholarly** truths with my edified falsifications. Such are the times: fiction is more real than reality itself. The place for the absolutely free, although truly paid for in blood. You see, for hundreds of years I've known that, when the time is ripe, Grossman will begin scheming. He's been working his transparent trickery for quite a while and now, using his piecemeal theory, he will begin to appear with his words when I make a pause, he'll gossip about me, babbling nonsense, and I won't be able to oppose him because my relative omniscience isn't the same as omnipotence, although as I deepen my absolute powerlessness I am drawing closer to that ideal one inch at a time. But even if I achieve it, I will have no use of it. When one is omnipotent, one desires to do nothing. Anyway, let's observe Grossman's infidelity from the literary-theoretical aspect. His regurgitations will freshen the narrative. Perhaps a wise word will be found here or there. Even the devil isn't completely dark. Especially not in relation to modern folk who have way outdone the devil's imagination. Something is said about that in the document, **The Devil's Epistle to the Great Whore of Belgrade**, in which Satan complains that he has been cheated upon. "Not only did they break their pact with God," he writes his madam, "but they also broke their contract with me even after I gave them rule on Earth. They managed to surpass even me in their greed. To create their own kingdom without God and without a devil, even more radical than me. The idiots. A man can become more like God or more like the devil or nothing at all. They chose the third. They undertook all means to turn Charles the Hideous's Rascia into nothing. They are destroying the hills and vales, giving away territories, pulling down the monuments, hanging plaques on the empty spaces with descriptors: RIVER, BRIDGE, STREET, MONUMENT, etc. Knowing in the depths of their rolled up souls that they will vanish from the face of the earth like shadows, they cannot stand the idea that anything will remain behind. All of those Illyrians, Vandals, Visigoths, Alemanni, Tungusi, humanists, liberals, and communists. They gave themselves all rights. They placed their signatures, stamped it, confirming history and sitting down to rule and eat, to multiply and thus increase the nothingness." That's exactly what the Devil said. No matter how evil he is, he still has a certain sense of moderation. Which could not be said for the people populating the territory of my former empire. Hell, as it is, is just a commonplace province for them; in order to host them properly, the devil will have to undertake detailed renovation work on his flaming assembly lines. Even I myself am defeated by the power of the insipidness of these generations. See, not even two hundred years will pass and they will return to the darkest barbarism, into the umbra of complete oblivion. If I'm not mistaken, the bastard who will design the future Pantheon has already been born. The means for construction have already been put aside from the funds of the IMF. That temple of atheism will be erected right in the middle of town, and its dimensions will cover 6 x 2 kilometers. In the interior, they will place statues of the new gods, Zeus—Freud, optimi, maximi . . . The god of drunks, Humphrey Bogart, the patron saint of whores, Cicciolina, instead of Ares Von Clausewitz will be strutting around, instead of Bacchus, the protector of drug addicts, Timothy Leary, and an entire constellation of local demons, revelers, adulterers, and prevaricators of that crappy Olympus. O tempora, o mores! And I, as naïve as I am, intended to liberate the entire kingdom from the ballast of the material and profane, and to incorporate it into the Heavenly Jerusalem. Where did I get such an idea from? Thomas More still hadn't written *Utopia*. Judging by all things, I wasn't cynical enough. The Hegumen of the St. Panfucius monastery advised me wisely. "Charles, forget all that nonsense. That's vanity. The Lord saves whom he wishes, if someone wants to ruin themselves, they will do so and no one can do anything to change that. Adhere to the fast, make your confession, pray, and secure your own salvation." I didn't pay him heed. Out of my vanity, which has now become metaphysical although no less uncomfortable, I'm rotting away in limbo. Twenty times or more I scheduled the general ascension of the kingdom. In vain. It was enough that the wretches I call subjects just leave their jobs, to observe a moment of silence or two and not think of anything, the rest would be taken care of by the monks and mystics with the help of God and the incantation of a mantra. Yeah, right. There were always enough idiots to screw things up. "I just have to milk the cow." "I just want one more glass of brandy." "I just need to sleep once more with my wife." Thus are the reasons that blocked the road between heaven and earth. Common human weaknesses. Feelings of duty and lust. But enough about all that. Grossman has already begun speaking, inserting his words there among mine and, since I can't stop him because there is not the least bit of continuity "here," let's listen, if we're lucky enough, to the kinds of hogwash which will be pronounced by my disloyal majordomo.

***

I wasn't sleeping through all these centuries, as the self-anointed king believes in his conceit. I pretended to think that my eyes were closed and that lulled him into the illusion of my absolute subservience. He too, at times, would be overcome by sleep; no one can resist that, he can say whatever he wants. This cannot be seen in the printed text because of typographical technology, but hours and hours would sometimes pass between two of his words. In addition, with time limbo has filled up with the presence of other apparitions that Charles chose not to notice because of their plebeian origins. I once hinted to him something about our beginnings back in that lousy pub, but he wouldn't even hear of it. "A kitchen boy in our time is more noble than a margrave today." So he said. The fool. He could have learned plenty of things and thus filled up volumes of his imaginary **History of the World**. For example, imagine all the things that the Marquis de Sade could have told him. I noticed shocking similarities between the two of them. Except that the Marquis was not a hypocrite and didn't claim to be the protector of truth and Christianity, either in his life or in his death. I don't know where he gets the strength to stand fast in his role as a benefactor and to wear the mask of an insulted and misunderstood saint. For example, his marriage to Queen Margot. In his version, he blames the devil and the spiritual delusion of poor Margot's blue eyes. However, at the time there was not a single demon in the kingdom. He had run them all out on the basis of a royal decree he actually proclaimed on Sinai, and all evil came from it. He figured: I'll repent and no one will be the worse for it. Like hell! Once the Hideous was out for a walk, I can bear witness, I was actually present, and he saw a little girl beside a stream. It was Margot. He immediately stopped and asked the chaperone who her father was. They brought around a fellow named Valdemar, a weaver, the poor guy had gone dumb with fear. Charles gave him a silver coin and some change, and proclaimed his intention to marry the man's daughter. "Your majesty," cried out the poor chap, falling to his knees, "that's an unbelievable honor for me, but Margot is only eight years old." The Hideous didn't care about age. He immediately took the girl along, summoned the hegumen, quickly going through with the marriage and adjourning to the bedroom that same evening. Over the following months it was awful to hear the screams, the grunting and heavy panting that were coming from the boudoir. He neglected his official business. He appointed his double to do it, a tin contraption slapped together by that heretic Ferrarius, and which sort of resembled him because he didn't look like much of anything. That scarecrow passed judgments, published

decrees, doubtlessly with the help of black magic and the archfiend. When he had satisfied his animal passions to an extent,
he came down from the boudoir all puffy and threw a banquet.
In order to reestablish the somewhat diminished discipline, he
randomly ordered the execution of twenty-odd nobles, and had
their corpses sent to the scientists for study. "There is no authority that doesn't spoil the one who wields it," he mumbled,
"but it must be executed over those who are already sinful. And
everyone is sinful, isn't that what it says in the Bible? Does it
make any difference, then, who should be executed?" On such
principles he founded his famous **Code**, about which the hacks
have scribbled page after page, praising it as just and progressive
for the era in which it was proclaimed. A law that **prevents**
crime instead of punishing it. Yeah, right. He proclaimed such
decrees: let so-and-so kill such-and-such; the wretch who suffered under Charles's wrath had no escape; how can you refuse
the king's command? And then the Hideous began boasting
that he could see crimes in advance. He killed his own son! In
his *Memoirs*, he lays out his fantastic narrative of how Margot,
ostensibly, gave birth to "the Devil's son, an everlasting tyrant,"
conceiving him with the Archfiend while he was off on a military campaign, perhaps against the tin soldiers of Sultan Bayezid
the Thunderbolt. The truth, however, is quite different. His son
did not look like him. He wasn't hunchbacked, he had both eyes,
so the Hideous poisoned him. The only truth is that he buried
him, in a completely unmarked grave. Who knows why? Yeah,
and then he fasted for two days and was done with it. Then came
the execution of Queen Margot, the Baron von Kurtiz and many
others. Perhaps the swindler had good intentions at the beginning, at the time when we were working our asses off in the pub,
but later he became depraved; he got disfigured by all the wine,
debauchery, and roasted venison. After gorging himself, getting
drunk and hearing his fill of lascivious songs, he would come to
my room, wake me, and force me to write down his thoughts,

from time to time bashing me bloodily about the head with his scepter. That's how I wrote down the famous **Code**. I learned it by heart and now I will write it down literally for study by law students, lawyers, and judges . . .

THE CODE OF KING CHARLES THE HIDEOUS

IN THE NAME of God who resides in the attic of my court, I, Charles the Hideous, do publish this Law for all: aristocrats and peasants, the married and the monks, the publicans and kitchen boys, the vagabonds, thieves, lepers, lechers, and the hordes of other rabble who inhabit this Kingdom of mine.

1. No one has any rights whatsoever. Every action is a violation and, only thanks to human imperfection, which is not able to classify crimes in their entirety, most people live out their lives unpunished. Therefore, every day without punishment should be celebrated as the mercy of God, and one should abstain from all vanity. Earthly laws are, likewise, lawlessness because they suspend the law of the Lord. The perfect code should be as far-reaching as the kingdom for which it is published.

2. This Kingdom is ruled by me, Charles the Hideous, autocrat, sovereign, and I will rule over it even after death by means of my double made of iron who will make decrees, pass judgments and new laws. In my presence, everyone is to fall to their knees, breathing halted, until I say: arise. I receive my subjects every day and all times of the night, and everyone has a place at the table in my court and straw in the stable to sleep upon.

3. My views are far-reaching. Whoever wishes to be a good Christian, let him sign this charter. Whoever wishes to be a sinner, let him be so. Christians and sinners are not to mingle. The righteous have a right to a home, a piece of land, an ox, two cows, and ten sheep. Sinners, debauchers, gamblers, whoremongers, drunks and the like have the Pub and the surrounding forest available to them.

4. If a Christian is caught in debauchery, adultery, gambling, or excessive drinking, may he be properly lashed. If caught again, his beard is to be singed off. If he sins a third time, may his ears be cut off.

Sinners caught in the mentioned evil deeds are to be let go and may they answer to God alone.

5. Good-looking lads and lasses, truly handsome men and seductive women are to be seared on the face with a red-hot iron and they shall have two fingers cut from their left hand so that they will not introduce scandal and confusion among the people of this, my Kingdom.

6. If someone cuts off the hand of another, let him cut off his own hand as well. If he refuses, let him be executed.

7. Women caught in adultery are to be assigned to the Pub as fornicators, and all the money from the sale of the adulteress's body, after covering the necessary costs, shall belong to the royal treasury and used for public works, the building of roads, monasteries, and endowments. Thereby will sin be harnessed and operate for the good of all.

8. Men, on the other hand, caught in adultery are to be castrated. So castrated, they are to be handed over to the sultans as eunuchs. All income from the sale of eunuchs likewise shall belong to the royal treasury.

9. If someone kills another, let him create another man in place of the victim. If unable to do so, let him be executed.

10. If someone goes to see someone at home on business and finds him not at home, the absent one is to pay a fine of one gold piece for the time lost by the visitor, and a fine of another gold piece to the royal treasury because of indolence.

11. If someone loses something, let him pay a fine of one silver piece because of carelessness.

12. Priests caught in adultery or debauchery shall have their beards singed, they shall be properly lashed and exiled for one year in Interim Hell.

13. Perjurers, liars, and slanderers are to be lashed. If someone loses their life because of perjury, lies, or false accusation, let the perjurer, liar, or slanderer cut out his own tongue and pay a fine of ten gold pieces. If they refuse to cut out their tongues, let them be executed. If they have not the coinage to pay, let them again be executed for they are not worth even half the sum.

14. If the corpse of an unknown man is found, let someone be killed from the village surroundings where the body was found.

15. The right to hunt is had only by the king—his entourage and the hunters of the state. Poachers are to be properly lashed, they are to pay a fine of three gold pieces, and to fast for the rest of their lives.

16. The death sentence is to be carried out in the following ways: women are to be decapitated; men are to be hanged; serious offenders are to be quartered by horses. Those guilty of infanticide are to be drowned. Those guilty of patricide and infidels are to be burned at the stake. The costs of execution: ropes, executioner's fees, wood, kindling, and tar are to be paid for by the family of the executed. If they wish the executed to be buried in the Christian cemetery, they are to write a request and bequeath fifty gold pieces.

17. Witches, elves, partakers of bestiality, and wizards caught in the territory of my kingdom are first to be interrogated in the monastery in order to bring the Devil's slyness to light. Then they are to be executed, cut to pieces, the pieces are to be dried and ground into powder. The powder is to be scattered in the fields.

That will be all. Many laws are the same as many offenses. Dura lex, sed lex. I, Charles the Hideous, retain the right, being the only judge, the Lord's sworn deputy on earth, to pass judgment more strictly or kindly, depending on the case, than I have prescribed in this Code. Never can I be mistaken. My law is the wisest and most enlightened because it foresees crime in its entirety, in the close relationship of the killer and victim, the robber and the robbed. For, if a bandit kills and robs a wealthy merchant, he commits a sin, but murder and robbery would not have occurred if the merchant had not succumbed to the mortal sin of avarice. Sin attracts sin. All the troubles someone bears are deserved a hundred times over, and thus I do not recognize the institution of appeals, nor the disgusting breed of lawyers, devil's advocates, the defenders of lawlessness. In the name of the Father, Son, and Holy Ghost, Amen!

That would be, so it seems, Grossman's version. I'm not impressed. Imagination, which he was lacking even when he was alive, has completely dried up in limbo, and that supposedly bloodthirsty Code of mine seems to me sad, naïve, especially for an audience at the beginning of the twenty-first century, accustomed to the far-reaching and totalitarian laws under which they live. I've already mentioned once that my Code was for suckers; I passed judgments exclusively according to my conscience, depending on my mood and the amount of wine I drank for lunch, while the massive book of my Code was only a part of the stage-setting; it was filled with troubadours' ditties, remedies for gout and boils, bills for wine, meat, and wood. The illiterate masses saw the letters and the horrifying sketches and lived in awe. But, as I said, democracy has its advantages, and I'm not sorry that I let Grossman babble on. You know, when I remember Interim Hell, that formidable project which I, who knows why, have completely forgotten. Yes, in the cellar of the court, I had a faithful copy of hell built. That was quite in keeping with the symbolism of the court, just as it was imagined by the mass of beggars I called my subjects: God was in the attic; that's what they thought, not me, as the sinister Grossman would have you believe. It was only right that hell was in the cellar. Between the heaven and hell in my residence was situated a hall with a throne where I passed decrees and made judgments. One afternoon, as I rocked in my chair it crossed my mind: why shouldn't I make a copy of hell? For purely pedagogical reasons. Instead of cruelly punishing my subjects, indeed mostly those who had no luck since each and every one of them was equally guilty, it would be better to prove to at least some of them by means of clear teaching that crime does not pay. I hired builders from Dubrovnik, and Ferrarius also helped me until he fled with his company. I had to read a heap of literature about the morphology of inferno, about the types of punishments for certain sins, so after some ten years of work, hell was ceremoniously opened on All Souls' Day. Interim Hell, I swear, filled up quickly. Sinners were placed in a room where all the excrement and all the swill from the court cloacae, the stalls, and washrooms emptied out. Up to their necks in that foul-smelling mass, they had to listen all day to sermons about debauchery read to them in shifts by deacons. They ate there, how they slept I don't know, some even drowned there. Nonetheless, those who would exit into the light of day were unable to ever again look at a female and vice versa. You see, that's what it means to join the good with the useful: to solve the problem of sewerage and teach lessons to sinners. This could also be said of the other department, in which those condemned to Interim flames were languishing, before the eternal one. Underneath an enormous kettle, they lit a fire with sulfur, coal, the hooves and horns of slaughtered bulls, so that the heat was unbearable and the stench awful. They only received a little water and some salted fish for food. And water from the cauldron was, through a system of pipes, used in and around the court, of course for the proper remuneration. The greedy were, on the other hand, locked up in a cage where every Free Citizen could approach them, to torture, denigrate, and insult them, as long as they remained alive. There were several other small rooms and hovels, but I'll talk about them some other time. It is important, now, to mention that this idea of mine was usurped a few centuries later by the Evangelical Bicyclists when they were designing the Grand Insane Asylum. Indeed, everything begins and everything ends in the library. Nothing exists outside of books. Even though mine have been burned, they were born again in another time, just like those which I wrote were the reincarnations of other books. For, the meaning of books is not to reveal things to the masses but to conceal things from them and protect the spark of invisible light. God appears in the world only through books. Is this not why the book-burners are placed among the most damned, because they forestall God himself who will, on Judgment Day, set fire to the Library of Babylon, separating out those written with internal flame from those written with falsehoods? Since, not knowing orthography very well, I dictated my books to Grossman's quill, the flame is mine, and the lies are Grossman's. He interpolated a lot of stuff. That I am, ostensibly, the patron of the rise of tinsmiths and lathe operators for royal thrones. To be fair, he says indirectly, because learning of my example and hearing of my rise, they themselves came to the idea of tempting fate, and later removed me from history, erasing me from all books, while they retained two or three copies in the basement of the Comintern Archive.

Here there's plenty of interference from that compiler **down below** to whom I am dictating these pages, and he renames my children and claims to be their father. That is, after all, what I did as well. I'm not jealous. Our cooperation is good. Much of what I see I would not be able to articulate clearly since I'm not well versed in modern terminology; on the other hand, how could he know that generations of women physically always look like what the erotic preference of future generations of men will be? This the Archfiend set in motion, changing the gene structure, just so that lust and debauchery would continue unhindered. Men love voluptuous breasts and asses, but their sons, miraculously, love skinny, thin chicks without asses or prominent breasts. And then, there's that crowd of the Archfiend's collaborators, producers of perfumes, aphrodisiacs, mirrors . . .

Of all those things that destroyed a myriad of souls, including that whore, Margot. Women! The Devil's most terrifying trap. And again, who could resist that, the most real of all illusions. I didn't manage to either. Nor did St. Augustine before me. However, let's look at the urinary-genital tract of women, and everything will be clear to us. The vagina is not an absence, as I naïvely thought in my existential phase. No, it is actually quite a presence, it is nothing more than a *penis inversus* which isn't just flopping about externally like it does with us, unsophisticated men, but is tucked inside, and together with the fallopian tubes and ovaries it makes up the split member of the devil, so that a woman is having sexual relations with herself each and every second. And, since the penis is inside, *mutatis mutandis*, her soul is, a pale animula, on the outside. That is why women are more beautiful than men; and that's why the most spiritual and most soulful of men are ugly. This is important. Grossman, wake up. Write down what I just said.

Now, all of this can be seen as clear as day in the instructions for every package of O.B. tampons, and also even in the biology textbooks, in another context of course, but back in the day . . . Who dared to dissect and pluck around inside the belly? Even the slaughterers of pigs and oxen had to do their work blindfold-ed, with a lot of scruples. Not without reason. It's better if no one has a chance to see blood. That creates either melancholics or murderers. So, now—write this down, Grossman—a woman is made up of the following: the thin wrapper of the soul hides a monstrosity and the rotting flesh on the outside; on the inside: flesh and bones. Seen from a bird's-eye view, actually our per-spective, it looks like this:

Among men, it is different, in fact. The soul is inside, and around it is a butcher's inventory:

You're wondering, surely, why I am telling you this. For the sake of science, Grossman. There you have the explanation for why 87.5 percent of all specters and ghosts the necromancers call up are feminine in gender. After death, the male soul shoots like lightning into heaven or tumbles helplessly into hell, depending on affinities; with the female soul things are not the same. Diffuse, hollow on the inside, it lolls about in the twilight, in ravines, and if some idiot is found to conjure it up, it can hardly wait, tortured by its vanity. But, Sire, you also had the custom of holding necromantic séances from time to time. Hush your mouth! Those were, in the first place, the dark Middle Ages. That's the first thing. Second, my necromancers were not amateurs and parasites but masters of their trade. And third: the souls of the greats were conjured up; we weren't just satisfying our curiosity, we were working in the name of science. And even you know that the living at that time were not interested in anything except gluttony, drinking, revelry, and Mammon; the threat loomed that many useful things would slip into oblivion, so from time to time I would call up one of the smarter corpses to repeat his teaching to me, and for you to write it down. Like hell would the writings of Plato have reached the present day if he hadn't been so kind as to occasionally come down into the earthly cave and recite to us *Timaeus, The Republic, The Defense of Socrates* . . . Then I took the liberty of giving the texts to the amanuenses to replicate them in a certain number of copies and to spread them about here and there in libraries, musty cellars, and catacombs. Time took care of the rest. All of that became worn, took on the patina of the antique. Now I can see that it was a waste of time. Who reads Plato? I can feel that Aristocles turns about in the World of Ideas, cursing me: "Charles, you idiot, Charles, you idiot . . ." Well, what's done is done. My intentions were good. But, Sire, weren't the intentions good of that Dictator who . . . Hush, you idiot, don't say another word, the agents of the Secret Police are searching through the compiler's drawers. Please, Sire, I beg your pardon, but would you please explain to me the phrase "agents of the Secret Police." Hmmm, well, that won't be easy, but let's give it a try. First of all, you have to know that the countries of today are not stable creations like they were back in our day. Remember, my kingdom was my property; God and the laws protected it. It is no longer so. Now, countries can be taken away from you, so rulers no longer live in certainty. They have turned their backs on God, broken their contract with the Archfiend as well. Such countries must be protected. Each of the subjects has a guard assigned so that those in power can sleep peacefully. So they are, if I understood your majesty well, guards like guardian angels. They look more like devils, but let's say you're right. And those agencies themselves, so it seems to me, are meant to replace God. Yes, Grossman, you actually understood something for once; you comprehend evil things quickly. That agency is something like a crazed god who sends everyone to hell one by one.

And what would happen, Your Majesty, if one of the necromancers decided to conjure up the two of us? Nothing, you idiot. Certainly, you can hardly wait to show up anywhere with anyone, you would give all of your former self to immortalize you with the help of their silly paraphernalia. Nothing more than that. Get that out of your head and realize once and for all that you are dead. At your service, Sire. Go back to sleep, Grossman. Don't try to pretend. Sleep, soon the archeologists will dig us up and you'll have the scientific verification that you lived. There. Now I can say a word or two about the Strategic Plan to Defend the Eastern Roman Empire passed at the Seventh, secret, Ecumenical Council, held in Trabzon while I was still alive. The Hegumen of the monastery of St. Gregory Palamas was my emissary. Actually, at the Council it was decided that the empire would be best defended if it were not defended at all. The barbarians were invading from the east; nothing could stop them. Thus, by imperial decree, the territory of Byzantium was raised to a height of a thousand fathoms, and the barbarians occupied a barren land. Thereby, the church fathers believed, no one would be able to desecrate the imperial institutions. Armies will come and go, they will slaughter each other in their conflicts, they will carve up the country and divide the properties. In vain. "Drought and heat consume the snow waters, so doth the grave those which have sinned. The womb shall forget him; the worms shall feed sweetly on him . . . and wickedness shall be broken as a tree."—as it says in the **Book of Job,** 24:19, 20.

***

I will interpose in Charles's soliloquy here as a warp into the weave of our afterlife saga. The pauses between his individual words are longer and longer, and anyway he keeps repeating himself, so I will take this opportunity to say a thing or two. For the sake of ontology. Because he keeps babbling; he's conceited, as God made him, constantly talking and only when he addresses me with one of his usual insults, he conjures me up from nothingness for a moment. The bragger. Mystifier. He says: the necromancers conjured up Plato's soul so that he would dictate *Timaeus* and the rest to them. Plato would never show up in that lair of debauchery and superstition, at the miserable court of Charles the Hideous, in his kingdom about which I will offer a couple of observations. That he had a kingdom—well, he did. However—although he admitted that it was small—he never actually mentioned the facts about its size. The land area of the kingdom amounted to, if I'm not mistaken, 8.62 acres, calculated by today's units of measurement. To be fair, he paid for the land outright. But no one recognized his kingdom: not the Pope, not the Ecumenical Patriarch, not the kings. They'd hardly even heard of him. A totally anonymous guy who, with the aid of magical techniques he learned while living, is now afterwards searching for his small place in history, and further-more he is accusing me of that. A clown who cheers up the simpleminded crowds and intrigues naïve critics. An eternal Jew from the other world, about whom one could read more in the volume "Kurze Beschreibung und Erzälung von einem Juden mit Namen Ahasverus [A Short Account and Narrative from a Jew Named Ahasver]" (Leiden, 1602), if only it hadn't been burned. He believes he will manage to convince someone of his ghastly view of history. Asinus!

Maybe the monkey is right. He is not right. It would be bet-ter for him to raise the lid on the septic tank of his brown-nosing soul than to occupy himself with the ex post factum measure-ment of my kingdom. Oh, all right, perhaps I exaggerated a bit in terms of its dimensions, but what is history other than exag-geration, inflation, spicing things up, and telling big ones? I shall repeat: the size of the kingdom does necessarily correspond to the size of the king. The blindness of materialism has infiltrated even here/nowhere, and Grossman—who tends to do that—is measuring everything, quantifying things, as if he were being paid per word. From the point of view of a clerk at the cadastre office, my kingdom was negligible, but my mission was not. Again I say: I didn't strive to expand my borders, to conquer other lands, to build up deserted lands and horde treasure. No, the dumbass will never get it into his head. Inspired by the Spirit of God, I just intended (and still intend) to indicate the existence of a conspiracy whose goal is to transform the world into nothing. It is fairly advanced on its way. And in that case, what use is there of size, of expanses, if one day they will simply evaporate. To turn into nothing. Into an abstraction like me. Yes, and also that Christianity which forces you to love the worst cad and biggest vagabond, including Grossman himself. God simply strikes you with a cudgel about the head and you no longer have a choice. Did any of the prophets wish to prophesy? Was there an application process for the job? Didn't Jonah flee when the Lord sent him to Nineveh? Oh, cruel fate! Does Grossman, that elective Christian, think that I took joy in this for a single moment? Ever suffering, both when I did good and when I did evil, ever before me stood a rather large quantity of the past and an even bigger hunk of the future. For example, I know this novel by heart, word for word, but I won't recount it because that would be distasteful. In the end of all things, courtesy demands that others participate as well. Although I thought it all up myself. As did my predecessors. Not in order to establish a hierarchical relationship—it's too late for that; not even Grossman in his most pious days managed to understand that. No, but to remind people of it.

He accused me of imagining that I was corresponding with Angelus Silesius, in the margins, of course, clandestinely, many years later when he discovered certain chronological discrepancies. He never learned of the secret that Ferrarius confided in me long ago, **that it's all a dream** and that time exists only for those who, in the splitting of minds, divide that dream into two vessels—the real and the unreal. What else could time be than the pouring of content from one vessel into another, even though the water is the same? Yes, the Little Brothers are neither in one vessel or the other, they are the water and they know that the vessel does not exist, that in reality nothing flows, that there is nothing before and nothing after. What is the point of this useless sermon? He died and never came to his senses. The deceitfulness of my Margot and the stubborn scholastics of my majordomo could not be cured even by death, so how then could I cure them? Silesius could snap back at God because he lived without vice. He could say, "Listen, you, let the Black Forest be moved to Silesia." And that's what would happen if Silesius cared about mountain ranges. But he didn't care about anything, and that's why he had the right to do so. I don't. Torn apart by passions, I would often feel the blows of God's cudgel. Then I would hit Grossman, Grossman would strike the commander of the guard, the commander of the guard would then strike the guards, no, the guards came later . . . He would strike, as I was saying, cuirassiers, the cuirassiers would scatter about the kingdom and whip the serfs, and through that transmission throughout the land the fear of God was spread, the beginning of all wisdom, the very essence of the hierarchy where it was known who was who. Just one asshole bigger than the other . . .

JOSEPH KOWALSKY'S LETTER

Dear Mr. Basara,

I'm certain that you will forgive me for the fact that, while reading it for the second time, my letter will be significantly different than the original version, written in disappearing ink and withdrawing behind the true version. That temporary version served to create confusion and to send the agents of the Secret Police down the wrong path. Now, when the microfilmed copy is stored in the archive (which says a lot about the trustworthiness of **documents**), I can lay my cards on the table: I am in no way M. Dimitrijević—that name, as you have guessed, was a part of the act of mimicry—I am indeed Joseph Kowalsky.

A few months ago, I read your "novel," ***The Cyclist Conspiracy***. Although I knew practically every word of it ahead of time—in fact, I've read forty-odd versions of *The Conspiracy* by various authors—my curiosity was boundless. I am sure that you will not be unpleasantly surprised when I tell you that as many as thirty-eight authors have written that same novel (the same arrangement of chapters, same facts, same characters); I must admit that there have been stylistically more successful attempts, but in the end your version was chosen to be printed. The justification was the following: in it the relationship between fiction, farce, mystification, esotericism, and ultimately serious historical facts is offered in the most acceptable ratio for the average reader. The remarkably successful version of the Mongolian writer and dissident Changlozhudin Chonglordan was rejected because of the rigidity of the Ulaanbaatar publishing house and because of the significant distance from the territories of Europe. I am likewise convinced that you also don't know that

The Conspiracy was written twice in the nearer and more distant past. The first time was in 1792 when, at the recommendation of the Marquis de Sade, the entire print run was destroyed even before it left the printing house. A similar fate occurred also to the second version written in 1920 in Moscow, when the signatory for burning the book was none other than L. D. Trotsky. Of course, the slow but unavoidable hand of heavenly justice caught up with both of them.

Those "novels" under the same title as yours were intended to prevent the French and Soviet revolutions, but they were unfortunately thwarted. Judging by all things, the times were not ripe for the message of the Little Brothers to be understood as anything other than an abomination. As you can see, the path of the Evangelical Bicyclists is not the road of constant success. Whatever the case, *The Conspiracy* saw the light of day at a time in which it is, perhaps, futile, since the **Librarians' Conspiracy** is nearing its apex.

As I intend to die next autumn (I am already eighty-seven years old), I feel obligated to communicate some of my knowledge about that conspiracy and to explain the "black holes" in my own biography (the period from 1943 to the present day) for the sake of the logical foundations of the first part of the trilogy. You should be aware that, just like the previous incarnation of **this** letter, it will be a provisional version which will change as time goes by, only to have the true one appear on the day of the Final Judgment.

About the **Librarians' Conspiracy** there is a long oral tradition, handed down from generation to generation by the members of the Little Brothers. Orally, for if it had been brought out in written form it would long ago have been falsified, ransacked, and made profane. And yet, today profanation has reached such a high degree that practically nothing can be profaned. In other words: when a lie grows strong and begins to feel omnipotent, it begins to impose itself as the truth. Nothing easier. But, just the same, in accordance with dialectics, when it imposes itself as truth, then it begins to suffer from the same weaknesses as truth itself—it becomes vulnerable. Accordingly, we hold forth the truth as a lie, and the lie accepts it as such. That is how cracks are formed in the supposedly omnipotent construction of deception. That's the thing which the Librarians overlooked in their otherwise perfectly designed plan.

Their conspiracy stretches far back into time, to the very beginnings of literacy. First of all, through skillful manipulation, they took the letter **alef (∀)**, the symbol of the beginning, the openness of the human soul for emanations from above, and turned it upside down **(A)**, into a symbol of a man standing on earth, closed off within himself and destined to ruination. The sanctity of the original **alef** will be clearer if we note that it is actually the lower point of the star of David (Magen David), disengaged because of the Original Sin, but still connected by the lower line of the vertical triangle to the Divine and opened to receiving the Spirit:

Picture one: Magen David, the unity of heaven and earth

Picture two: Alef, fallen man with the Divine spark

Picture three: The upside-down alef, man closed off within himself

(About all of this you can inform yourself in great detail in the short text by Gershom Scholem, *Magen David*.)

That was the first falsification of the Librarians. The second, no less subversive, is indeed—the insertion of vowels. As is widely known, in early times only consonants were written. Through patient seditious action, they affixed the putrid flesh of vowels onto the solid skeleton of consonants. At the time, languages did not differ from one another like today; people could, according to the similarities of roots, understand one another. At first glance, especially ours, accustomed to reading that way, the addition of vowels seems to be progress, but—like everything else that seems to be progress—it was anything but that. That innovation, ostensibly useful, opened up the way to the multiplication of languages and to falsifications of myriad kinds. Let's take a random root—**s(h)mn**, for example—and we will see that by the addition and permutation of vowels we can produce a whole series of combinations: shaman, shemen, shomon, shumen, shomun, etc. The Librarians took serious advantage of that, creating an entire series of superfluous words, words indicting non-existent things, simultaneously suppressing the originals.

But they didn't stop there. The next bit of treachery was to change the direction of writing. Instead of right to left, as it was in the beginning, they reversed the direction of writing from left to right, which made possible the later creation of profane texts. You will write in more detail about that in the new soliloquy of King Charles, he has a lot more to say on that topic.

Of course, in all times there have been people who saw through conspiracies and sought for ways to elude them. Plato took refuge in his esoteric texts and myths; the greatest never wrote a single line. Many people used pseudonyms. The Librarians, in fact, can do nothing if they know who the author is but do not possess the text, just as they are powerless if they have the manuscript but do not know who the author is. For, I must warn you, writing is always an aspect of the Cabala; whatever is written—it produces a certain influence, perhaps a crucial one. That is also why the first volume of *The Conspiracy* is conceived to cause an even higher degree of dissolution within a particular Falsified Creation—Yugoslavia—by anticipating the construction of the Grand Insane Asylum. At the same time, the Librarians become incapacitated; *The Conspiracy* itself is a falsification, and thus they could not counterfeit it and turn it to their own advantage. How useful is that mimicry into which the narrative *I* retreats, is testified to by that sloppy intervention of Secret Police agents at the beginning of this book: they found nothing; they obtained a naïve version of this letter for their archive, and they were used as an effective beginning to the novel, all the while being exposed to the disdain of the democratic reading public.

Be forewarned, that initial success should not make you proud and reckless. Counterfeits in this world are more perfect and convincing than the truth. That does not sound encouraging. They are like movies—two-dimensional. Even those people who are slaves and servants are treacherous like movie posters, but they do not seem to be so because of the imperfection of the sense of sight, and also because of habit, which make us see them in three dimensions. The worst of them are not even two-dimensional but are **collections** of diffuse, scattered parts, the shards of the body and refuse of the soul, which still—because of the abovementioned aberrations of the senses—take on form and even manage to impose themselves on the masses as "real" people. They are full of so-called love and understanding for their loved ones, kind toward their family and children, they are actually the opposite of those about whom the Savior says, "Whoever does not hate his father and mother, and his spouse, shall never enter the Kingdom of Heaven." They are, therefore, given the this-worldly kingdom and they are at a great numerical advantage. Strictly taken, there are only 144,000 real people on Earth; all the rest are counterfeit. Not everyone, however, is destined for ruination; God is generous. If any of them shall repent, the Lord will grant him ontological foundations, repairing his soul and giving him a new name. But such people are rare.

Where, then, do they come from? How do they come into being? That question is not hard to answer. People-counterfeits come into being through literature. They create one another with the aid of magical and Cabalistic formulas. Describe some sort of monster today and he will quickly be born. Man, even if he too is falsified, is always the image of God and can do anything God can, in truth one thousand times less (like Adam) and moreover reduced by the root whose coefficient is equal to the current number of people on Earth. But even that negligible ability can create something from nothing. It is not enough to say "fiat," and to have this or that come into being, but if that is written down enough times, new things do appear. Reasonably, it is not foreseen by Providence, and thus it necessarily creates confusion. That is why Plato meant to cast poets out of his ideal state. Unfortunately, that did not work out for him.

The Golden Age of falsification came about after the Library of Alexandria burned down. That fire swallowed up thousands and thousands of irreplaceable books. Never again were people to see the marvelous pages of **The History of Atlantis, The Expulsion from Eden,** and many others of which not even a mention has been preserved till today. The tradition of the Evangelical Bicyclists states the position that, after the fire that was set by the Librarians, not a single authentic book is left in the world. After the devastation, the evil-doers took on a rather ambitious task: they rewrote all the destroyed manuscripts, but in doing so they added and took out things. They falsified Plato, they falsified Aristotle. They removed the warnings of Egyptian black magic priests from the walls of the pharaohs' graves, came up with new hieroglyphics and composed texts intended to mis- lead everyone. They did that knowing that—citing the authority of the manuscripts—future philosophers and writers would also unknowingly introduce the embryos of nothingness and deceit into their own works as well. And they were not wrong. Yet, no matter how perfect it seems, a delusion is always hollow on one side. They could not foresee that all the key books would be rewritten. And they, at the end of this world, have been written indeed. They do not, in fact, remember their earlier incarnations, but they unmistakably find specifically defined readers.

It is difficult to imagine, much less comprehend, the terrible breadth of the falsifications. Once they eliminated all the manuscripts that connected the Iron Age with the traditions of the bronze, silver, and golden ones, they had *carte blanche* to do whatever they wanted to. The world no longer had any sort of history other than the one the Librarians crafted. Through patient effort, with the aid of many tricks and a handful of corrupt astronomers, they managed to get people to accept the heliocentric system; they removed the Earth from the center of the universe and put it just out there somewhere, and this produced a sense of disorientation among the masses. Believing that they were far away enough from God, they began to reshape the land and seas in accordance with their sinister intentions. They made some countries larger, some smaller, made up new ones. Just like that. Ordinary, everyday magic. They would draw a map of a country giving it the shape they wanted, and soon thereafter the territory itself would adapt to the assigned form. It is not as mysterious as it seems at first blush; matter is formless, inert, and it only takes on the forms given to it by human observation. Only recently was this deception by the Librarians unraveled. Professor Arno Peters, a member of the Little Brothers, who is also a lecturer on universal history at the University of Bern, wrote a study about the geographic deformations and made a new Map of the World which shows the objective sizes of the land masses. However, there is little chance that the map will ever be accepted. The Politburo of the CP of the USSR simply would not hear of Peters's projection, because the territory of the USSR is fifty percent smaller than on Mercator's map. Acceptance of Peters's projection would mean the reduction of cities, tanks, airplanes and mineral wealth by the same percentage. (See Illustration 1 in the enclosures to this letter.)

The Grand Masters of our brotherhood reflected long and hard about how to oppose the Librarians' Conspiracy. At the Third Ecumenical Council of the Little Brothers, held in 465 in Jerusalem, they decided to accept a modified version of the Taoist doctrine of WU WEI: **do nothing**, do not directly oppose the falsification, moreover contribute actively to the flood of counterfeits at a reasonably ironic distance. But the Little Brothers did not come up with a single godless or Satanic doctrine or heresy; those all originated from fictitious individuals. We just inserted our own people in the falsifying institutions, and thus not a single deception was **conceived** in the soul of any of our members. Our, let's call them, agents, just led falsifying to a paroxysm, eating away from the insides of all subversive projects and causing them to fail. The methods they used in doing so were not always to the liking of the secular **morals**, so many members of the Order are remembered in history as negative characters.[2] As such, we rendered several important popes, theologians, writers, philosophers and common to all of them is that they are characterized as obscurantists. Still, our path is not a series of successful undertakings. Far from it. For example, we did not manage to forestall the penetration of Islam into Europe or to stop the French or October Revolutions. But we did cause the First and Second World Wars. You will probably wonder why

2 Here's an example of one of our falsifying agencies, which, partially, is of interest to you as well. It has to do with Charles the Hideous, one of the key figures in *The Cyclist Conspiracy*. Although it is known for certain that he existed, there is no tangible evidence of him whatsoever. Keeping that in mind, the Grand Master of the order in 1798, having read the "novel" (our Library, in its integral form, lies beyond; in the world books appear adapted to the time and in succession) made the decision to create a falsification of the ruins of Charles's court with all the details, not far from Negotin. That was, under the guise of searching for minerals, done in 1804. So that the "novel" would gain the illusion of having a documentary character, the "site" will be "discovered" at the proper time.

I count those two mindless slaughters as a success of the Little Brothers. It will be clarified for you.

It is a huge prejudice that war is necessarily a bad thing, and that peace is always good. On the contrary, wars often bring a halt to greater evils than they cause. Concretely, if it were not for the First World War, Austro-Hungary would have conquered the Balkans, and then Turkey. That had to be stopped. A boring bourgeois empire, standardized in kitsch, depressingly punctual and self-sufficient, it was not a threat just to the world order, but to the heavenly one as well. Predictability, comfort, and punctuality make people godless, sufficient unto themselves. Humankind is always on the edge of sinking into material torpor. If it were not for the plague, misfortunes, and wars which sporadically shake people up and warn them that they are after all ephemeral, the Archfiend would rule the world. As I was saying, it was necessary to stop the Austro-Hungarian expansion. The conclusion was reached that the most efficient way to start a war would be—the assassination of one of the members of the royal family. In the first version, Franz Joseph himself was supposed to be the victim, but difficulties of a technical nature arose; namely, at the time of his birth breech-loading rifles were used, but they had become outdated, and the munitions of the times couldn't kill someone from a previous epoch. So, instead of Franz Joseph, the heir to the throne, Franz Ferdinand, was selected instead. Still, even though he was assassinated, even though he died, the Bicyclists were not even indirectly at fault for his demise, though the order for the shooters to act was passed on by my father, Witold. Because if he had not been killed in 1914, the heir apparent would have had to die from galloping tuberculosis as early as three years before, in 1911. By sentencing him to death, we extended his life; he had to wait for the bullet. Those who die from a bullet are not hit by just any bullet, but by a specifically defined one. In the war which followed, the Serbs utilized a Byzantine tactic, the same one by which they arrived in their lands from the Apennine peninsula and with which they defended themselves metaphysically from the Turks: they left Serbia. A country is made up of people, not territory; if the population leaves the country where it belongs, behind it nothing remains. It is actually that **nothing** which necessarily eats away at the conqueror, weakening him from the inside and forcing him into destruction. That is how the K.u.K monarchy ended. That will be the end as well for all other states that expand beyond the borders that Archangel Michael, upon orders from God, drew on the **Celestial Map of the Lower World**. Most certainly, it would be naïve to think that the conspiracy against the Eastern Roman Empire was cut down at the root by this. Far from it. The detritus of Austro-Hungary (in fact the country reduced to its true, miserable size) will continue its subversion up until the very last day. That is necessary for two reasons: so that they could be judged and that we, absent our enemies, would not sink into comfort, predictability, and punctuality, becoming like them and falling into destruction with them. Because of this, in no way be upset if they make fun of you, humiliate you, and gossip about you; it is a sign of God's special favor. Do not return it to them in kind. "Vengeance is mine, thus sayeth the Lord."

In order for us to cause the Second World War, we had to use subtler methods. That war was unavoidable. If they had not started it (and lost it), the heathen could have won it by peaceful means. To that end, several archetypical dreams of power, among others the dream of Alexander the Great, were adapted to twentieth-century sensibilities and relocated to the territory of Austria where it should be dreamt by a suitably unstable person. For, in order for a dream of power to be effective in reality, it is necessary that it be dreamt by a dreamer with an endless feeling of low self-esteem. Such a person was quickly found, a certain A. Hitler, a painter by profession. Driven by delusions

of grandeur, with the aid of A. Rosenberg (inserted member of
the Evangelical Bicyclists) he composed a syncretistic doctrine
founded on the supposed superiority of the German race. As
a symbol of the party, the **swastika** was chosen, the archaic
symbol of the collapse that comes about as the consequence of
distancing oneself from the Center. Thus, the inglorious end
of that movement, which stepped away from civilization and
sought for its roots in the mythology of the Germanic tribes
(which is anyway a pure mystification written by the Librarians),
was anticipated from the outset; the conquests, the wild imagin-
ings of world rule, are indeed nothing more than the centrifugal
yearnings of desacralized people and nations. Exit from the center, from rest, has only one result: removal to the furthest circles,
to the chaos of determinism from which returning is most often
impossible. That is why the swastika is nothing more than a
desecrated version of the primordial bicycle wheel:

The Primordial Wheel   The Swastika

In order to present it more clearly, I must use elements of
Bicyclist iconography. In that light, God can be understood as
a bicyclist who turns the pedals and who is, understandably, the
transcendental axis of the driving wheel, an unmoving point
in which one finds the mystics, the righteous, and the saints.
They, based on observance of the transmission chain, can only
conclude that the entire machine is moving forward, that there
is a goal and nothing else. There is no way for them to prove
that to the multitude inhabiting the large number of circles
inscribed inside the wheel, but they believe and thus remain

in the hub, while the unbelievers are cast out onto the tire and disappear, crushed by the friction between the tire and the road. According to that analogy, the front wheel symbolizes Satan, God's monkey, the impersonator. As we can see, he is illusorily equal to God, but he has no drive of his own; he is driven by God's energy and can only go in the direction God wants him to, which is clear from the position of the steering mechanism placed above him. There is an ancient legend saying that in the beginning the world was in the shape of a bicycle with one wheel, a unicycle, like the ones used today in circuses, and that only after Adam's transgression was the front wheel added as well. Moreover, orthodox Bicyclists, followers of the most ancient cult, present all of humankind's psychophysical makeup in the form of a velocipede:

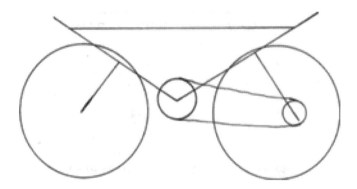

Certainly, that is only a symbolic representation. Construction of the bicycle, its mass production, and the change of the name of the brotherhood into the Evangelical Bicyclists, was a necessity caused by the advanced stage of dissolution in which everything must be represented in an obvious and tangible fashion. In that presentation, the man-bicycle is turned with the wheels down, thus bringing the frame into the position of the primordial **alef**, open to divine emanations. Thereby, the drive wheel is located on the right side and symbolizes the spiritual in man, while the left wheel, parasitically dependent on the right, signifies selfishness and conceit. Things become much clearer when the projection of the man-bicycle is fit into the Tree of Life, where one can observe man's place in the structure of the universe. The human being is the conjunction of two sephirot, of **Hod** and **Netzah**. The left wheel (Hod) is the center of ephemerality, desire, childishness, and the right symbolizes eternity, servitude (in the positive sense: obedience) and youth. It is up to human free will whether one will ascend along the sephirot to Kether or if one will collapse into Malkuth:

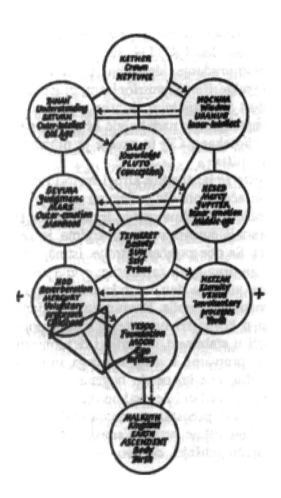

As it can clearly be seen on the graphic representation of the Tree of Life, the totality of humankind is composed of the principle of HOD and the principle of NETZAH. The waking state is dominated by HOD (ephemerality, willfulness, lack of masculinity), and the state of sleep by NETZAH (eternity, youth, obedience). If HOD dominates (which is most often the case), the human being falls under the authority of YESOD, the world of sub-lunar emanations, egoism, tribal myths, daemons, and a faulty eternity. The dotted arrow connecting HOD and YESOD continues to MALKUTH, the lowest degree of creation, where history and falsification begin. MALKUTH symbolizes the kingdom, Earth, the body and birth, ideology, and thus all movements characterized by expansionism, health care, obsession with material goods, the corporeal, and increased natality, are inspired personally by Satan through the Librarians. The goal of this conspiracy is to transform the universe into nothing.

Now you will be surprised: we lost the Second World War. Do not pay too much attention to the yapping of historians and the memoirs of brave soldiers; the war was lost because almost all the people dominated by NETZAH died in it. On both warring sides. In fact, plenty of the others died as well, but remember: all of them were destined to die on the day and hour when they were killed; God never kills anyone. The balance was definitely shifted in favor of the falsifiers, the sons of the killed who, believing in the stability of the material world and of determinism, little by little transformed everything they could lay their hands on into nothing. But, in the name of comfort, there really was not much of value around; all the valuable things had been evacuated into more spiritual times and they were allowed just to destroy ruins, to inhabit forms lacking any kind of meaning, to—thinking that they were constructing a thousand year Reich—build THE GRAND INSANE ASYLUM, the grandiose dream of megacomputers, which will ultimately destroy the world.

That process is now in its advanced phase; already about sixty-nine percent of the entire cultural heritage has been microfilmed, recorded on audio and video tapes, ostensibly to be preserved, but in fact so that it could be transformed into photoelectric and electromagnetic impulses and thus handed over to the mercy of the whims of nature. Fortunately, all of those everlasting acts did their jobs on the inside, in the souls of people of all centuries, and they have long since been archived in the heavens where "matter" molded to the temptations of this fallen world is being used to construct the New Earth and the New Jerusalem, whose architect and mayor will be the Son of God. Only the power of spiritual inertia allows us even today to perceive the world around us as stable, solid, large, and unexplored. According to the latest research, the actual size of the Earth's radius is no larger than 1.5 meters, although it seems to be infinite in our eyes. But that is a matter of perspective. From a distance of some one million kilometers, it looks like a dot.

Therefore, you as the compiler and editor of *The Conspiracy* are not required to make a book for eternity. If you do your job well, you will be given the opportunity to obtain eternal life, just as that opportunity is offered to all people. Using the sand of this-worldly deserts, you should make a book of sand, a disposable and temporary book which will, as time goes by, dissolve, disappear, return into something inarticulate so that it will make room for other books, just as the dead make room for their heirs. It would be largely incorrect for you to believe that it is actually **your own** work or to think you own the copyright to it, because everything good in it has only been **given** to you to use, as a temporary gift. One might say: it exists more for others than for you, and thus I direct you, without shame and authorial envy, to use and insert the texts of the earlier editors of *The Conspiracy* into the book as well.

P.S. Enclosed, I am sending you **my** version of the biography, then the correspondence of a certain John Smith, whose name means nothing to you but who, at the end of the war as a lieutenant in the American army, was the assistant investigator at the war crimes trials in Nuremberg, and a copy of the investigation which Mr. Smith attended, and which will certainly be significant material for the further plot of the novel.

Sincerely yours,
Joseph Kowalsky

Joseph Kowalsky
APPENDIX TO MY BIOGRAPHY (1943-1983)

HONESTLY, I AM not dissatisfied by the description of my life from the previous volumes of this book. The material is easily readable, at times exciting, without exaggeration or cardinal mistakes in chronology or factualness, which—as you will see in one of the footnotes—saved me from countless unpleasant situations. Imagination and intuition, among other things, have an incomparably better **influence** on the past than vain attempts by empiricists who attempt to impose the yoke of documents and facts upon it. "Documents and facts are nothing," my father Valdemar Kowalsky (you mistakenly called him Witold) used to say; but your mistake had a positive outcome: it allowed that charming drunk—by the way, he was not my real father—to avoid several unpleasant arrests.

Let us take things in order. If I'm not mistaken, on page 175, with a bit of hedging you wrote that there are several different versions of my disappearance. Not a single one of them is correct. That night when the commandos of the Traumeinsatz came for me, I did not, as it says, "climb on to a bicycle and disappear in a cloud of dust" that enveloped me. There was no sort of mysticism in it. At least not that sort. I used a simple trick described in my story, "Bicyclism and the Theology of Valdemar Kowalsky": I stopped my brain waves, became invisible (both in reality and in dreams), and when all the dust had settled, I went to the cemetery. I chose a half-empty grave, lay down inside it, and brought myself into a state of death. Please note: death, not catatonia. Since biography should not be too much like Hoffmann's improbable stories, I am bound to offer an explanation of how I did so.

If someone, namely, concentrates on a given thing, it becomes real to that person, as real as things actually are all around us—mountains, rivers, cities—in everyday situations when we are not concentrating. So, I lay in the grave, stopped breathing, slowed my heart rate to a minimum, and quickly died. Without too much of a risk. No one can ultimately die before his time runs out, so I could wake up of my own will several months after the war was over. I mastered that siddhi of temporary death in a short course with a certain yogi during my stay in Dharamsala. The yogi claimed that anyone can master it. For understandable reasons, it hardly ever crosses anyone's mind to use it unless really necessary. But if it might offer you comfort: it's not really that bad; life abounds with creepier situations. No one bothered me, except once when someone died from the grave owner's family. It all ended quickly, they noticed that there was an extra corpse in there, but they didn't raise a stink because the dead are still shown at least a little respect.

Thanks to having died, for a certain time I saved on food, water, air, and months of languishing about in all sorts of warehouses, cellars, and attics, with the ever-present companions of criminals of all types. In addition, I studied death, preparing myself for the real thing, the final one, which will—as I wrote in my letter—soon have the honor of happening to me. I killed time to the end of the war in long conversations with the still unborn[3] and long since dead members of the Brotherhood, and

---

3 If you remember your story "Memories of the Football Season 1959-1960" (Peking by night, Prosveta, 1985) in which you mention my name the first time, in it you write that you and I met on the bank of a river somewhere and I taught you breathing techniques. Don't be shocked: that really did happen. Of course, not on the Oder or the Nisa, not in any place in this world. You weren't even born then, I was dead, which comes down to the same thing, and I really did teach you a special breathing technique, which is a

I found out a lot of particulars about the past and future. A multitude of things that are available only to the dead. Among other things, I had extensive conversations with our old acquaintance, King Charles the Hideous, a good lad who sometimes likes to spice things up, here and there, and to twist the facts, but he is also knowledgeable of a lot of interesting stuff. He was constantly besieged by that obscure Marquis de Sade because, listening to all kinds of obscenities from the magician Cagliostro while he was still alive, he decided to ingratiate himself to the shrewd king in order to learn from him how to be born again. The Marquis's situation was truly desperate. From limbo he was forced to watch—that's the expression he used—a film of the endless monstrosity of his crimes and the endlessness of his future redemption, ever anew, on an endless tape, so that in addition to all of his hellish sufferings, one more would be added: boredom arising from the fact that he would learn them by heart.

The Marquis sent a variety of ultimatums to God, searched around a hell full of Cabalists and magicians for someone who could show him the fissure between the worlds through which

---

common practice in the Brotherhood. Remembrance of that prenatal event many years later intruded through your artistic imagination, and you thought it was a mental creation. That's how things go. But not just that: You wrote my biography, ending in 1943, that is with the date of my temporary death. I lived through that as well, safely guided by your writing skills, through all the temptations of this stormy life. I believe that this does not confuse you much, the fact that I could live through something that you had written when it had already happened. This is indeed where the secret of our strength lies: The life of all Evangelical Bicyclists is defined by events from the future, not from the past, from the sequence of things, so in that way we are saved from determinism and achieve superiority over our enemies. **They attempt to influence the future** and thus, jousting at windmills, fall under the rule of the past and sink into ruination with their undertakings, dissolved within the whims of that sublunar world.

he could drag his evil soul and be born again, so that he could finish his work in progress: the destruction of the divine order. Several times, he claimed, he managed to slip out, but nowhere in the world could he find such a sinister couple whose coitus would make it possible for him to see daylight again. The only one who knew the secret—Charles—would have nothing to do with it. He thought the Marquis was an upstart, like all the others who long to be born again. The Prince of Darkness did not want to help him with his plans. He no longer needed him. In the times that had come, there were plenty of more skillful and more evil characters around. He rejected him like a washed-up boxer. Like a bicycle tire with a hole in it. Charles told me, and later I saw it myself, that, toward the end of the century, the prince of this world will withdraw all his demons from the environs of Belgrade, because they will no longer have anything to do, outdone by the members of the secret Union of the Sinister who will come to power.

As I was saying, in October, 1945, I rose from the grave like Lazarus. I shook the dust from my clothes and headed for the closest pub to have a beer. I was terribly thirsty. Additionally (at first I thought it was because of the years spent in the grave), I noticed that the world had begun to vanish and dissipate, and that freshness and joy had started to disappear from its face. This is familiar and obvious to you because you were born in those surroundings, but the devastated landscape, the semi-transparent houses and expressionless faces of men and women left a terrifying impression on me. I thought: perhaps I didn't come back to life; perhaps I was sentenced from one limbo, full of interesting folk, into another peripheral one, among the pariahs of the dead. But it truly was **this** world, I quickly became convinced, because in order to get ahead of non-reality, which was eating away at everything, the members of the Union had used a lot of canvas and paint in order to beautify the general impression by means of the written word. I realized that, during my absence, the Librarians' Conspiracy had only become more advanced. As if dreaming, I walked down the streets where it said that those were **streets**; beside houses and buildings that were hung with inscriptions about what was inside them and glaring instructions about how people should behave, like: COMRADE, DON'T FORGET TO TURN OFF THE LIGHT WHEN YOU LEAVE THE BUILDING.

But, alas, to make the absurd even worse, the bazaar at the edge of town was full of specters who, upon command, shouted that Trieste was ours and, quite entranced, like in the paintings of the Old Masters (only much more surreal and crude), they danced some sort of round dance that looked like the *dance macabre*. It could be seen that they believed that it would all last thousands of years . . . That none of them would ever die. How great was the power of self-deception to which those unfortunate creatures had succumbed? "Why," I thought, "do they think that the world has to exist at all? Where do their arguments for that come from? There is no reason in the world itself for it to exist; it's all just the good will of God." There, in one of those dark streets, as if in a fog I saw the title of your novel, but I forgot about it at the same moment because I was rudely stopped: three members of the People's Militia stood before me with German machine guns over their shoulders (the same as those used by the commandos of the Traumeinsatz), demanding to see my documents.

I showed them my papers from the former Kingdom and was immediately incarcerated, actually roughly shoved into the dilapidated police headquarters where they locked me up in some sort of oubliette, and the patrol leader, locking the door, said threateningly, "Tomorrow you will certainly sing about all the **things** you know, and **those** you don't." However, fate had other plans. As soon as they slammed the door behind me, I fell asleep and, of course, woke up the next day in my apartment in Lausanne. Day broke on the empty cell, so the patrol commander and two policemen were shot that very evening as collaborators with the people's enemies, because in the meantime—having received a dispatch that Kowalsky had been arrested—some of the top dogs of the Secret Police had arrived from Belgrade.

As for me, I shaved, tailored myself a new suit, registered at my bicycle factory again, got married, joined the Social-Democratic Party, and applied myself to the construction of a new generation of bicycles with a higher gear ratio. That might seem to some, after all, to be nonsensical. Wrong! Besides the prayers of the monks on Athos, the spinning of the prayer wheels in Lhasa, riding a bicycle (balancing oneself and turning the pedals) is one of the last things that keep together the incomprehensible pile of counterfeits in this multifaceted deception, at least until the fullness of time and until all of the elect are saved.

However, in error is anyone who believes that things on this side of the Iron Curtain were any better, that the world was more real. The world is one, the Earth is a ball, if I may paraphrase the mystical saying, "WHAT IS UP, THAT IS DOWN—AS IT IS IN THE EAST, SO IT IS IN THE WEST." Moreover, I would say that the mechanism of deception functioned much better in the countries of Western democracy and that the people who languished under communist regimes got the better deal because "Whomever God loves, it's him that He screws." In the changed circumstances I was forced to write my own biography, so that's what I did. In order not to stand out, I decided to get married in 1957, to get divorced in 1960; in great detail I established the schedule of my supposed rises and falls, weaknesses and virtues, business successes and failures, and I stuck to it religiously. I worked out the conditions under which I would meet with and befriend Mr. René Guénon and Mr. C.G. Jung, but also with several bums, drunks, and outsiders. Namely, in the face of the growing solidification of the world, facing an onslaught of rabid materialism, it was ever more difficult to seek for asylum in dreams. Here's why: as the world became more surreal, dreams became ever more real; I mean to say: the same rules of the game applied on both sides, subtlety was disappearing in all spheres available to man. Just as the face of the Earth was flooded with hordes of reckless tourists, so occult spaces were occupied by esoteric dilettantes of all sorts. I was forced to build, as they say nowadays, an image of perfect averageness so that I could quietly work on things that interested me.

And thank God, I had plenty of time. Through certain pre-war friends and antique dealers, I bought up a myriad of lesser known medieval manuscripts so that they would not fall into the wrong hands and be profaned. That was how, in an unknown tractate by Bombast Paracelsus, I found a confirmation of my long-held suspicion: using the poor spread of literacy and the small number of books of that time, the Librarians, Paracelsus says, calling them **Pagoium**, set out to destroy whatever existed but was not mentioned in the manuscripts. That was the beginning of the genocide of gnomes, trolls, fairies, good woodland sprites, against the white wizards and witches, against the countless numbers of those tiny creatures that are natural conjunctions of nature and man, just as angels are the connection between God and people. They intended to lord it over nature without an intermediary, but nature, it turned out, lorded it over them.

In that enterprise, they only partially succeeded. Because of the high percentage of nothingness in each of us, the human being is not able to destroy anything entirely, just as we are not able to create anything lasting. All of those miniscule and fragile creatures, driven from their forests, received asylum in the other world, and the Librarians began to fill the void with classifications of the remains, the shards of the world, and with the multiplication of their tomes constantly doing away with everything and everyone that might endanger their project. I'm sure that this seems shocking, but the facts are incontrovertible.

Even to this very day, for example, the burning of witches goes on unhindered. To be fair, it is not done with pomp and fanfare, but here and there, and in the newspaper you read how a girl was burned up in a fire. The experts take care that it always looks like an accident. Yeah, right. Or, why are there no longer any saints and why don't holy men do miracles anymore? Because the Librarians make sure that a child with a predisposition to be a saint very quickly disappears from the face of the earth. They have infiltrated everywhere; most often they are unaware of their mission. In fact, they are unconscious of the rules. A doctor makes a so-called mistake in diagnosing a newborn, a pharmacist makes it worse by giving medicine with counter-effects—and the little saint leaves this world without too much trouble and tranquilly goes to grow up in the peace of God. It is completely futile to cite evidence for such cases. I don't possess any whatsoever, but it isn't even necessary. No matter how hard we try to imagine it, it is not possible to get anywhere close to exposing the grandiosity of the evil which the Librarians have done, nor is it possible to **come up with** a single evil that they have not done.

And so, try to come up with a few. Don't be afraid of the endlessness, or better said bottomlessness, of the imagination. Since the Librarians started off destroying the world by means of books, the world can also only be saved by means of books. And you, by the way, if you continue heading through the streets of the labyrinths of this novel whose map is falsified (like the maps of Moscow), in one of those streets you'll also find the name of this second volume on an incidental storefront. I already know it, but I won't tell you. Do it yourself. And one more thing: at the moment when you start loving something, try to destroy it or lose it as soon as possible. Remember that, not because it is wise or important, but because it is an exceptionally effective end for this chapter, my dear Mr. Basara.

New Jersey, September 9, 1980

Dear Kowalsky,

A few weeks ago I got your letter where you expressed interest
in the fate of von Klosowsky, the higher German officer, whose
hearing I attended at the trial of war criminals in Nuremberg.
Because of my obligations, I could not satisfy your curiosity
immediately, but I hope that you will understand.

As soon as I had the chance, I wrote an acquaintance who
works at the archives of the US Army, and he kindly sent me a
copy of the transcript, which I am sending to you in a separate
envelope. As to the circumstances under which Klosowsky was
arrested, it happened in the following way: in April, 1945, I was
with my unit near Kassel. One afternoon, a patrol captured, or
more precisely came across, a high-ranking SS officer in a state
of complete shock. Since all SS officers were exposed to a careful
procedure to determine whether they were perhaps responsible
for war crimes, I immediately informed Major T. P. Wood (he
died three years ago), so we interrogated Klosowsky together
and wrote up the transcript, which was later the cause of great
headaches for both of us.

Namely, the story told to us by Klosowsky, in spite of certain
incontrovertible facts, at best seemed like a chapter from a fantasy novel. He consistently stuck to that version. The mention
of **your** name interested me personally, so I—in spite of my
skepticism—insisted on details.

However, the committee for establishing responsibility did
not want to hear the esoteric war narrative of Klosowsky, so
they sent him for a psychological checkup where it was established that he was a sane person. Ultimately they concluded that
Klosowsky was pretending to be insane, so he was sent to trial
where he answered for his indirect guilt in the death of several
dozen Jews. He was sentenced to ten years.

Before returning to the United States, I visited Klosowsky

several times and inquired about his condition. He left on me the impression of a calm, though slightly depressive man, and the prison guards told me that he spent most of his time sleeping; he sometimes did not wake up for as many as ten days.

That was also how he passed away. In 1950, he fell asleep. Accustomed to his long intervals of sleep, the guards did not wake him. They became suspicious when his cell began to smell of decay, so that his real date of death has never been established with certainty.

Kindest regards,
J. Smith

STATEMENT BY OBERSTURMFUEHRER KLOSOWSKY TO THE INVESTIGATORY COURT AT THE WAR CRIMES TRIAL IN NUREMBERG

(transcript)

Klosowsky:

My name is Klaus von Klosowsky. SS Obersturmfuehrer (Senior Assault Leader). In terms of education, I am a doctor of psychology. As a convinced national-socialist, I joined the SS units in 1937. In June of 1939, an emergency call-up was suddenly delivered to me. Together with Captains Dietrich and Kluge, I was to report to the Reich Chancellery because of a special assignment that was not specified in the call-up. We were received by the Reich Chancellor himself, who emphasized that the upcoming assignment was top secret, the existence of which was known only by, apart from the Fuehrer, a few of his most trusted officers. Without further ado, quite understandable when one takes into account what he was to tell us, the Chancellor informed us that a decision had been made at the very top to establish an SS unit, later to be called the **Traumeinsatz** (the Dream Force), for campaigns in the dream world and in occult and parapsychological situations.

Major T. P. Wood:

Mr. Klosowsky, how do you explain the fact that the existence of such a unit throughout the war remained a secret to the allied intelligence agencies?

Klosowsky:

Simple. My unit was not a secret at all. During the war it was stationed at Tubingen and your intelligence agencies kept track of it as a reserve infantry brigade. Because of the nature of its dealings (dreams, occultism, magic . . .), its real activity was never discovered. In fact, at the very beginning of the war, the Russians were a bit suspicious. However, because of the rigidity of the Soviet generals, they never saw beyond our experimental stage.

The very idea for establishing the unit no doubt came from Adolph Hitler, whose affinity for astrology and the occult sciences is fairly well known. The party ideologue, Alfred Rosenberg, having read my doctoral dissertation "The Three Dimensions of Dreaming," and having insight into my earlier research on the phenomenon of dreams, proposed to the Fuehrer that command over the unit to be established be given to me. In doing so, he remained silent about the fact (or perhaps he did not know) that, in the period between 1919 and 1923, I corresponded and met several times with Dr. Sigmund Freud, a fact which could have gotten me into a lot of trouble . . .

Major T. P. Wood:
Trouble?

Klosowsky:
Freud was a Jew.

Major T. P. Wood:
Oh, that. So, you accepted the assignment?

Klosowsky:
Yes. The deadline for preparing the Traumeinsatz for battle was very short: six months. In that time, I adapted a purely academic, theoretical doctrine for practical, battle conditions. I had to find 850 soldiers of exceptional psychophysical constitution, to organize theoretical and practical training, and then to lead them on several trial operations. Only after two years, at the height of the war, did I indirectly find out the real reasons for the establishment of the Traumeinsatz. Namely, I

came across a confidential party report about a subversive group, some sort of Gnostic sect of the Evangelical Bicyclists of the Rose Cross, followers of an ancient Near Eastern tradition who also acted through dreams, creating nightmares for members of the Wehrmacht and thus introducing panic. From 1942 to the end of the war, most of the assignments of the Traumeinsatz were aimed at them, and it must be admitted—with very little success. According to some later data, the high masters of the Evangelical Bicyclists **projected** the Fuehrer's dreams which, interpreted mistakenly, accelerated the downfall of the Reich.

Major T. P. Wood:

Major Klosowsky, you must admit that your claims sound a bit strange. Are you faking insanity, or are you pulling our legs?

Klosowsky:

Neither one. I am simply telling you my story. You can hear me out if you want to.

Major T. P. Wood:

Go on.

Klosowsky:

Captains Dietrich and Kluge were of inestimable value in organizing operations; I had enough time to concentrate on the domain of my specialization: the research of techniques for battle dreaming. In the meantime, the unit got its own insignia: a black circle with a silver owl inside and the motto: flectere si nequeo superos, Acheronta movebo.[4] In those first days, the biggest problem was the selection of soldiers and officers. The

---

4 In the margin of the original stenograph, Lieutenant Smith (who, with his unit, captured Klosowsky) left this note: "How cruelly does fate sometimes play with people! Is it just a coincidence that the same maxim (if I cannot reach the heavens, I will change the course of Hades) was used by Sigmund Freud for his book *Traumdeutung*."

criteria for acceptance were exceptionally strict. They all had to be above-average sensitive people, intelligent and extremely patient, with no affinities for vices or superficial entertainment. I visited a large number of barracks and selected 1,800 candidates of whom—after two weeks of testing—800 remained. For the headquarters of the SS Traumeinsatzkommando, I selected Tubingen. Not in the least accidentally. Centuries of developing idealistic philosophies in that university town had created an irreplaceable habitus for oneiric training.

Lieutenant Smith:
Can you give us some more detail about that training?

Klosowsky:
That was actually my greatest difficulty. How does one report on unfathomable things? How does one convince 800 young and reasonable people that things which they consider to be impossible are actually possible? By then, I had already completely mastered the skill of dreaming. I could go to sleep and wake up not according to the natural cycle but by my own will; I could move about in the third dimension of dreams at will; I could appear in the dreams of other people and determine their course . . .

Major T. P. Wood:
You mentioned the third dimension of dreams . . .

Klosowsky:
Yes. There are three dimensions of dreams. You might have been able to learn more about that from my dissertation **On the Levels of Dreams**, published in Zurich in 1925, if the entire print run had not been destroyed for security reasons. The levels go in this order: light dreams, dreams, and profound dreams. Certain mechanistic psychologists place profound dreams before dreams. This confusion has come about because of the

backward flow of time in dreams. Namely, when we go to sleep we do so in the present, but when we wake up, we awaken from the future, that is really important. It is incorrect to understand this as time flowing backwards; the closest analogy to this process is the face and its reflection in the mirror. From a lack of experience and inherent indolence, most people are overcome by the third dimension of dreams in which one loses the feeling of the profane ego. But with disciplined practice it is possible to **wake up**, just like that, in the third dimension, which is not, as it is mistakenly believed, the space of nothingness, but **the region of higher reality** in which things, although very subtle, can be seen more clearly and where all the laws of physics are suspended. What laymen believe to be dreams are only the threshold of the world of objects, preparation for reality; returning from the regions close to the true human homeland, into which we depart to renew our strength, and return to a foreign place. Rare are those who can withstand that return and not think that they have been nowhere at all.

Lieutenant Smith:

Major Klosowsky, it seems you are avoiding the question. In what way did you manage to wake up in, as you say, the third dimension of dreams?

Klosowsky:

With the aid of the subtle body. These bodies of ours which are nonsensically conversing are just residences of our subtle bodies, abandoned embassies in nowhere land. Within the profane body, a person's finer body is placed . . .

Lieutenant Smith:

The soul?

Klosowsky:

No. The finer, subtle body. The soul is inside of that, but I don't know anything about that. I would dare to say, it is that body in which we will be resurrected. Now you are seeing it for yourselves. Everything I am telling you had to be somehow explained to the recruits, without shocking or frightening them, and without having them start thinking that I am crazy, just as you are thinking at certain moments. So I had to proceed with caution. During the first weeks of training, mostly physical exercise was done, and only later did I introduce the theoretical part. The preparations were, I must admit, exceptionally difficult. If it's barely manageable for even a single psychophysically trained individual to master the technique of waking up in the third dimension of dreams, with a larger group things change from the ground up. Synchronizing the dreams of several hundred people is no simple task. Especially because people act in their dreams like they do in reality: automatic, whimsical, undisciplined, and egotistical. That is why we first synchronized the unit in reality. The recruits were subjected to an exceptionally strict, carefully planned training regime. They all got up at the same time, did exactly the same activities, and read identical texts. From four in the afternoon, they just had a little free time till supper, and they spent that time in solitude. In the evening, they were charged with noting down in their **Training Journal**, to the tiniest detail, everything they thought and wished, everything that made them happy, sad, or angry.

Lieutenant Smith:
What was the point of that drill?

Klosowsky:
The elimination of excess reflection; obtaining complete insight into the events of their "conscious" state so that they could master their reactions in their dreams. In the beginning, those were simple dreams: waking up in the third dimension, leaving the barracks, and mustering at the gathering point. We quickly managed to muster the entire brigade in its dreams in

just a few minutes, after they had gone to sleep. The rest of the training was done **there**. Because, it's worth mentioning, the dream (especially its third dimension) is in no way a place devoid of danger; except for ephemeral ones, caused by physical discomfort, dreams are not the products of the consciousness of this or that dreamer, but are entities unto themselves. They happen to the dreamer and if one loses concentration, it can easily occur that the dreamer gets lost in some labyrinthine dream. During training, we had several losses: twelve soldiers lost their minds and were dismissed as incapable, seven, as the committee determined, disappeared without a trace in the depths of Nebuchadnezzar's dream.

Major T. P. Wood:
A moment ago you mentioned the Evangelical Bicyclists of the Rose Cross. Can you tell us something more about the structure of that esoteric organization?

Klosowsky:
Unfortunately, no. I don't know enough about it.

Major T. P. Wood:
Can you tell us the names of some of the more prominent members?

Klosowsky:
Some of them, yes. But I doubt that most of them will mean anything to you.

Major T. P. Wood:
Go ahead and name them.

Klosowsky:
Eugene Ionesco, Emil Cioran, Mircea Eliade, Eduard

Sam (liquidated), Andrija Hebrang, Miloš Crnjanski, Rastko Petrović, Dragiša Vasić, Aleksandar I Karađorđević, Slobodan Jovanović, Nikolaj Velimirović, Joseph Kowalsky, Joseph Vissarionovich Jughashvili, Geca Kon (liquidated), Milovan Đilas, Edvard Kocbek, Živojin Pavlović (liquidated), Dobrica Ćosić, Svetislav Veizović . . .

Major T. P. Wood:
If I heard correctly, you mentioned Stalin's name. Are you certain that he is a member of the Evangelical Bicyclists?

Klosowsky:
Quite certain.

Lieutenant Smith:
If I may ask, isn't that in a bit of a contradiction with Stalin's ideological orientation?

Klosowsky:
Stalin's ideological orientation was nothing more than a mask. That so-called leader of the "world revolution" is one of the prominent members of the Evangelical Bicyclists. And not only was he not a communist, but he was assigned to be the annihilator of communists and communist ideas.

Major T. P. Wood:
That's incredible!

Klosowsky:
Not so much if we look back a little and study the list of prominent revolutionaries Stalin liquidated in the last decade. Russia was never, ever, nor will it ever be, communist. If any true communists do manage to appear, they soon vanish from the face of the earth. All of those masquerades on Red Square

are nothing more than a smokescreen. Germany lost the war against Russia, but you must carry on with it. That's the only way you will save Western civilization.

Major T. P. Wood:
Where do you get that information from?

Klosowsky:
Early in 1942, a group of Traumeinsatz commandos interrogated the subconscious of prominent Soviet leaders and generals. They learned some discouraging facts. Although in a waking state they believed in determinism and the historical role of the proletariat, deep in their souls they were Byzantines, iconodules, and they were unconsciously living out the idea of the Eastern Roman Empire . . .

Lieutenant Smith:
In what way?

Klosowsky:
By turning the Soviet Union into an enormous monastery . . .

Major T. P. Wood:
Let's go back to the details related to the actions of the Traumeinsatz.

Klosowsky:
Whatever you want. The second phase of the training included the following elements: movement, concealment, infiltration, scouting, elimination of the enemy, and safe awakening. As you know, in a dream it is enough to just think of a place and one can instantly find oneself there. But in the military, precision is necessary. So, when they were awake, the soldiers learned maps and terrains by heart, city maps, so that they could orient

themselves. As I already mentioned, synchronicity is of vital significance here; it is enough if just a few soldiers don't appear at a designated place at the designated time, and panic takes hold of the others, which could result in all of them ending up as the ephemeral dream of a wood merchant from Transylvania, and dispersing into nothingness after he wakes up. That is why the entire brigade never went into battle at the same time. A third of the company always remained in the barracks in a semi-conscious state where they observed the development of the situation. If they noticed anything unusual, they would quickly get up and wake the rest of the men.

Lieutenant Smith:
When did you undertake those first battles?

Klosowsky:
Immediately after the deadline of six months passed, the one set by the Fuehrer. At first we searched for hiding Jews. You know that a great number of Jews hid from the Gestapo. The procedure followed by the Traumeinsatz was quite simple. Every night, one battalion would head off to monitor dreams. Relatively easily they detected the Jews' dreams; there are differences between Aryan and Jewish dreams . . .

Lieutenant Smith:
What kind?

Klosowsky:
Jews, with understandable variations, even when they are atheists, always dream one and the same thing: the return to Jerusalem. The Traumeinsatz would just locate the places where the fugitives were hiding. The Gestapo did the rest. In any case, we had more important things to do: the battle with the Evangelical Bicyclists. Officially it was thought that they

are also a para-Jewish organization, but my later experiences in battle with them do not support that thesis. On the surface and from a distance, I became familiar with the unusually complex structure of their hierarchy.

Lieutenant Smith:
Tell us something more about that.

Klosowsky:
For a start, the example of Stalin is enough. Even though he is the dictator of an empire, he is subordinate to a certain Aziz, a seemingly feebleminded beggar from Istanbul. Moreover, the Grand Master of the Evangelical Bicyclists is a certain Joseph Kowalsky, a bum, alcoholic, and mystifier. In a nutshell: the higher a member of the brotherhood is on the hierarchical ladder of the Bicyclists, the lower he is on the social ladder of the society in which he lives. Several times we tried to liquidate him; throughout the war he lived in occupied Serbia. In vain. Kowalsky is uncatchable. The Gestapo hunted him in reality, the commandos of the Traumeinsatz in dreams. Without success. They say that he was detained briefly by Feldwebel Krantz, but it turned out to be just a dream. On another occasion one of the most experienced units of the Traumeinsatz got onto Kowalsky's trail; they realized too late that the trickster had deceived them. Fleeing through a labyrinth of dreams, he led them too far away; too late, they realized that he had slyly led them into reality. They found themselves, as they reported by radiogram, on a deserted island swathed in fog. They were never heard from again . . .

Lieutenant Smith:
From your story it turns out that the Evangelical Bicyclists had better mastery of dreaming.

Klosowsky:

Unfortunately, yes. In addition, they outnumbered us; all members of the sect were fighting in their ranks, both those from the most ancient times and those who are yet to be born.

Major T. P. Wood:

Can you explain that?

Klosowsky:

Couldn't be easier. Don't you sometimes dream of your friends and relatives who have died?

Major T. P. Wood:

Yes, yes, go on.

Klosowsky:

The subtlety of their dreaming techniques, perfected for centuries, was incomparably superior to ours. I already said that training had been done quickly. And still, even if I had had much more time at my disposal, we would have accomplished nothing. I don't have any material proof of it, but I got the impression that they knew all of our movement's intentions ahead of time. It made it possible for them to change the landscape of dreams at will, to set unexpected traps, so that in a relatively short period of time we lost almost half of our soldiers.

Major T. P. Wood:

When was that?

Klosowsky:

In the spring of 1942. After I filed a large number of exhaustive reports, the Fuehrer finally approved of the reorganization of the unit and allowed soldiers to be brought in from the ranks of a certain number of battle-tested units from the Eastern Front.

Those men had lived through the hell of the Russian winter, through horrible conflicts, so that the worst nightmare could not have been much of a surprise to them. The Traumeinsatz at the time numbered around 2,500 soldiers and officers, not counting the additional instructors we took on for all sorts of occult skills.

Major T. P. Wood:

What was behind the sudden change in the decision-making of Adolph Hitler?

Klosowsky:

There's no longer any doubt. Judging from the interest in all things related to my unit, Hitler had the ambition of totally controlling all of reality, and not just the realness of the physical world. He decided to do so after he read, in the reports of the intelligence units of the Traumeinsatz, that Stalin was controlling the dreams and subconscious of his own collaborators and subordinates, and that he was being shown the future by the Evangelical Bicyclists.

Major T. P. Wood:

We didn't know that Stalin was a psychotherapist.

Klosowsky:

He certainly wasn't! But that would be the reason for your failure. The decline of Western civilization. Nobody got rid of Stalin out of a whim or because of paranoia, as the hacks were quickly to begin claiming. No. All of those who disappeared in the purges had, in one way or another, the intention of overthrowing Joseph Vissarionovich. It was their misfortune that they did not know of Stalin's secret ability. Hitler had a much better ear for such things than your generals-pragmatists. He started with the routine supervision of the dreams and subconscious minds of his generals, the party elite, scientists, and prominent citizens. How do you think he avoided all of those assassination attempts?

Lieutenant Smith:
Did Hitler stop there?

Klosowsky:
No. He ordered the attempt to establish control over the world of the dead. In one underground laboratory somewhere in the Norwegian mountains, the party necromancers worked day and night on evoking the dead warriors of German mythology, on conjuring up the spirit of von Clausewitz and attempting to manipulate it.

Major T. P. Wood:
What was their goal?

Klosowsky:
They were planning the invasion of England by spirits to create complete chaos. The undertaking required no material means (transport, weapons, equipment), nor were there any risks or casualties; the RAF would be completely helpless. It is a well-known fact: the dead cannot be killed again. Who knows why the spirits (even though they appeared often, about which the documentation is all in order) weren't especially interested in Goebbels's propaganda machine, though attempts continued— as far as I know—all the way to the end of the war.

Major T. P. Wood:
How did the further activities of your units develop?

Klosowsky:
During that time, I tried to come up with a plan for a final showdown with the Bicyclists. During earlier operations, an

enormous astral construction had been noticed, far away to be fair, which seemed to be the headquarters of the sect. We concluded that a successful attack on the enemy holdout would turn the battle in our favor. Of course, we avoided rushing into missions in spite of the Fuehrer's impatience and ever more frequent insistence that "the Cabalistic, Jewish ruse be destroyed." We first had to perfect in detail some of the occult skills necessary for doing battle in dreams. Here I primarily mean mastering the ability of **substantializing**, that is, transferring objects from dreams to the waking world and vice versa.

Lieutenant Smith:
And how far did you get in mastering those skills?

Klosowsky:
Quite soon we established that the second process isn't possible because objects have no conscious state, since they are also in reality just a projection of the soul, in dreams they become completely useless. With substantialization from dreams into reality, things were much better. When waking up, if the dreamer focuses his attention on an object in his dream, it somehow wakes up with him and appears in the external world. As time went by, we gathered a rather large number of those objects, among them for a while even King Arthur's sword held a place of honor in the brigade's muster room. Among other things, there were also a few manuscripts of the Evangelical Bicyclists. In one of them, I read that the Bicyclists do quite the opposite; it said there that they take things from the face of this world to the very boundary of the third dimension of dreams, where those objects are taken over by angels and carried into the spirit world. That's how, for example, confronted by the onslaught of the Turks and heathens, they executed their *coup de grace*: during a single night, with their collective strength, they moved the Byzantine Empire into the heavens so that its holy land can be saved undesecrated for the Day of Judgment.

Major T. P. Wood:
Wait a second. It's hard to follow what you're saying. That is completely absurd. What do you mean—they moved the Byzantine Empire into the heavens?

Klosowsky:
Now, after all is said and done, knowing a lot of things which I didn't at the start of my adventures, I can say: The Bicyclists, whoever they are, from their inception have "stolen" everything valuable and real from the face of this world of already impoverished reality. I don't know how the Bicyclists moved Byzantium; if I did, Germany would have won the war. In the manuscript it says, and I believe it because I have quite substantial reasons, that they raised the Byzantine Empire into the heavens. The territory, of course, remained illusorily untouched, but quite quickly, lacking its ontological foundation, it disintegrated into a multitude of abstract little states which showed a tendency toward further atomization. In order for that tendency to reach fruition, the texts foresee, in the near future they will have to think up a few new nations and several languages. It seems that the Bicyclists are consciously aiding and abetting that process to speed up the end of the world.

There was also a rumor about some mythical King Charles the Hideous who intended to raise his entire (in truth tiny) kingdom from this world, through dreams, into the other world. About the success or failure of that attempt, there was no mention.

In terms of those, let's call them **otherworldly**, objects, they showed strange characteristics. Even though they were tangible, it was impossible to possess them, to actually keep them in one place. During a routine operation, I found myself with my unit in an area covered with unusual crystalloid forms. Upon returning, I took one of those glowing objects. When I woke up, I saw it right next to my bed. If my memory serves me correctly, it looked basically like this:

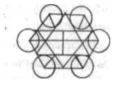

Not a week passed, and the object disappeared from my office. I reported the case to the Security Office, and they interrogated the subconscious minds of my collaborators, but the investigation produced no results. To make things more interesting, in the next letter I received from my wife, I read that a strange crystal had appeared in our house (830 km away). From the description, I realized that it was actually my fugitive war trophy. In her next letter, Greta (my wife) told me that the crystal had been stolen. But I already knew then that it was not stolen.

Major T. P. Wood:

Mr. Klosowsky, are you aware that your statement is highly improbable and that I cannot appear before any judge with it?

Klosowsky:

I completely understand the disbelief that my story causes. Not even I can believe most of what happened to me. In fact, I try to, I pretend that I don't believe it because only in that way can I somehow stand the terrible memories that obsess me.

Lieutenant Smith:

Excuse me, Major, but maybe it would be better for us to hear Klosowsky's statement to the end.

Major T. P. Wood:

Yes, go on, Major Klosowsky.

Klosowsky:

Somehow at that time, near the end of 1944, the Bicyclists started a counter-offensive, in fact a psychological one, since one of the complicated rules of their Brotherhood forbade them to start a battle first. They made use of the most devious of means. They revealed the future to the members of the Traumeinsatz. That introduced horrible confusion and the collapse of fighting morale into our ranks. A man can function only if he does not know the future. Actually when he does know it, and everyone faces the same certainty—death! That is the reason we go on functioning; we hope, hate, go to war, we do everything possible to turn our attention away from and to forget that unbearable certainty.

To some, actually, the past was revealed. It is known from psychology that a large number of people have a completely mistaken conception of themselves. In their blindness and partiality, they literally make up their lives. When faced with their true self, they experience a breakdown. In short, no matter which of the two methods they used, the Bicyclists succeeded in their intentions. Suicide, desertion, and nervous breakdowns became an everyday occurrence. There was nothing I could do. We had to go for all or nothing. That's why, on the night between December 22 and 23, 1944, I set off with the entire unit into the decisive battle although I knew beforehand that we would lose it.

Major T. P. Wood:
Why did you do that?

Klosowsky:
I had no choice.

Major T. P. Wood:
You didn't have to give the order to attack.

Klosowsky:

I repeat, I had to issue the order although I knew the consequences would be disastrous.

Major T. P. Wood:

That, I can't understand.

Klosowsky:

Please allow me to ask you a question. Maybe things will be somehow clearer then. Let's say, for example, that you're drowning in a river. Are you aware of the fact that you're drowning?

Major T. P. Wood:

I suppose so.

Klosowsky:

But you are unable to do anything except wave your arms about and, by the way, make your situation worse. I found myself in a similar situation. Generally, when you get involved in events, when you get emotionally attached to things, you have no choice at one point but to be a common, everyday straw in the rushing flow of their stream. Let there be no mistake, you also, together with the lieutenant, are up to your necks in the stream.

Major T. P. Wood:

I don't doubt it. But now, can you tell us something more about that fateful battle?

Klosowsky:

In order to protect my family from unpleasant consequences, a month before the final battle I sent them an official telegram announcing my death. I could give myself over to fate with a clear conscience. I already knew for certain: in our charge, when we damage one wing of the Astral Cathedral, an unearthly hurricane will begin to blow, and scatter us into the unknown.

Major T. P. Wood:
Do you mean to say that it was the wind that defeated you?

Klosowsky:
In a way, yes. I don't remember seeing any of the Bicyclists nearby. At one instant, I saw my loved ones in black, a guy named Borges in Buenos Aires, far from the heat of battle, writing out the pages of the short story "Aleph," dedicated to the place where I actually was at the time . . . I saw myself in the rhythms, lost in the mist; I saw the face of Lieutenant Smith and the faces of his soldiers; I saw this room and you . . . I saw myself speaking the sentences of this statement . . . And that is where the memory stops. From the day when we went into battle, to the day of capture, so an entire six months and four days, there is a blank in my memory. I don't know where I was, or what I was doing. A total blank until the day I was captured. It would not surprise me that I was "spared," meaning returned from the void of the third dimension of dreams, just in order to be used for one of the dark vagaries of the Evangelical Bicyclists, the real sense of which will be clear only in the very distant future.

Nuremberg
4.10.1945.

ATTACHMENT 1
THE CONTENTS OF THE DESK DRAWER

INVITATION TO THE New Year's ball in an envelope with the letterhead of the Republic of Marina (Republica de Marina Embajada), one. Copy of Hitler's book *Mein Kampf* in the original, with the dedication of the author to a certain J. Kowalsky, one. German-made calculator, broken, one. Photograph of S. Basara with the rock singer Nina Hägen, one. Photograph (montage) of him with Stalin, one. Folders with manuscripts, letters, and press clippings, four. Figurine of the Buddha, with a hammer and sickle drawn in on the stomach, one. Plastic jar of rheumatism cream, two. Hand grenade, American-made, two. Copy of the book *The Philokalia*, one. Piccolo harmonica, one. Pelikan fountain pen, one. Photos of nude women, pornographic, twenty-three. Photograph of the Serbian Academy of Sciences and Arts "Memorandum," one. Bullets, 7.62 caliber, sixty, no clip. Crystalloid object of strange shape which inexplicably disappeared during the investigation, one.[5] VATROSPREM fire extinguisher, one. Postcards, catalogues, various invitations, fifty-two. Dagger, old-fashioned with engraved cross and inscription IN HOC SIGNO VINCES, one.

---

5 The inexplicable vanishing crystalloid was, if my memory serves, roughly in this shape:

ATTACHMENT 2
PHOTOGRAPH OF THE DESK DRAWER

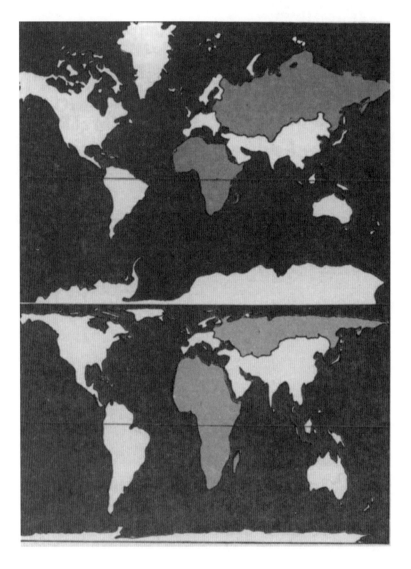

The false size of the world (Mercator) and the true size of the world (Peters). "Peters's Projection," *Duga*, 2.2. 1990.

1. Latin alphabet version of J. Kowalsky's letter

2. Facsimile of the Cyrillic version

Note:

The miraculous letter of J. Kowalsky was legible in the Latin alphabet for the even dates, Cyrillic version for the odd ones. The facsimile of the Latin alphabet version was photocopied on August 18, 1989, and the Cyrillic one on August 19, 1989. A chemical analysis of the paper and ink produced no results at all: the paper and ink were ordinary. Graphologist A. D. confirmed that the handwriting of both versions belongs to the same person.

Klaus von Klosowsky (marked by the X), commander of the
Traumeinsatz, Commando with a group of officers. Tubingen, October 1942

A VISIT FROM MRS. GLOVACKI

AFTER ALL, LITERATURE is just a little bit better than life. Perhaps only every thousandth situation escapes the forms of the general enervation that Radbertus of Odensis condemns in his work *De vanitate mundanae*, presupposing its solitude and removal from the illusion of this-worldly changes. Is there a more bizarre subject than an unknown woman who shows up at the door? And yet a middle aged woman did appear at my door and asked if I lived there. I answered affirmatively, invited her to come in and sit down. Obviously under the influence of too many American melodramas from the 1950s, she sat on the edge of the bed, without taking off her coat or setting down her purse. Then, she corrected herself. Realizing that **sat on the edge of the bed** would bring up certain associations among the readers, she got up and moved over to the armchair where I wanted to sit, so I was left standing. Then she, as the rules of the genre dictate, lit a long menthol cigarette (which they haven't been making for ages now), cleared her throat, and began speaking.

"Please allow me to introduce myself: I am Ana Glovacki. You see, sir, against my will I have gotten caught up in your novel; indirectly, it goes without saying. I am, namely, a medium; to be honest, a fake medium. Until recently I didn't even believe that spirits exist at all. Simply, using the credulity of sentimental souls, I hold spiritualist séances in order to make my living . . ."

"My dear madam," I interrupted her, fearing (unfoundedly, it would turn out) an endless, syrupy self-justification, "you are no exception. A great majority of people make a living by deceiving other people, and still they are members of respectable guilds and fraternities, and they are honest people. Let us take things in order. For example, priests convince us to accept certain teachings of which they themselves are, strictly speaking, unsure, and which they don't believe in at all in extreme cases. Yet, do we want to say that God doesn't exist because of that? Not in the least. Or, let's take the example of politicians. Those crafty liars try to convince us that we will, if we just give them our trust, all together experience an unimaginable material and spiritual transformation, which is the most common of nonsense; page through any textbook on history and you will see that every order ends up in the chaos of the invasion of barbarians; the barbarians quickly become civilized and likewise get overrun by new barbarians, and in the meantime, the first ones, the civilized, have now become barbarians, and thus the process goes continually on. Shall we say that there is no advancement because of that? Of course we will say so, but there's nothing we can do about it. Or the example of the producers . . ."

"But, sir," Glovacki interrupted, "I didn't come here to listen to a lecture on history. I'm here for a concrete reason, one slightly discomforting for me."

"Well, go ahead then, say it . . ."

"So, my troubles started one evening when a **real spirit** appeared to me for the first time. I had just started practicing my act for an upcoming séance when the chairs began bumping around the room; the doors and windows flew open, the drawers flew out of their places . . . Objects were hovering about in the air. I was overwhelmed by the fear of death. I thought I would die at any moment. In the terrifying howling of the wind, screams could be heard; then, for an instant I saw in the corner of my room," here Mrs. Glovacki paused, "no more or less than three German soldiers and an officer. They were in full battle gear. 'Was ist das für Traum, zum Teufel!'[6] the officer shouted. Then I heard an indescribable voice, 'Klosovski, get the hell out of here!' Then he said something to me . . . This makes no sense.

---

6   What kind of dream is this, dammit! (German)

No one will believe me."

"Take it easy," I told her. "This is, conditionally speaking, a novel which is categorized as fantasy, and you can say whatever crosses your mind. Actually, it indeed exists so that it could be an asylum for improbable things. Everything rejected by the disbelief of the world is welcome here. Just go on."

"So, the voice addressed me, saying, 'And now, slut, listen to what I am saying! You're the last person on earth I should be talking to, but since there's no one better, you'll have to do. For your information, I am Camael, the angel who rules Wednesdays. Now, a specter will appear before you, Jean Jacques de Malvoisin, a respected Parisian who the Jacobins killed right at the end of the First Republic. Take a picture of the ghost. Material evidence is important. Such are the times. Then, write down every word Malvoisin will say. You'll deliver your notes to this man (here, he gave me your name and address), and may God protect you if you don't do exactly as you've been ordered.

"Then Camael fell silent, and the room was filled with a sort of semi-darkness in which some strange forms were moving about. Quickly I spotted the face of the aforementioned de Malvoisin. With trembling hands, I took several photographs, only one of which was even partially successful. Then he dictated a text to me. It is in this envelope." Mrs. Glovacki offered me the envelope.

"I almost forgot. So he didn't have to climb the stairs, the mailman asked me to give you this letter as well."

Then she fell briefly quiet.

"Camael said that he would return, and that we have to stay in contact."

"If that's what he said, then we don't have much choice." I saw Mrs. Glovacki to the door, and then opened the letter that had come through the regular mail. In it, there was an invitation.

THE MUSEUM OF THE REVOLUTION

invites you to the grand opening of the artistic exhibition of

NENAD ŽILIĆ

Wednesday, March 21, 1990, at midnight

The Gallery of the Museum of the Revolution. Lenjinov bulevar, page 104

I crossed myself and opened the envelope that Mrs. Glovacki gave me.

Jean Jacques Marie Antoine Geffroy de Malvoisin

A COURTEOUS LETTER TO MR. BASARA,
THE COMPILER OF THE ETERNAL NOVEL
THE CYCLIST CONSPIRACY

MOST RESPECTED MR. BASARA,

I dare to write you through a person who will introduce themselves under a dubious name, an obvious pseudonym by means of which she is concealing her deceptive activities. Pay no attention whatsoever to her stories of ghosts, the angel Camael, the spirits, and the entire atmosphere of the bazaar. Specters who remain entrapped in that sub-lunar world do not possess any sort of intelligence, nor can they tell you anything except their incoherent wishes. Never has a single member of the brotherhood of the Evangelical Bicyclists of the Rose Cross ended up in those spheres. There are those who have vanished into the gorges of hell, that is true, but we are people of extremes, are we not?

Despite everything, Mrs. Glovacki's version has elements of truth. Namely, she believes that things happened just as she described them. In fact, it was all a dream; she dreamed that the chairs moved about, that the door opened with a slam, that Camael appeared, along with my ghost and—proof of the dream's authenticity—Obersturmfuehrer Klosowsky with his adjutants. Those precautionary measures were necessary and unavoidable; if she had been **aware** she was dreaming, Mrs. Glovacki would not have taken the dream seriously, and then I would not have had the opportunity to write you. That is why **the illusion of an illusion** was created, which Mrs. Glovacki could believe, at least indirectly. The lines you are reading she wrote in a state of complete catalepsy, in French which she does speak, which only increases her conviction in the supernatural character of the events she participated in.

You are certainly aware that I compiled an earlier version of *The Conspiracy*, the publication of which stopped the Marquis de

Sade because one of the chapters in the novel was dedicated to shedding light on his evil activities and biography, which were so different from the version placed in various tattered volumes and studies written by naïve bunglers. Since, in your times, there will be attempts to rehabilitate that arch-scoundrel and atheist, I am giving you access to my twelfth chapter, because of which I lost my reputation, my property, and ultimately my head.[7]

Yours sincerely

Jean de Malvoisin

7 Indeed, that same year (1989) when I began working on putting together the second volume of *The Conspiracy*, the selected works of the Marquis de Sade appeared in an edition of "Rad" in Serbian (edited by **Jovica Aćin**). Through subtle manipulation, my friends were enticed into working on the publication of de Sade's works, members of the Evangelical Bicyclists of the Rose Cross, **Milojko Knežević (as a translator) and Branko Kukić (as an editor).**

That detail drove me to turn my attention to some of the details of the graphic form of "Rad's" publications. Above all, the name of the publishing house is a colloquial anagram of the word "DAR" [talent] which is a symbol of refusing God's mercy and the attempt to achieve everything through one's own "work" [RAD]. The emblem of the company is a circle in which there is a sitting figure with an unwound scroll on which is written RAD and in which there are several lines—a simulacrum. **Only at first glance.** Under a strong magnifying glass, one can clearly see the saying ERITIS SICUT DEI. Further, on the covers of the magazine DELO (published by RAD) from edition to edition, an application is printed. The so-called subscription of the form "SIGN UP TO FOR DELO [WORK]". It doesn't say for what. The little devil on the left side, as if he is hinting at a certain possibility.

The Emblem of "RAD"

Copy of the subscription form for "DELO"

CHAPTER 12

On the false report that the scoundrel Marquis de Sade died in December of 1814; on the magical transfer of his soul into the body of an innocent male infant and the desecration of Teresa of Ávila; on how, with the help of his scoundrel sidekicks, he attempted to destroy nature, and how he set up the writer of the lines that follow.

IN MID-DECEMBER 1814, the rumor spread around Paris that Donatien Alphonse François Marquis de Sade died in an insane asylum in Charenton. The writer of these lines was ultimately doubtful about that news, knowing that the great scoundrel gladly and skillfully used mystifications and half-truths like those—which will enter history as indisputable facts—that he spent time in the Bastille although he actually only appeared there from time to time, so that he would be seen and—without personal investment—offer a demonic example to the future revolutionaries. And truly, it turned out the rumors were only partially true. De Sade really was supposed to die on December 2, 1814, and after a fashion he did, however on the basis of one clause of his Contract with the Devil, he had the right to extend his earthly life by twenty-five more years in order to expand his insight into the *Mysterion impietatis*, and to attempt to do that which no one has ever managed: to completely annihilate God's work, his very own soul.

His first great defilement is relatively well-known: the exhumation of the body of Saint Teresa and the attempt to blackmail God. Here is what Pierre Bouchard has to say: "April 15, 16, and 17 (Germinal 25, 26, and 27). On the night between April 14 and 15, de Sad and Ricardo Strezzo dug up the body of Saint Teresa of Avila, who by the mercy of God was not only perfectly preserved in spite of death, but even showed signs of becoming more youthful. Teresa's face, peering out from under a cap of rough cloth, appeared to be like the face of a beautiful young woman of about thirty. They wrapped her up in a blanket, they placed her in a post-office chaise and departed, rushing toward France. On the sixteenth at dusk, they crossed the border at Pertuis and on the seventeenth, at twilight, they reached the Château de Lacoste, in Vaucluse, which is the Marquis's property. They left Teresa's body in the chapel and went to drift into a refreshing sleep.

"After a good night's sleep and a hearty breakfast, de Sade and Strezzo returned to the chapel. Strezzo, using secret methods that he owed to Cagliostro, breathed life into Saint Teresa. Waking from a two-hundred-year sleep, she sat up and learned, from the mouth of the Marquis, that she was now his prisoner. One of the maids took her to the boudoir of de Sade's wife, not present at Lacoste, where she was to be enslaved.

"That same evening the Marquis throws a banquet in Teresa's honor, attended only by the captive and Strezzo. At the end of the meal, raising his glass of champagne, the Marquis made a toast and spoke to Pascal's God, not the God of faith but the God of the **gambit**, informing him, if he exists, that he, de Sade, would hold Teresa as a hostage until God himself appeared for trial. So, the God of the gambit (. . .) would have to save de Sade, so great were the sins of the latter, because if he didn't do that, de Sade would shame her name irreparably and drag her into hell with him.

"That very night Strezzo had a dream in which he saw his own damnation. In the wee hours of April 19, he woke up, went into Teresa's room, and sent her back into death. God intervened and sent Teresa's body straight back to the Carmelite cemetery in Avila, where she took her place among those at rest waiting for resurrection. Strezzo left the chateau, jumped on a horse and returned to Italy. Nothing was ever heard from him again."[8]

---

8 Cf. "Književna kritika" [Literary criticism], 5-6, 1989 (editor's note).

This failure does nothing to weaken de Sade's resolve. Sensing that death was nigh, he organized a spiritualist séance where he conjured up Cagliostro's ghost and asked him advice on what to do. Cagliostro turned his attention to the aforementioned clause in the Contract. But, the great magician warned him, no one had ever dared to do that. De Sade, roiling with anger toward God, agreed to the possibility of the **complete** obliteration of his person; he rolled the dice and decided to desecrate the **Tree of Life**.

But, if he wanted to extend his life over the boundary set by God, Cagliostro told him, de Sade must undergo a beastly Assyrian ritual which the Savior himself put on the list of sins forbidden to human beings. The ritual consists of the following: at the moment of his **first** death, de Sade's adjutants had to kill an innocent male or female infant so that, with the aid of magical incantations, the Marquis's soul would take over the other body. The Marquis agreed. His endless vanity was soothed by the knowledge that he was doing something that no one after Christ's birth had done and that would be done just once more, before the end of the world (unsuccessfully, among other things) in foggy Ljubljana, in order to extend the life of the Great Heathen, about which there is a prophecy in the **Fraternitatis Saga**.

At the proper time, the beastly ritual was carried out. Successfully. His decaying body was buried in a grave without any sort of marker. Now completely ephemeral, imbued with evil completely, de Sade studied the texts of secret societies, trying to find out which of them was undermining the forces of evil. Plotting, he learned of the Little Brothers, a respectable member of which was my ancestor Enguerrand de Aubrix-Malvoisin. Sensing the danger, the Great Master handed the Rosenkreutz organization over to the laymen (to whom it was supposedly a secret), but he undertook measures to adapt the Brotherhood and its activities to the New Age, the era of great discoveries that was peering over the horizon of the nineteenth century.

His intelligence finely whetted by evil, unhindered by the troubles and discomforts of the foreign body in which he was and which he did not care for, de Sade attained the ability of seeing the future so that, in a Parisian bookstore, he stumbled on this book, at the time still unwritten, read it at one sitting, and tailored a hellish plan; in fact, from the novel he simply took the description of the orgy which was about to happen, composed by one of the inserted brotherhood, Jean Bitor, who was later cruelly put to death in the cellar of the Marquis's chateau.

"Most honorable Mr. Malvoisin," the unfortunate Bitor wrote me, "The scene I saw in the luxuriously lit underground room froze the very blood in my veins. The rabid Marquis had a giant copy of a wooden bicycle built, a machine you probably see now and then on the streets of Paris, but which was invented by Mr. de Sivrac. The apparatus was lying on the floor so that the huge wheels could freely turn, driven by the strength of about two-hundred strong servants. The inside of the wheels, their entire surface, was filled with naked scoundrels, torture machines, food and drink. On a rise, the Marquis was standing in the body of the twenty-year-old young man who his evil spirit had possessed, and before the beginning of the orgy, he gave this speech.

Friends,

All of you who cannot stand the presence of this world and the hypocrisy that rules it. Our time has come. If you energetically and earnestly struggle with and screw each other, if you joyfully slaughter these innocent maidens who have been set apart for our goal, if you truly learn to hate and are ready to become worse than animals, turning these wheels which symbolize YOD and TIFERET counter to the direction in which God sent them, we will put an end to the nonsense.

Nature, in fact, attempts to renew its strength by sometimes destroying entire peoples with disease, cataclysms, wars, strife, and criminal actions, but it thus only plays into the hands of the secondary nature that man also possesses, and which is controlled by the laws of metempsychosis; and when it sends powerful criminals or great misfortunes that are able to destroy that entire secondary nature, it only exhibits its lack of power; because, in order for everything to disappear, nature must destroy itself, but such an act is not in its power. It needs our help. And we will offer it, regardless of the opinions of hacks, like the stiff-necked de Malvoisin whose weakness is thus more obvious, if one keeps in mind that I have done everything possible to outlaw his miserable pasquinade even before he writes it, and to sentence him to a humiliating death from which he sought gentle comfort in the auspices of God.

With his murders, a criminal not only aids Nature in its goals that it wouldn't manage to fulfill, it also aids with the laws that maintain our secondary nature from the outset. I say from the outset in order to make it easier to understand the act that we will carry out tonight, since there was never a beginning to creation because nature is eternal, and the beginning, or that is the movement, exists as long as there are beings. If they were no more, there would also be no "beginning" moves, which would create a place for new moves by nature which it longs for, and which it begs to attain only through the total destruction toward which crime actually leads: It is thus logical that a criminal who is able to endanger secondary nature by destroying all its layers and productive abilities would be the one who is best serving nature.

If we give our all, if every atom of our being is given over to the passions of annihilation, the liberated energy will force the others to get involved as well. So, let us begin . . .

About the further developments at the Satanic gathering, I can report nothing definite because the Marquis's aids discovered me, whipped me, and decapitated me, most likely doing many other indescribably wicked things to my mortal remains.

I remain your loyal and obedient servant,
Jean Bitor

Fortunately, no matter how great it is, evil is always limited and destroys itself. It was as if he himself was aware of that, writing in the *System* **of Pope Pius VI**: "On earth, never will enough crime be committed as the unquenchable thirst of Nature demands." His hellish plan failed even despite the unimaginable number of beastly acts carried out over seven days and seven nights of surrendering to unspeakable transgressions. In fact, using the aforementioned abilities, the wicked Marquis made this other version of my novel impossible by manipulating the lack of comprehension of the modern audience, its absence of understanding for meta-prose approaches in which dead people write letters and the protagonists of novels depart into the future in order to read about what they should do in the past, losing their heads thereby. However, such is the fate of all those who are ahead of their times, and I am patiently enduring it, waiting for these lines to be resurrected in the future and testify to the horrible injustice he inflicted on me, *e pluribus unum*, that scoundrel Donatien Alphonse François de Sade.

THE PHANTASMAGORICAL EXHIBITION OF
NENAD ŽILIĆ

IT TOTALLY SLIPPED my mind that on March 23, 1990, in the building of the Youth Committee of the Communist Party in Bajina Bašta, the exhibition of Nenad Žilić was being opened. I remembered it only around ten in the evening, when the last bus was already long gone, so I rushed mindlessly out in the hopes that I would find some kind of transportation. There was no need for me to hurry: in front of my building, a long black Lincoln was waiting for me, with *Corps Diplomatique* license plates. The chauffeur was standing beside the car, the back door was open. "We were supposed to leave around six," said the driver, "they were waiting for you there, but we can still get there on time." "Who was so kind as to . . .?" I almost inquired of him, but then I realized that it was pointless, that people on the silver screen, in truth, do move, speak, pass on messages, they do everything we do, but it is impossible to ask them questions. Anyway we wouldn't hear him. They don't even see us. Nor do they know we exist. They just do their jobs, driving us around in silence and then returning us from our history into the History of Film.

He must have taken some sort of new road—I couldn't see where we were going because of the tinted glass on the windows—because, no matter how good the car is, one doesn't exist that could cover a distance of 42 km on a winding road in less than fifteen minutes, which was how long it took us. He stopped at the very city limits of Bajina Bašta. I was amazed at how much it had changed in the little less than a year since I had last been there. In the places where gloomy, secretive gardens with ivy covered fences used to be, there were now expansive squares with statues of four of our local Partisan heroes. Each square held one. I noticed that the statues had been changed; since they had grown old in the meantime, they had new ones cast, frowning even harder, their faces even more wrinkled. And all around, where there used to be dark little shops with colonial goods, flour and grain, and the small school supplies shop (in that order), brightly lit Duty Free Shops, second-hand stores and video rental shops were now standing. For thirty years not a single change, and then so many in just a few months . . .

"Time really is nothing," I thought and set off with my eyes closed, walking blindly, using only my sense of smell along the road I had taken so many times in my childhood, orienting myself by the hints of scents: cinnamon, vanilla, coffee, SOKO STARK candy, shoe polish, cheap cologne, flour and newspaper. But there were no more little stores, and I felt like an airplane that has lost its navigational equipment. Regardless, I kept going with my eyes closed; one who is not able to find his way in his hometown is lost anyway, whether looking around or not. Suddenly, I had the opportunity to be aided by my sense of hearing instead of my sense of smell; from somewhere, muffled, I heard the familiar strains of the melody "Lady Jane." "O," I thought, "this will surely take me to one of the good old places," so I went on following the words, "O, my sweet Lady Jane," step after step, "When I see you again," and soon I was in front of a small café that I had never seen before. It must have been built in the meantime. It was called NOSTALGIA, except that the name of the business was all in blue, neon. I went in. Inside, in clouds of tobacco smoke, were all my childhood friends, every last one. And just like the Partisan heroes on the squares, they had also gotten older. They were waiting to appear in the novel. Not because of vainglory—literature never really interested them much (and I allow them that right)—but so that we could all together be saved by fiction, just as Kowalsky wrote earlier.

As usual, they were drinking wine and listening to the Rolling Stones' *Greatest Hits*, recorded on a looping tape. In fact, that was not a tape, but a **Machine for Stopping Time**, which worked quite simply. The never-ending revolution of the music tape-recorded in the sixties in conjunction with the energy of their nostalgia and with the semantic definition contained in the name of the café—NOSTALGIA—caused time to run more slowly. The second hand on my watch was rapidly making circles, while the second hands on their watches had hardly completed a single revolution. Indeed, inside it had just struck nine, there was plenty of time till midnight and I could have a drink or two and tell them the real version of this paragraph, which I had falsified so that I could make room for introducing the **Machine for Stopping Time.**

The real version goes like this. The **Machine** was constructed by Jovan of the Rain, a poet who we came up with in the enduring boredom of youth so we could dilute the grayness of socialist realism, the dominant way of life at the time. We fashioned a story about a young man who studied philosophy in Jena, who wrote poetry and ultimately contracted tuberculosis and returned to his homeland to finish off his life. On one of the abandoned headstones of the city cemetery we chiseled in his name and the date of his death (1903). I wrote some twenty love sonnets, we gathered up yellowing daguerreotypes of some old heroes, here and there we found an old letter or two written in thick, old-fashioned handwriting. We all "lost track" of that stuff in the attics of pre-war houses, between the covers of the albums and herbariums of our grandmothers, so as time went by a rumor was created and people actually began to talk about the poet Jovan. Not long ago, after all these years, an **authentic** manuscript appeared, written by the person we had **thought up**. Grateful that we had created him from nothing, making him into an ethereal golem, in hardly visible handwriting, Jovan wrote instructions for us about building a hiding place where we could at least sometimes escape the hurricane of accelerating time which, there outside the café, was razing everything to the ground in front of it, rushing to its own end.

However, this slowed time had only an internal value and was not accepted on the scoreboard of the official time, outside. No matter how much I wished the opposite, it was already five to midnight and I needed to be going. But I still hadn't had that drink . . .

"What'll it be?" the guy behind the bar asked me.

"Mezcal."

In order to reach the building of the YC of the CP,[9] I had to pass the house of the late Svetislav Veizović, a hotelier from Bajina Bašta, whose profession was simultaneously his cause of death, because he was shot in a firing line by the local cads as one of the bourgeoisie in the name of the future and communism into which I, again, his grandson, was to be born twelve years later. On the corner of that house, there where the north and east wings of the building join in a **Г**,[10] near the very bottom, there is (and any passerby can check this) a bronze cylinder stamped onto the skirting, on which is engraved "1.7 G." Like that cylinder on one of the squares of Madrid where it says "0 Km" and the inscription ORIGEN CARPENTERRAS RADIALES, and signifies the zero point according to which Spaniards determine their distance from the heart of their homeland. A special committee of the Evangelical Bicyclists marked the spot in 1939 where the distance between the surface and the center of the

---

9 See the same author, *Phenomena*, Užice, 1990.

10 My grandfather liked houses built in the Cyrillic alphabet.

Earth is the shortest on the planet, the place where the Earth's gravity is highest, equal to 2.5 Gs.

As I approached the building of the YC of the CP, I noticed that it had grown smaller with time, that it was in fact ugly. I entered the empty entryway, confused by the absence of the babbling crowd, which is customary just before the opening of an exhibition. "Maybe there's been a mistake," I thought, "whoever heard of an exhibition opening at midnight . . ." But at that moment I saw to the left, over where the Event Planning Department used to be, a trapezoid of yellowish light which indicated that somewhere near its end there must be an open door. But there was not. And yet, the light leaked in from some sort of hallway that disappeared in the distance, but right at the front of the hallway was a small poster and the inscription EXHIBITION, OPENING AT MIDNIGHT confirming that at the end, or somewhere before that, the exhibition must actually be located.

That hallway was unnaturally long. In any case it was incomparably longer than the real length of the building, but there were no windows so that I could look outside and confirm this. In the end, I didn't really care. I sped up and, what do you know, a few feet ahead of me, in a niche in the wall, I saw an old, but upright and healthy fellow. He was dressed ridiculously, like an athlete from the 1930s: high-topped soft shoes, knee socks, pantaloons, a thin-tailored waistcoat with countless pockets, and a Sherlock Holmes cap with aviators' glasses.

"Excuse me," I said. "There's supposed to be an exhibition opening somewhere around here. Do you perhaps know . . ."

"I do," said the man, and a foreign accent could be heard in his voice. "I do know, and actually it's you I've been waiting for."

My heart began to race.

"Are you . . . Are you maybe Kowalsky?"

"No," the man said. "My name is Ernest Meier."

So, he returned from the Pilgrimage to Dharamsala. He survived all the dangers and difficulties and now he was here, walking beside me in an endlessly long corridor, which quickly began to branch out both to the left and to the right. So, that means, I calculated, if he was a college freshman in 1928 when he asked Dr. Sigmund Freud for help, he couldn't have been older than nineteen; 28 − 19 = 9. According to that calculation he must have been born in 1909, and now it was 1990. Ernest is eighty-one years old.

"Wait!" Meier said. "Here, I'm supposed to give you your Decree of Acceptance into the Order of the Little Brothers of the Evangelical Bicyclists of the Rose Cross."

Then, from one of his countless pockets he took out a yellowing slip of newsprint, obviously ripped from the margin of a newspaper, and handed it to me without a hint of a ceremony. It said:

GENS UNA SUMUS
SVETISLAV BASARA Member.
Grand Master E.B.R.C.
Signature illegible
In the corner, in block letters:
Cumhuryet, 23.3.1930

"Now, place your right hand on your chest and look up," Meier ordered, he checked if I had done what I was instructed and then suddenly began singing:

Iesus dulcis memoria,
Dans veram cordi gaudiam:
Sed super mel et omnia
Eius dulcis praesentia.

Nil canitur suavius,
Nil auditur Iucundius,
Nil cogitatur dulcius,
Quam Iesus Dei Filius.

Iesus spes poenitentibus,
Quam pius est petentibus,
Quam bonus et quarentibus!
Sed quid invenientibus.[11]

"Good," Meier said. Obviously, he was satisfied with what we had done. But I was not. I asked him if that was the entire ceremony. He indicated that I should shut up, yanked the little paper from my hand with the Decree of Acceptance into the Order of Evangelical Bicyclists and set it on fire with some sort of antediluvian lighter. That was going too far.[12] Still, out of

---

11   *Jesus, the very thought of Thee*
        With sweetness fills the breast!
        Yet sweeter far Thy face to see
        And in Thy Presence rest.
        No voice can sing, no heart can frame,
        Nor can the memory find,
        A sweeter sound than Jesus's Name,
        The Saviour of mankind.
        O hope of every contrite heart!
        O joy of all the meek!
        To those who fall, how kind Thou art!
        How good to those who seek!
        But what to those who find?

Through the kindness of Mrs. K. D., translator of classical languages, I learned that the author of the hymn which Ernst sang was Bernard of Clairvaux (1090-1153). Except for the coincidence that the author died exactly 800 years before my birth, I could find no other symbolism. (Author's note) (English translation of the hymn by Edward Caswall)

12 By setting fire to the piece of paper with the Decree, Meier left

respect for his considerable age, I refrained from protesting. Then again, there was one more thing: the corridor was getting more and more interesting. In passing I saw that its branches led to large halls; I caught glimpses of spiral staircases, niches in walls, but because of the speed of our gait, all of that was as if in a fog, so I decided to be patient and wait for the further course of events.

I didn't have to wait long. Ernest Meier suddenly stopped and pointed at a window (or a monitor) on the wall, some 50 x 75 cm in size. I saw a bearded man at the keyboard of a personal computer.

"Mr. Umberto Eco," said Meier.

But then, seeing how shocked I was, he put a patronly hand on my shoulder and explained, "We are on the above-ground floor of the Grand Insane Asylum. Yes," he went on, "we are in the Grand Insane Asylum."

"And Eco?"

"Eco is writing one of the chapters of this novel. Don't be conceited. Kowalsky wrote you and let you know that you are just one of the authors, and that your name is on the cover because of the geopolitical situation.

"In the first volume you were undercover, but from now on, since you have been accepted into the Order, you have to go

---

me without a tangible document which could testify to the fact that all of this is not fiction or something even less understandable and tangible. Yet, from our later conversation, I realized that he did that with the best of intentions. The Bicyclists are, above all, opponents of all forms of documentary, of all facts, and they are believers in blind faith. Besides that, depriving me of that document, he consciously was counting on the greatest possible improbability of the story which would then repel adventure seekers and the curious who might even set off in the markedly dangerous search for the entrance into the Grand Insane Asylum. Ultimately, I could always just falsify the document and comfort myself that there are so many authentic documents that perfectly correspond to fictional ones, only proving that the thing we call "reality" and that which is fake—are actually one and the same.

public."

I protested in spite of my decision to be patient.

"Did anyone ask me if I wanted to be a member of the Order?"

"Why would anyone ask?"

"Because it's about me. No matter how insignificant I am, I was still one party in that contract."

"You don't understand," said Meier. "You had no choice. It's your fate. Or, let me be clearer: it's the plot of the novel. Earlier, while you were writing those unreadable stories . . . Did your protagonists have the possibility of changing the course of their actions?"

"No."

"So, what do you want?"

"What do you mean, what do I want? That means that I have no free will."

Meier stopped again.

"That's nonsense. You're a member of the Order just because it is your duty to put together two or three books that will serve a certain purpose. Everything else is in the domain of your free will. You can be good, you can be evil; you can decide about whatever you want and you alone will bear the consequences and responsibility for it."

That was already a little more acceptable.

"And what about the exhibition?"

"We've arrived at the opening. There're the first pictures, to your left."

And truly, I saw a painting by Bosch I knew quite well. At that spot, the hallway of the Grand Insane Asylum was straight again and the paintings were hung on both sides at regular intervals; this can be faithfully rendered in the novel if the reader supposes that the even pages of the book are the left wall, and the odd pages are the right, and that the line where the pages meet at

Nenad Žilić, Untitled, oil on canvas

the point where the parallel sides of the hallway merge (of course, illusorily) into one.

Thus, instead of reading to the side, from left to right, one must read **forward**, as if we were walking down the street, and this could be represented on the **Map of the Novel** like this:

Up until the **Exhibition** the plot was running in one direction and then it made a ninety-degree turn, and this must be marked off so that misunderstanding can be avoided, since **at this point** a crossing occurs: The reader goes on, on the next page (A), but Meier and I continue forward in an uncertain (at least to me) direction (B) until our paths meet again in some suitable sentence.

"Do you like these paintings?" Ernst inquired.

*Nenad Žilić, **Untitled, oil on canvas***

"I like them. If I didn't like them, I wouldn't have organized in the novel this impossible exhibition that drives me more and more into a dilemma. But, I would rather ask you something else: can you tell me something about the Pilgrimage to Dharamsala?"

Meier burst out in laughter.

"You are mistaken," he said, wiping away the tears. "You think that I am that Ernest who was suffering from neurosis and who knew Freud. No, my friend, I am Ernest Meier II."

"I don't understand."

"It's a simple thing. Members of the Brotherhood who are exposed to high risk are born in two copies, moreover at different times and in different, often very distant, places in the world. Just in case something happens. If everything goes well, the second one never (or never completely) learns that he has a double. Otherwise, as in

Nenad Žilić, Untitled, oil on canvas

my case, if something happens to the first one, then the double comes into play. Ernest Meier I disappeared somewhere in the expanses of Asia Minor, so I took up the job. But that's not why we're here."

"Then why?"

"So that you could see it all, make some notes, so that you would try to remember as many details of the Grand Insane Asylum as possible. Open your eyes wide, take in every detail, and I will, as you do, try to fathom the meaning of these paintings, though I don't have much affinity for modern art."

Ernest Meier went on walking down axis y, and I turned down the x-axis, thus dividing the readers into two parties: the party of those who love art (who can look at Bosch's paintings with Meier), and the party of those who love fantasy literature who will go with me. To tell the truth, I didn't know where to go; without the calming presence of my fellow traveler, I felt

Nenad Žilić, Untitled, oil on canvas

insecure. Suddenly, I was overcome with the knowledge that I was in the third dimension of dreams, that Meier had inconspicuously led me into that world about which I had only read and heard up till then.

The specificity of that dimension, as I soon figured out, was the extremely diminished significance of the dimensions of time and space. Stated simply, it can be compared to a video-recorder: when the action gets boring, it can be fast-forwarded; if something interesting appears that deserves careful examination, it can be slow-motioned, and even completely freeze-framed. I decided out of professional curiosity to return to that window through which I had seen Umberto Eco. I found myself there at the very same instant, although, it seemed to me, Ernest Meier and I had spent several minutes heading toward Bosch's paintings. But it wasn't a window, rather some sort of monitor. Eco was pacing the room.

Nenad Žilić, Untitled, oil on canvas

"Of course," I thought, "this is indeed the principle of the Grand Insane Asylum: absolute control. Probably there is a monitor somewhere here where I can see myself writing out these lines." I wanted to see what Umberto Eco was writing; as if drawn in by a telephoto lens, the first lines on the terminal appeared. I read the first one:

And then I saw the terminal.

I could not read the rest. I decided to go back and find Meier. Then I heard a muffled sound like the clanging and noise of a construction site. In one spot, the corridor had a sort of balcony, and so I went out onto it: way down deep, they were building a New Bajina Bašta, a faithful copy of the one through which we entered the first circle of the Asylum. Everything was in its place: every street, every tree, every hole in the road . . . "That's how it will look," I thought, "one day, and that day is close, judging by all things, the Librarians will just pull a switch and

Nenad Žilić, Untitled, oil on canvas

we will all find ourselves down there and have no idea that a change has occurred." It dawned on me that the Librarians were on the threshold of their greatest undertaking: the construction of a copy of the entire World with each of its details, but the World turned upside down.

At that moment, somebody laid a hand on my shoulder and I cried out in fear.

"Hush!" Meier said. "Just as the readers can hear you but not see you as well, **they** can hear you, but not see you.[13] You've stared at stuff enough. We have work to do."

"Why didn't you tell me that we're in the third dimension of dreams?"

"You had to figure it out for yourself. If I had told you, you would be thinking about that, and we would get nothing done.

"We might even have been exposed to danger as well. The

---

13 Probably an intervention by the falsifiers. It is supposed to say: "they can see you but not hear you as well."

passage from the first to the second to the third dimension of dreams is not sensed. That comes from the fact that we exclusively notice ephemeral phenomena while the essence of events, though the easiest to notice, escapes our attention."

I felt profoundly disturbed.

"I had no idea how far the construction of the Grand Insane Asylum had progressed," I said.

"I don't understand why in the world you were chosen for the order of the Little Brothers. This is not the present, this is the future; you wrote so much about how dreams are timeless, how it is possible to reach the beginning and end of the world in them, and you didn't even realize that we are in the future. To be fair, that hasn't been the distant future for a long time. That's why you are here, in fact. To gather material for the novel. So that you could describe and possibly frighten some of the chosen, if there are any more such people."

"Why are you such a pessimist?"

Nenad Žilić, Untitled, oil on canvas

"Because I'm dead!"

I almost woke up.

Just then we arrived at the last painting in the exhibition. "Your friend has an interesting painting style," Ernest said. "That's what people actually look like. Like cockroaches blown apart by a small explosion. And that's also how rotten they are. They're all faggots, including women and even small children. Demons, if they're not better, at least they are more polite and cultivated. Just look around you: there's a guy going to meet his dear-faggot on a date with a bouquet of roses, and another guy is timing his misfortune. He stops to drink a beer, he's a little bit late and—boom—the lover turns into something that looks like Žilić's canvas. He becomes two-dimensional. What can the dear-faggot do? Complain? No. True, there will be tears as needed, but what do tears mean, every day he also pisses but no one is surprised by that. Why does grief for the disappearance of a dear person not get expressed by pissing? At least that would be for life. The only thing a man is consistent in from birth to the grave—that is pissing.

"And now, my friend, leave all this dream business behind, go rob a bank, flee to Brazil or Paraguay, surround yourself with beautiful young chicks (making sure that they're not faggots in disguise), read comic books, and drink Black & White."[14]

Ernest unbuttoned a couple of buttons on his plaid vest and gave me a rather thick file folder. It was faded, tattered around the edges. Who knows how many years he had carried it.

"Here you have several manuscripts that can be used for

---

14 During the final proofreading of the pages of the novel, it turned out that part of the text, starting with my supposed question to Meier (about why he is such a pessimist) up until ". . . read comic books, and drink Black & White", had been inserted later, obviously by one of the followers of the Librarians. In our hurry (the novel had to go to the printers) there was no chance to peruse the entire text, and this it is not to be excluded that there are more of these falsified passages in the novel. (Editor's note)

the novel. It's up to you to find translators and to fix up the text stylistically."

"Ah," I said, "so many times I dreamed that I was writing and I would always, when I awoke, forget what I had written. I don't believe that I will remember this time either."

"There will be no need for you to remember. I told you already that this is **the third dimension of dreams**. If you're careful and concentrate in **the second dimension**, the boundary lands, you will bring these manuscripts into reality. Now, I've got to go . . ."

"Aren't you going to show me how to get out?"

"I'm sorry, but that's impossible."

"Why?"

"Because I'm dead! I can't return to reality anymore."

"That means that you're actually Ernest Meier, the one who went to Dharamsala, who knew Kowalsky . . ."

"Of course, that bullshit about the duplicates of important people among the Evangelical Bicyclists is just the Librarians' mystification. Go now. You'll find the way, if you don't look for it, of course."

I set off at random. I turned right, then right again. I quickly realized that I had reached the cellar of my apartment building. Hardly dragging my feet, I climbed the stairs to my apartment, opened the door and saw the agents of the Secret Police looking through the contents of my desk drawer. I remembered what Ernest told me: "They can hear you, but not see you as well." So, I tiptoed through the door for the astral body,[15] entered the room, sat on the edge of the bed, sighed, and thought: "Thank God, this

---

15 Doors and windows, since they are voids, empty spaces, necessarily have their twins so that they can exist in the first place. Just as a physical body enters and exits through the empty space of the door, so does the astral body pass through the substance of the twin, which is located on the right side, just next to the opening and it is of the same size. Astral bodies and their spiritual beings can also pass through a wall, but then there is a danger that they will be imprisoned, which actually happens to many inexperienced ghosts. From those imprisoned ghosts come all those mysterious nocturnal poppings and scratchings in the walls of old houses.

too has come to an end." I wanted to take my clothes off and go to bed—I put the folder on the nightstand—and then it occurred to me that it was a trick, that the Librarians wanted to deceive me and keep the manuscripts from appearing in reality. Quickly I grabbed the folder, sat back down on the edge of the bed, and waited. The night dragged on. Just before dawn I was already starting to dream the usual nonsense, followed by the face of an unknown woman, my anima, standing beside the bank of a river. Then I woke up. I looked at the clock. It was midnight. I might have slept an hour, two at most . . .

With both hands I was tightly clutching to my chest the faded folder that Ernest had given me.

THE FILE FOLDER
SMUGGLED
IN FROM DREAMS

JUST A FEW comments on the texts in the folder.

In the middle of 1936, a pamphlet entitled "The Devil's Epistle to the Great Whore of Belgrade" was circulating in Belgrade. In the prewar uproar and the general lethargy and hedonism (common, among other things, just before great disasters), hardly anyone paid any attention to the plain-looking flier. The few who read it thought it was some kind of **joke**. The only ones who took it seriously were certain esoteric circles and the communists. The latter because, in "the class of the deceived," they recognized themselves in the interpretation of the Secret Police. The underground survivors of that period say in their remembrances that, at meetings of the Party cells, the pamphlet was considered to be a typical bourgeois fraud. The few esotericists, however, thought the pamphlet was a metaphorical announcement of the coming Anti-Christ's arrival, and they took it quite seriously.

An examination done by the prominent Parisian Satanologist, Gerard Levi-Marten, maintained that the authenticity of the pamphlet was not to be excluded, but if it was not authentic then it was written by a well-versed Satanist, since the Secret Police (or some sort of evil-doer) could not have known that the signature at the bottom of the pamphlet—X—meant nothing less than: "whoever signs his name with an X": ABRAXAS.

The same Gerard Levi-Marten claims that today there are only two original copies of the pamphlet, and that one is preserved in the Comintern Archive, the other in hell.

The "Auto-da-fé of Joseph Vissarionovich," supposedly the post-mortem confession of Stalin, is a photocopy made in the library of the Great Orient Masonic Lodge in Paris, and thus its authenticity is not guaranteed. The interview with J. Kowalsky, given to a correspondent from *Time* magazine, is an original document. Its publication was prevented by the American Masons.

Through the kindness of the author himself, we received the

short story that is one chapter of Umberto Eco's larger fiction (which will not be published) in which a cleaned up version of Meister Eckhart's story appears in an indirect way (the **remake** of which you wrote in **Phenomena**).

At the end, here is also the continuation of the story by Sava Djakonov, "Pilgrimage to Dharamsala," whose counterfeit version you published in "Phenomena," with the addition of Borges's striking introduction. The true version, carefully preserved in the **Archive of the Third Dimension of Dreams**, is of great significance for understanding the novel.

The few pages of the book, *The Three Dimensions of Dreaming*, by our old friend Klosowsky, were a huge problem to obtain. Just a few days after the book came out in print, Claus von Klosowsky withdrew (who knows for what reason) the entire print run from the bookstores and destroyed it or hid it. As far as we know, four copies were sold. One of the purchasers was Alfred Rosenberg, later an ideologue of Nazism. These few singed pages found here belonged to that copy and were irreparably damaged during the bombing of Berlin.

Who the other three buyers were has never been discovered. We suppose it was the libraries of the Vatican and Comintern. It is not to be excluded (moreover, it's highly likely) that one of the copies was bought by the Masonic Lodge of Buenos Aires, and that later, in the sixties, using the knowledge of von Klosowsky, Carlos Castaneda composed a series of books, ostensibly anthropological, in which he describes Klosowsky's travels in the third dimension of dreams, combined with the magic of the Mexican indios, presented as his own research. Those books aroused enormous interest, especially among the young, and they had a great subversive influence in the sense that they strove for a negative spirituality.

However, for the novel it is most important that von Klosowsky actually appears in it without our approval; the last sentence of the passage unambiguously testifies to the fact that he was stalking us (or is stalking us) while we were looking at the paintings of Nenad Žilić. The fact that he is long since dead can cause doubt only among the most naïve.

THE DEVIL'S EPISTLE TO THE GREAT WHORE OF BELGRADE

OH, MADAM, WHO represents me in the damnable town at the confluence of the Rivers Sava and Ister,

I command you to summon all the devils and evil spirits, demons and household sprites, the knights of the secret doors of the East, the knights of the great construction, the knights of the Pharaonic pyramids, witches, warlocks and wizards, gamblers, whores and debauchers and all those who bow down to me and kiss my ass on the Sabbath.

Say to them:

Thus speaks the One whose throne is in the north:

God has turned his back on this land. But that does not mean that our time has come. Behold, a new class of the deceitful is on the move, new men are coming who have broken their contract with God and with me. They will not even hear of me, the father of all schismatics, the protector of rebels and plotters.

They believe that they came into being because apes became people through long-suffering labor. They fantasize that millions of years went by so that they could appear. What kind of times are these? Sodom and Gomorrah were razed to the ground for far less evil deeds. Does a higher devil exist, of which I know not, who is plotting behind my back? Or is that just one more of the evil deeds God is doing to me?

Because as soon as they stop believing in him, they also stop believing in me. They think that we are all superstition! They lie even more than we do, and we are powerless.

How many souls have been sold in the last three years? Eighteen. It's shameful! How many followers have left our lodges during that same time? Four hundred twenty-nine. Even worse. Those simpletons, those earthworms, are convinced that apes strove to perfect themselves over thousands of generations, yeah right, that these monsters would appear—they are usurping my following. O tempora, o mores!

You reported to me that they are offering more. What are they offering, I asked you, and you held: that they can do whatever they want. Don't I offer the same? Yes, earthly goods, power, fame, the opportunity to commit evil deeds. But, you maintain, they don't want to give anything in return. They have pulled out of the world order, killed emperors, kings, and princesses. They betray each other, kill each other, and do all sorts of villainy.

Announce the *urbi et orbi*. To all my servants:

Go wherever your eyes lead you. Attack the few remaining hermits. Do what you will. Their blood is on their heads. You have nothing else to seek here. The few elect will be saved whether we like it or not; the rest are far too damned even for my taste. They break the rules of fair play that God established and which we all have to respect, as it is in heaven, so it is for us down here.

But, lo, the day is coming when their rage will reach its end and when they will long for the comfort of my hell. I can see ahead and behind and I know that—instead of the thing they intend to construct—they will build a hell for themselves, the Grand Insane Asylum in which they will torture themselves, world without end.

Quod dixi dixi.

X

René Guénon
THE POVERTY OF
ESOTERICISM

STRICTLY TAKEN, WHEN we speak of secret societies, we certainly do not mean any of the numerous "rose cross" and para-magical collectives which, as a faithful witness to the decline of spirituality, are sprouting up every day, striving for primacy and laying exclusive claim to the preservation of unbroken traditions. We would not be mistaken if we subsume all of those phenomena under a single descriptor, **charlatanry, fraud, and dilettantism**; a truly secret society must include complete anonymity outside the (most often close inner) circle directly dedicated to the secret.

Truth be told, we cannot deny the existence of a mystical European brotherhood whose spirituality is certainly not authentically European, but is rather the heir of the Near Eastern tradition. Likewise, the exceptional influence of that brotherhood on events in the profane world is undeniable, but because of the unavailability of any relevant facts, we must be satisfied with an exhaustive analysis of **what that brotherhood is not**, and not with speculation about what it really is or what it might be.

As a starting point in the search for the truth of esotericism, for the lack of anything better, we must turn to its falsification—the aforementioned "heirs" to the traditions of the Templars, Rosicrucians, and Druids. Doubtless, in earlier periods those were ways of gathering true esotericists, yet with the passing of time (the corrosive nature of which inevitably leads to divestment) sooner or later the danger of infiltration by profane elements appears, from which the Grand Masters defended themselves by means of a, at first glance, defensive tactic: they would throw the doors wide open to the onslaught of curiosity-seekers enchanted with insubstantial rituals void of content, and have the core of spirituality transformed into a higher form of organization, sufficiently concealed from the public that it could carry out its this-worldly mission unhindered. Therefore, it is a huge (and dangerous) mistake to pay homage to one of the "public secret societies," and especially to take seriously their ostensible profundity or the supernatural powers of their members. After all is said and done, since man is not just a natural being, with a clear conscience we can say that every man is supernaturally gifted. In any case, it is better to leave those potentials untouched, in their latent state, rather than to boast that a high level of initiation has been achieved because this or that "magus" can communicate with some sort of guru in India. Measured by such a criterion, the everyday telephone is an adept of a higher degree, because it also has similar abilities. Moreover, the telephone is magic *sui generis*, to one who does not know about ritual actions, dialing a number is completely useless. But magic that becomes everyday soon ceases to be considered magic, which surely does not mean that its negative influences are thereby eliminated.

Therefore, with a definite degree of certainty we can claim that the Secret Society (we will call it thus for the lack of a better name) quite painstakingly avoids all manifestations of paranormal phenomena, and that its membership consists mainly of people who we would describe in everyday life as "quite average and non-descript." Especially absurd are the claims that some sort of esoteric texts exist, and every such text, without a single doubt, is nothing more than a falsification. Because genuine esotericism always has to do with a higher, unchangeable sphere of mental emanations, while writing is just a weak link with the traditions of the past, in any case of dubious credibility. Insofar as they do influence reality, which they definitely do, esotericists make use of subtle methods and exercise that influence by means of seemingly profane media: works of art, printing, and film. [It would not be amiss if we digress here and note the rigidity with which the so-called totalitarian regimes (in fact, the organized powers of solidification) cope with literary and artist works whose content exceeds the strictly regulated canon and which deal with topics outside of the mediated, subhuman state of material existence.]

Numerous serious researchers point out that, unable to **stop** the influx of raw materialism (and the subsuming of the masses under the authority of idols), the Secret Society sets, at first glance, an absurd goal for itself: the acceleration of the process of destruction. Such a conclusion arises from the knowledge that the rather advanced degree of entropy and nihilization of the world does not favor the primary powers' distancing themselves from the idea of the Center, so for the purpose of catalyzation, they willy-nilly organize counteractions masked in the form of a variety of ecological movements, so that we can say with a clear conscience that, out of those "landfill" utopias, the fascism of the 22nd century will come into being, if there ever is a 22nd century.

For that purpose, the Annihilation Centers support all sorts of human gathering, as long as that is not gathering around the Savior, or at least not around the idea of a transcendental God. The feeling of insecurity, so characteristic of this era, is neither an obsession nor paranoia; man **is** endangered, but that endangerment is ontological, internal; its causes are certainly not in the world of objects, where they are most often sought (and found), to the detriment of all.

Therefore, if the Secret Society's principle of action has to be defined, then the most adequate expression would be WU WEI, the Taoist principle of non-action, certainly not literally understood as the complete turn to the self, or to absolute introjection, but non-action in the sense of non-participation in phenomena which the illusion industry produces. Or, perhaps this is a more suitable expression: giving up on any kind of organized action, the goal of which is to improve the existing state of things.

Giving signals through art that it exists, the secretive members of the Brotherhood ever and anew skillfully avoid the traps of profanation, withdrawing ever deeper into passivity, and allowing the spirit to . . .

(the rest of the text is missing)

Translated from the French by *Milojko Knežević* [16]

---

16 The text "The Poverty of Esotericism" is written as a special chapter in the book *The Crisis of the Modern World*. For some unknown reason, it was not placed in either the first or second editions of the book. Likewise, we do not know whether it was left unfinished or if the missing part of it was later destroyed. (M.K.)

Claus von Klosowsky
THE THREE DIMENSIONS OF DREAMING
(fragments)

(. . .)

ALREADY DURING THE second phase of my research of dreams
I came to the conclusion that Freud's theory is completely un-
tenable, incorrect, and possibly even harmful. Namely, as to
what Dr. Freud considered to be the significant content and
symbolism of dreams, after studying medieval manuscripts, I
established that it was peripheral, confusing, capable only of
misleading, certainly not indicating a clear path to analysis. It
is almost as if we would expose the expansive settlements of
Pericles's Athens to study, ignoring the Acropolis and Pantheon.
Because that phase, I would more like to call it *dimension* of
dreams, strictly speaking, is not a dream in a true sense but only
its surface, a warped mirror which reflects the muddled contours
of the deeper layers. So, Dr. Freud, following his "empirical"
method, found himself in the position of those people in Plato's
cave, staring at shadows on the wall.

In a letter sent to Freud, I laid out the results of my research
which, in truth, were in the early phase, and the respectable
doctor called them, with carefully chosen words, poetic and
fantastic adventures in imagination, useless for even the least
serious clinical work. That was where our correspondence came
to an end. Though a bit shaken by the dubiousness expressed
by his authority, I didn't doubt that I was going in the right
direction even for a moment. I went on with my experiments. In
order to reduce the influence of external events to a minimum,
I avoided going out, and I stopped receiving guests altogether.
The hypothesis, supported by the text of a little-known sect from
the Middle Ages according to which what laymen call "a dream"

is only the gate for entering the deeper (they called it "higher") regions of dreaming, attracted me irresistibly and gave me the strength to not give up.

Briefly stated, the thesis of the *Purgatorium somni* (written in horribly broken Latin) claims the following:

A man who is in a waking state would not be able to stand it long; he would soon wear himself out and die. (This is also known from clinical practice.) Now, God, they say, for that reason gave us sleep so that people can renew their spiritual (and thereby physical) strength. But since very few people can stand the crossing from the physical world into the spiritual one, he set it up so that this takes place by removing consciousness, temporal-spatial prejudices, and logical sequences. And this, again, they justified with the impossibility for a living man to see God and not die, quoting Exodus (33:18): "And he said, I beseech thee, shew me thy glory. And he said, I will make all my goodness pass before thee, and I will proclaim the name of the Lord before thee, and will be gracious to whom I will be gracious, and will shew mercy on whom I will shew mercy. And he said, Thou canst not see my face: for there shall no man see me, and live. And the Lord said, Behold, there is a place by me, and thou shalt stand upon a rock: and it shall come to pass, while my glory passeth by, that I will put thee in a cleft of the rock, and will cover thee with my hand while I pass by: And I will take away mine hand, and thou shalt see my back parts: but my face shall not be seen."

Understandably, the anonymous writer (or several of them) of that text did not think that the dream is the departure to see the glory of God; all the same, they believed that the average human being cannot (at least not without harsh consequences) pass through the "gate" and confront the world of higher reality. But they did believe that specially gifted and trained adepts could pass through the "gate," which is protected by the most terrifying phantasms (the second dimension of dreams, of which we only see the reflections in the mirror of the first) and rush headlong into the astral world of the third dimension of dreams.

The unclear, allegorical, and furthermore awkward style of the text made it impossible for me in my efforts to uncover the techniques by which adepts mastered the passage through the "gate." I had to depend on my intuition and my own strength. Soon I realized that I must first become disciplined in reality. I composed an exceptionally precise daily schedule that I followed down to the last detail. I thought: a man who cannot master himself in the conscious world, in normal situations, will hardly be able to deal with things in completely uncertain and unknown places. Later, I was convinced that I was completely right. In one passage from Meister Eckhart, which I was reading in those days, I came across an idea, formulated approximately like this: "If anyone wants to be like God, then he must be ready to bear all difficulties (anyway, the most efficient way of getting all the difficulties off your back is to simply bear them) and become impervious to everything happening around him." That's what I did.

Later I moved on to experimentation with the first dimension of dreams. Namely, I had to not allow the variety of the contents of my dreams to distract me, dull me, and then unconsciously take me to the place I intended to go completely conscious. That variety is nothing other than a means of hypnosis. In that vein, I began to plan my dreams. For example: this evening I will dream that in the evening I am walking along Lake Geneva carrying Goethe's *Faust*. I will stop by a bench where I usually sit, and open it to page 137 and begin to read.

At the beginning it wasn't easy. I needed a lot of suggestions so that I could start dreaming at all about the given topic. But one night, I dreamed that I was walking along Lake Geneva. I tried to focus just on my steps, paying no attention to the phantoms who passed by me on the left and right. That first night I reached the bench, and then I saw an unfamiliar woman next to the water and then it all melted into the most profane of dreams.

After three full months of practice, I arrived at the place where I sat down and opened the book. In order to read a particular page (the identicalness of the text in reality and in dreams confirmed my belief that I was on the right path), it took me six more months. Soon I completely mastered the techniques of dreaming; I could dream whatever I wanted, but I simply had no luck reaching my one true goal: to pass on to the third dimension of dreams. Finally, almost completely discouraged (I was already intending to throw in the towel), I accidentally came across an article by Dr. Freud on the ephemeral case of one of his patients, a certain Ernest M.

It happens that people with opposing opinions accidentally help one another. That is what happened to me. In laying out the case history of Ernest M., Freud states in one place that the patient believed he belonged to a sect ". . . whose followers gather in dreams." In Meier's notebook, verses were found—Freud believed they were made up—the initiation poem of the abovementioned sect. I offer here a copy of them:

When you fall asleep, die
To this world. Then arise from your corpse and go
Straight ahead regardless of the ghosts.
Know that those unfortunate beings exist only
When they trick you into believing that you exist, too.
Withstand, you must, the burden of death.
In your dreams it is always
Good to know that you are not you, and that you are far
From yourself. Neglected because you turned your attention
To the specters in hell. Do not connect yourself,
Either through pain or joy, to the illusions of reality
So that you also will not exist as they do.

Those two verses were fragments of the text of **Purgatorium**

somni, actually those which (among others) were missing from the damaged parchment. They were not difficult to decipher. "When you fall asleep, die to this world"—the key line—concealed the basic reason for my errors; thinking that it was enough to master the first dimension of dreams, I expected that things would develop further on their own. But in that first dimension, the relationships and logic of reality are still true, in fact slightly twisted, but still quite strong.

I needed to, that meant, fall asleep again in the first dimension.

Then arise from your corpse and go
Straight ahead regardless of the ghosts.

The two lines quoted revealed the nature of passing from the first dimension into the second. Arise from your corpse— in esotericism that means set off on an astral journey; in the secret tradition, like in alchemy, the corpse is a synonym for the unrefined physical body. The warning that one should pay no attention to the ghosts and illusions is related to the preparation for the encounter with creepy, semi-existing creatures, so called "guards of the threshold"; those monsters stop the uninitiated from entering the astral expanses where the dissolution of their beings would be fatal. Some of them were described by the adepts of black magic, Eliphas Levi and Aleister Crowley.

Know that those unfortunate beings exist only
When they trick you into believing that you exist, too.

These lines are related to the nature of the abovementioned creatures; they are, namely, basal projections of the repressed content of the psyche. But it would be ultimately wrong to view them as "illusions"; they really **are** full of enmity. All reactions related to one's biography, logic, and emotions in this **world** that come about in ultimate panic, make them even more real than the adept in those "places," so in the literature there are cases noted where the monsters coming about from the imagination of the adept managed to tear him to pieces.

Withstand, you must, the burden of death.

This verse is commonplace among initiation cults, starting from shamanism all the way to western magic. The same is also true of the second verse. The basis was this: fall asleep, then fall asleep once again—in your dream. I had the roadmap, but I needed a lot more practice. In my well-practiced oneiric milieu, there on the bench beside Lake Geneva, every night I tried, already asleep, to fall asleep once more. Without success. At one moment, a simple idea crossed my mind—*saneta simplicitas*—if I wanted to fall asleep twice—I needed to be really tired.

Thus, I began to wear myself out by sleep deprivation and hard physical labor. And it worked. One night, I fell asleep dead tired, hardly managed to drag myself to the bench on the shore, sat down, opened *Faust* to page 137 as was my custom, began to read and then imperceptibly sank into sleep. If that can be called sleep. Suddenly everything came rushing at me in some sort of spiraling abyss driven by an indescribable chaos. Already at the very start I was afraid, but I knew that I dared not resist at that moment. All at once, from all sides, monsters like those from Bosch's paintings descended upon me (Hieronymus must have had a similar oneiric experience), pinching and biting me (during which I felt completely **real** pain). "Go straight ahead regardless of the ghosts"—I repeated it like a mantra; I felt horrible fear (who would not), but I also knew that I could not give into it, no matter how long the nightmare lasted.

And then I found myself in the third dimension of dreams.

During my later experiments, I systematized my experience from the second, most dangerous dimension. First, no one without solid intentions should dare to set off on the adventure of entering that zone of horror. I managed because I threw the dice and gambled everything to reach the third dimension. That was the only thing that helped me to get past the horrors. Mantras and incantations are of no help here.

The second dimension of dreams is composed of seven spheres.

The first sphere is filled with the repressed contents of the soul of the person entering it. The creatures are the formative personifications of the vices and sins of the dreamer himself. As we already mentioned, as fear rises, the very existence of those revenants increases proportionally, and they do everything possible in order to completely frighten and enslave you, if one can say it like that, to take authority over you even after waking.

The second sphere is inhabited by the ghosts of the dead. Since they no longer have their own soul, and yet they survive in that world, it is understandable that they go after the dreamer with even greater passion and malice; that is actually how they feed themselves, and that is what maintains them in that aberrant semi-existence.

The third sphere is that of illusory bliss (this is forewarned by the line: ***Do not connect yourself, either through pain or joy, to the illusions***). The superstitious expose themselves to the danger of remaining forever in that sphere, at first enjoying indescribable satisfaction, but quickly turning into revenants even more ominous than those in the first two.

The fourth sphere is actually the sphere of those who were deceived in the previous one. Feeling enormous pleasures, with the possibility of "experiencing" them again, these specters are even more enraged, cruel, and malicious than the preceding ones.

The fifth sphere is inhabited by the astral bodies of those people who did not believe in the afterlife. One would expect that they would not be so terrifying, but that is a mortal mistake for those who believe in man. Liberated from all moral principles, fear of the law and punishments, those spirits are the most nefarious of all those hitherto. (Ultimately, are not all the preceding just forms of the refuse of human evil?) Those spirits appear at spiritualistic séances and sow confusion, increasing the chaos on Earth.

The sixth sphere, like the seventh, is filled with fallen angels and the souls of the great sinners. Paradoxically, it is relatively easy to pass through it (they are more interested in the souls of the dead); when those barriers are overcome, nothing stands in the way of passing into the third dimension of dreams.

***

What can I say about the third dimension of dreams? Words are completely useless. In my opinion, it is not a dream at all (it is a dream only for us) but is rather the Earth before the fall of man. Spatial-temporal relations do not exist. Roughly speaking: it is always **now** and always **there** where the dreamer wants to be. On one of those "journeys" I met Meister Eckhart. I knew that it was him; in the third dimension of dreams, everything is crystal clear because nothing is concealed. All things are transparent and they only represent what they truly are. I remember that Meister Eckhart warned me not to profane anything that I saw by publishing books or articles. But how could I deny the human race the knowledge that one of their members had seen the dream of King Nebuchadnezzar, the dream of King Herod, all the famous dreams, dreams from the beginning of the world as they continuously unwind as if on an endless tape in one of the regions of the third dimension of dreams. I knew that I had to write a book, even if it exposed me to the mockery of a nauseating type of scientists.

During one of those "journeys," wandering "here" and "there," I found myself inside of a strange building, in a labyrinth of endless corridors. Driven "by curiosity," I was walking along (the whole time having the strange feeling that I was part of some sort of text), and then in one of the hallways I saw two men standing in front of a painting of large format. One was old, really old. The other was middle-aged. A part of their conversation reached me:

"Hush!" said the older man. "Just as the readers can hear you but not see you as well, **they** can see you, but not hear you as well. You've stared at stuff long enough. We have work to do."

"Why didn't you tell me that we're in the third dimension of dreams?"

"You had to figure it out for yourself. If I had told you, you would be thinking about that, and we would get nothing done. We might even have been exposed to danger as well. The passage from the first to the second to the third dimension of dreams is not sensed. That comes from the fact that we exclusively notice ephemeral phenomena while the essence of events, though the easiest to notice, escapes our attention."

That was my first encounter with other human beings in the third dimension of dreams. I realized that they were obviously an adept and his disciple. In that sen . . .

(At this spot, the page had been singed. The rest was missing.)

THE AUTO-DA-FÉ
OF JOSEPH VISSARIONOVICH

SO, MY TIME has drawn nigh. On Spasskaya Tower, midnight
rings out. What does that mean? It means that the whores of the
Politbureau have prepared the poison. For years in the Kremlin's
dark corners, they've been colluding about how to knock me off.
For that purpose, they've come up with a special language composed of winks, finger movements, throat clearing, farting, and
burping, and I don't know what all else. A non-human language.
In my language, Russian, they didn't dare to squeak about me
even in their dreams. Vigilant guards from far away, the men
of my friend, the Great Knight of the Door to the East, Joseph
Kowalsky, carefully controlled those wretched dreams, bringing
me written reports, so that I knew what everyone was thinking
and dreaming about me at every moment. But more on that
later. Now, they've finally gathered their courage into a pitiful
pile of rags, and that is supposed to be the stake for Joseph
Vissarionovich. They've even come up with a communique for
the domestic and public audience. Supposedly, I died from a
stroke. They will skillfully slip me some poison, I will die, with
a smile on my face (which they will later describe as "sneering"),
knowing that I once again tricked the cretins, because I would
have died that day anyway. That is my destiny. And what follows
from that. What follows from that is that even when they lie,
liars serve the truth; the truth cannot be outwitted. Only those

who attempt such things, bring misfortune on themselves.

Then, why am I writing this confession in invisible ink, and also on invisible paper, simulating the letters of the Georgian alphabet with my hand movements? I have no intention of negating all of the previous, sycophantic and future, supposedly critical, biographies about my life. For example, that I cut the hours short. I am drawing the bottom line on my life. Like all other Bicyclists as well, my life has taken a completely different direction than the one I wanted. I studied hard at the Seminary in Tbilisi; at night, I knelt in the pathetic room of the dormitory and called upon the name of God all night. I wanted to go out among the Yakuts, Tungusic, and Chuvash peoples, to shed the true light of faith on the Siberian nomads. Then, one night—the room filled with light and an angel appeared before me. "Joseph!" he cried. "I'm right here," I said. And the angel went, "Leave the Seminary, study Marx thoroughly, and join the communists." Then the light vanished and I was left confused, thinking that I had been tempted by the Devil. A few days later, in the middle of the night, the same angel burst into my room. This time with a whip. A scourge of light, of course. Then he gave my ass a good beating. Eh, then I was convinced. Whoever God loves, that's the one God screws. The ways of the Lord are mysterious. Did he not order Hosea, "Go, take unto thee a wife of whoredoms and children of whoredoms: for the land hath committed great whoredom, departing from the Lord."

Soso,[17] I told myself, if Hosea could do it, so can you. And so I did. I was fighting at demonstrations, writing all sorts of articles (and poems, I swear), skirmishing with the police, just waiting for that angel to return and tell me what to do. Only in exile, in Siberia, did I have the opportunity for that. Every night, as soon as I would go to sleep, some people showed up and patiently held classes for me. They brought me into a state where I believed them unconditionally (which I myself would

---

17 Stalin's childhood nickname.

later demand of my collaborators). They told me the day was coming when the heathen would rule over the Third Rome and grow strong, threatening to conquer the whole world and erase the name of God, and then to hand the whole thing over to the Devil just like that. "You have been chosen to prevent that," two of them whispered in each ear, simultaneously. "To undermine that whole demonic affair from the inside."

I was prepared to do anything, but I didn't know how. How could I oppose millions, the "masses," as I was so fond of saying later, nicely and hypocritically. "Just do your job, and don't think too much," they told me. So, that's what I did. The heathens, to be honest, never act in their own interest. In the end, they always end up harming themselves, as will be seen. Little by little, and here came the revolution. If only you could have seen the radiant faces of the bums, whores, derelicts, swindlers, and imposters shouting, "Long live *tovarich* Lenin, long may he live, long may he live." They were already hoping: here it comes, the land of Cockaigne, we'll eat, we'll drink, we'll get laid. They all rushed wildly about, breaking, burning, killing, desecrating churches, in order to clear the place out as quickly as possible, in order to immediately clear a path to the Garden of Earthly Delights. But I could already see them in a couple of years, dropping dead of hunger, and a few years after that toiling in the camps, eating runny borscht and crusts of bread. And I smiled with a "sneer." I suppose that since then that smile has remained, which will attract so much attention from the hacks, the disappointed generals of the white guard, all the way down to my greatest devotee, later a liberal democrat, Milovan Đilas from some sort of Neverland called Montenegro.

Vsjotaki,[18] I thought. Sooner or later my time will come, and I will—like King Charles the Hideous did four or five centuries ago—raise my enormous country into the heavens, with the help

---

18 Whatever. (Russian.)

of God. God thought otherwise. What can be done? If Charles didn't manage with his 429 hectares, five or six churches, one monastery, and a few thousand souls, how could it be expected of me to elevate a sixth of the Earth's land mass, with all those steel mills and wide open Slavic souls? And then they killed the emperor and his family. The idiots. They didn't even realize that they were cutting the branch they were sitting on, committing an unforgivable sin by disturbing the Divine hierarchy; how in the world could those phantoms who drown themselves in vodka, munching on pickles and smoking burdock root even dream that if you kill the emperor, you cut off all communication with God. It's not important what kind of emperor he is, good or bad, a drunk or a nobody, he is the means of communication; if you remove him, the machine doesn't work and that's it.

Anyway, when the idea of raising Russia went bad, one night in my dreams I saw the Glory of God in a cloud, and the Lord spoke. "Listen, Joseph," he said, "Don't overdo it. Man is not allowed to do the work of the Lord. Come to your senses." I woke up bathed in sweat. I realized I'd gone too far, that God had other plans. And absolutely rightly so. What can be done with the expansive mass of wretches and horrible sinners? It should be done differently: turn all Russia into an enormous monastery with me at the head as hegumen, and make the rest of the Orthodox countries into small churches and give them over to repentance. This could not happen with rhetoric, argumentation, and sermons. No. But, if they wanted it easy, they'd have to do it the hard way; didn't the ancient Romans, or some other ancients, give us that wonderful thought: "Fortune leads the intelligent, it drags the stupid behind." How profound and simple that is at the same time. Well, now, who can they blame if they turned their back on God, becoming deluded with earthly idols and goods. Nu, harasho. If you want steel mills, you'll have steel mills; if you want cheap cafeterias, you'll get them. If you want a collective life—you'll have it, but according to my typicon, strict, Caucasian, cruel, I mean, one should use strong medicine when the illness is bad, as St. John Climacus would say.

But it will not go so simply. How to approach comrade Lenin with a proposal full of mysticism and theology? How to approach Bukharin, whom Marxism has so badly disturbed in his mind, that in the end his brain was placed backwards, the cerebellum in front, the telencephalon in the back, which was established during the autopsy and for which there is exact documentation. I had to act wisely. Byzantine. Marxist. *Kanyeshna*,[19] I had to learn Marxism in detail because that is an ideology which is unusually suitable for eliminating one's opponents. I couldn't, after all, call upon the Holy Trinity to remove the Devil's emissaries from the Kremlin. Like this: so-and-so has left the path (which is true, we have all left the path), he betrayed the people (also true: they have all betrayed the people), investigation, judgment, Lubjanka, *dasvidanya*! It was just necessary to let time unwind, no hurry, no panic, each one of them digs his own grave. It's true that Lenin wrote a note on his deathbed which sullied my name—he probably suspected something—but I understood that as a spicy detail from forthcoming history, thus as a completely unreliable thing, in any case unimportant. Speaking of spicy details, the fact that I threatened Nadezhda Krupskaya not to babble nonsense because I would have her replaced, that I would take away her rank as Lenin's widow and give my blessing to another, at least that wouldn't be difficult: it's a little known fact, but Lenin had a full 370 women, all over Russia and the world. It's interesting *a propos* that Marxism produces strange changes in the brain—during Vladimir Ilich's autopsy it was established that his blood vessels had turned to stone. That's what materialism leads to, you see: in the end you turn into matter.

Sending Lenin to hell, it wasn't hard for me to get rid of the

19 Of course. (Russian.)

other little Lenins. Their blood on their own heads, they got what they asked for, they just followed the thread of their silly fate and I myself cried sincerely at their funerals. One never knows. "Judge not that ye be not judged" and "Vengeance is mine," thus sayeth the Lord. That's why Vyshinsky was the judge. Isn't that nice. Everyone had classes in religion, they should have taken the Bible seriously.

My mission also demanded knowledge of the Cabala. I was taught the basic things by J. Kowalsky while he was residing in Moscow, but later I went on by myself. As Kowalsky said, yes, just how many times did the Librarians rearrange the letters, just how many times did they shake up every word. One should have steady nerves to enter into that kind of adventure. And plenty of time. Eh, at least I did have time. What can one do, how can one fill the long Moscow nights except with esotericism? Already at eight o'clock the streets are empty. Hey, gentlemen, drunks and debauchers, now Russia is a monastery; no more nightclubs, champagne, striptease, cocaine, music halls . . . Sit in your hovels and wait till you remember why everything is so vacant and awful around you. Nothing is as good as an obvious lesson. You're down here, God's up there, me instead of an emperor, but that's not that, I was not born to be an emperor, and I don't conduct electricity well from the heavens to the Earth . . . That's like when the fuse blows and the circuit is made with wire. God pushed me in there out of pity, so that all the connections wouldn't be broken and so that you wouldn't be plunged into the worst backwater bumfuck nowhere, into hell, which is actually where you belong.

Not for long, those who visited me in my dreams brought me lists. Of those who needed to be saved. For them, I erected special camps. Fenced them off from the world, from vice, from religious delusion, and from temptation. I separated the males from the females. Work, fasting, work, fasting. Only the heavens knew how many sins I prevented. Liberty, liberty; egalité, fraternité! Even to the outskirts of Moscow comes the grumbling of liberals, faggots and lesbians from all parts of the New Europe. This fashionable thing did not pass by our steppes either. Everyone wants everything, right now. They want to take their fate into their own hands. *Pazhaluysta*,[20] I gave them all their rights, the hacks wrote an excellent constitution, everyone could make decisions, to be whatever they want, *kanyeshna*, on the surface: under the icing, God's laws and God's justice rule supreme, and they don't have to correspond at all to the human conception of justice. They didn't want God, they got me, scourge of God. If you won't be led, you will be driven. So, like this: I am here instead of God, the Archangel Gabriel is the head of the NKVD, and then comes a whole series of the hierarchy of cherubim, seraphim, thrones, rulers, and simple angels, and the entire organization serves to disobediently discipline the tribes and teach them a lesson.

People want to go to the West. All of this was cooked up by that mason, Peter Komandor,[21] whom the Russians shout praises for even though he put them through the wringer a hundred times worse than I ever did. Well, *nevozmozhno*.[22] Theirs is to sit where they are, in a state of latent religiosity and to wait for their five minutes. What is there in the West? Atheism, madness, the return to barbarianism, to a tribal, or even hereditary order, as Engels would say. All right, people there are of good stock, they know how to be moderate, but give the Russians complete freedom, the way they are, fond of the worst kind of overdoing things, and everything would go straight to hell even before Providence could respond. If I hadn't enforced iron discipline, I swear to God, the world would have blown to pieces as early as 1946. The vessel of sins is not bottomless; when it overflows, that will be the end of the world. Here, for example, Roj Medvedev

---

20 Please. (Russian.)
21 Peter the Great
22 No way! (Russian.)

and the other historians, what would have happened if I had
been born, by chance, in England? What? I would have been a
priest just as I planned to be here as well, but because of higher
interests I could not, rather I had to spend my whole life reading
nonsense and writing reports about Donetsk coal and Ukrainian
wheat. Come on, tell me, is it possible that one man can force
himself on dozens of millions of people? Or did those millions
simply, as always, unconsciously push the dictator out of themselves, not in order to subject themselves to discipline, but to be
able to torture one another and to manifest all of the vileness of
their stinking souls to the utmost. Pure psychoanalysis.

Not that I'm justifying myself. I am a criminal, but I'm the
one on Christ's right side of the cross, the one who repented.
Why should I care, after all, about the opinions of students
and feminists, sociologists and political scientists! What the hell
do they know? Just what has been published in *Pravda* and
the *Entsikopediya*. The principles of secret societies require that
real activity is concealed and in that way the profane world
is offered the illusion that quite the opposite is actually happening. Yeah, the extent to which esotericism flourished in the
cellars of the Kremlin, while up on top, on the face of the world
on which God had given up, museums of atheism were built.
That's how, one night, just for fun, I made a Golem of Nikita
Khrushchev. How we did laugh, I and my Georgian adepts, who
never appeared in the light of day, at the first awkward steps of
the future General Secretary of the Communist Party of the
USSR. At any moment I could have wiped the Aleph from his
forehead and Nikitushka would have disappeared into dust, but
I didn't. I left it up to the wind, rain, erosion, so that Nikita
will "live" a long time. Just to continue my work. The extensive works, which later generations of critics will proclaim to be
nonsensical, which—to be honest—seemed to be nonsensical to
me as well, but it is theirs to fit into the project about which not
even I myself know anything. Something related to, at that time

undeveloped, electronics or some other such whatnot.

Now, I see, they say that I'm to blame for the early failures in the war for the Fatherland. I suppose I was supposed to draw my sword and stand at the front of a unit and lead them into a charge. I could have with ease of mind. Then I was already more than aware that I would not die before 1953. But I had smarter things to do. Anyway, why should I care about war? Let them fight it out, led by marshals who got degrees from marshal school in the evenings. I'm supposed to get upset by the war adventures of a Viennese aquarellist? How eternal is human stupidity. Nothing here could have been sped up or slowed down, things run their course. No one can conquer Russia. That's just the way God set things up. I don't know if he was right, but you cannot stand in opposition to God. What's all the hubbub about? That's what I couldn't figure out. I was sitting there, reading Dostoyevsky, and someone or other from my entourage was talking with the marshals and ministers; they never dared to look up and doubt that I was in charge. They were afraid of me like the Devil fears the cross (and that would actually be a fairly adequate comparison). You could have pasted a moustache on a broom, they would have behaved themselves and made their insignificant reports. Not even imagining that I am right at the bottom of the hierarchy of the Evangelical Bicyclists. I could have gotten promoted, but I was drinking too much and that dulled my spiritual abilities. But how not to drink when surrounded by a crowd of monkeys who thought that life is a Party assignment, who lived and died standing at ease, or what's even worse—doing a march. In the end, I never liked people who don't drink. They have absolutely no sense of humor, especially dark humor. They're serious, full of themselves, and that's the most dangerous kind of all. I remember, on occasion, at the end of the war I was visited by some sort of delegation of Yugoslav partisans. Out of pure curiosity, just to see those good-for-nothings myself, I didn't send Bakanidze in my place, nor did I order that my life-size deputy-mannequin sit at the table. I showed up in person. I saw: they truly seriously understood the situation, just waiting for my imprimatur, so they could take the thousand-year reich of communism back to their ravines. Harasho, I thought. We sat down. Nu, comrades, eat, eat. Then I grabbed for two hundred deciliters of homemade vodka, and the servants filled everyone else's glasses. "Long live the Red Army," I toasted and drank it down. They drank it too, the poor chaps, I don't remember their names. A little later, again I make a toast, of course, with two hundred grams. I drank it down, so did they. Their eyes already glazed over, their tongues were thick. But it was just starting. I made a toast every few minutes, none of them had the guts to refuse. Well, deep into the night, just when I had warmed up, I cried, "Dear comrades, I want to see and hear the songs and dances of your peoples and nations, the members of the great international community of victors of the Soviet revolution." They started dancing, I swear, knocking over chairs, breaking glasses, making true merriment. I wouldn't be me if I didn't make some sort of mischief. "What the hell is this!" I roared like a tiger. Dead silence fell over the room, they froze, not even blinking. I threw them all out. I ordered the drivers not to take them back to the hotel, but to drive them around, each alone, to a different part of Moscow, way out in the suburbs. And I sent special men from the NKVD to shadow them and see what they did.

They say you should have seen how those generals stumbled around Moscow. One of them looked for his hotel for three days. Another almost froze to death in a park when he sat down to rest on a bench and fell asleep. Let them see who the boss is. And that roasted chickens don't fall from the sky, as they fantasized at meetings of their SKOJ, or whatever they call their Comsomol. After that, I made it possible for them to have a rich cultural-entertainment life. To forget the unpleasantness.[23]

23 The Yugoslav delegation left for Moscow on January 4, 1945, and it included the following members: Andrija Hebrang, Arso Jovanović, Mitra Mitrović – Đilas, Rade Hamović, Srećko Manola, Branko Ob-

radović and Gojko Nikoliš. In his memoirs "Korijen, stablo, paveti-na," general Nikoliš presents a somewhat different version of Joseph Vissarionovich's reception: "About two hours had already passed since dinner had begun, and then, without any reason, Stalin addressed these words to our delegation: "Vot, Đilas denigrated the Red Army!" Knowing what Stalin was referring to (he spoke of Đilas' complaint against some of the Red Army men's unseemly behavior toward our people, particularly women, in Serbia and Vojvodina) and being aware of Đilas' best intentions regarding that matter, all of us, except for Hebrang, stood up, gathered round Stalin and started proving to him how much all of us, Yugoslavs, even Đilas himself, loved and respected the Red Army. Therefore, Đilas' intervention was not to be interpret-ed as an insult, but as brotherly advice that would help avoid the repe-tition of the same mistakes, adding that our soldiers died shouting out the Red Army's and Stalin's names, and so on and so forth. Through-out our plea, Stalin was sitting calmly, tapping the table with his index finger and snickering, and, finally, once we'd all settled down a bit, he repeated: "Vsjotaki, Đilas denigrated the Red Army." Once more, a bouquet of our hands appeared around Stalin's head, another attempt at defense, but it was in vain: "Vsjotaki, Đilas denigrated the Red Army." Unable to affect Stalin's conviction, we plopped into chairs and continued to eat and drink. Then came another round of toasts and praises, after which Stalin, like a bolt from the blue, burst out: "Vot, Bulgarian army is better than Yugoslav army!" That was simply too much. It felt like being impaled through the guts. Again we in-stantly surrounded Stalin as our hands thrashed around his head. You could no longer tell who was saying what. "Indeed, comrade Stalin, they eat better food and wear better clothes than we do, but did you forget, comrade Stalin, that just yesterday those very soldiers served Hitler as reservists, that they occupied and committed crimes in our country, how can you compare us to them? Comrade Stalin!" Andrija Hebrang was the only silent one among us. Molotov and Bulganin were saying nothing, so we looked at them vainly seeking their sup-port. Comrade Stalin, who was still tapping the table with his index finger and snickering, said: "Vsjotaki, Bulgarian army is better than Yugoslav army." It is noted in my journal, four times did we jump out of our chairs, four times did we make a bouquet round Stalin, and four times did the cold wind of Stalin's 'vsjotaki' lash our naïve Yugoslav flowers. The flowers would rise and fade, then fade and rise again. Finally, when Stalin quietly uttered his inexorable 'vsjotaki' for the fifth time, Arso Jovanović lost his composure and burst into tears:

But in terms of the charge that I liquidated the flower of Russian literature, that's 90% a lie. I did indeed, following Plato's edified doctrine, rid the State of a few mimeticians. But most of them were sent to gulags or firing squads by their colleagues. And then, again, I sent the colleagues. As a punishment. If they betrayed their brother in the quill, the next thing you know they'll betray the fatherland, their mother, father . . . There's no end to betrayal.

Strictly speaking, you can pick up any passerby from Arbat Street and send him to do ten years in Kolyma, and you won't be wrong. There are no innocent people in this world. Especially not in Russia. I ruled with that principle, and afterward they accused me of being a paranoid, psychopathic monster. Make no mistake, that is all true. But what does that mean? That means that everyone else is also paranoid, a psychopath, a monster, but the slimy bastards do no dare to be that way in public, so they always have to place the blame on the shoulders of an idealist like me. Be it so, then. I don't give a rat's ass about the babblings of future historians who would, if I were alive, write elaborate odes to my personality. They are equally awful both when they criticize and when they praise. I am following the example of my idol, Charles the Hideous; I pay no attention to the diversity of the world . . .

(Remainder of the manuscript destroyed by moisture and completely illegible.)

"Comrade Stalin, don't you understand, how can you even, comrade, comrade...", when our leader Andrija spoke for the first time, but not to join our defense, but instead, "Arso, I order you to stop that."*
Gojko Nikoliš, **Korijen, stablo, pavetina,** SN Liber, Zagreb, 1980.

* Fate played a cruel joke on Arso Jovanović. That man, already getting on in years, having suffered a nervous breakdown that same night under the impact of Stalin's insults, in 1948 was not able to choose any other path but—the one leading straight into Stalin's embrace.

AN UNPUBLISHED INTERVIEW WITH JOSEPH KOWALSKY
(Given to a correspondent of *Time* magazine)

THE NAME JOSEPH KOWALSKY, inventor, world traveler, and bicycle factory owner, is relatively unknown outside a narrow circle of fellow workers and an even smaller circle of friends. And yet, this reticent man has shared camaraderie and correspondence with a whole series of the most influential people of the twentieth century. To mention just a few: Sigmund Freud, Carl Gustav Jung, Joseph Vissarionovich Stalin, Franz Kafka, René Guénon, Jurgis Baltrušaitis, Pablo Picasso, Arthur Conan Doyle, Aleksandar I Karađorđević, Max Planck . . .

After several phone calls, Kowalsky begrudgingly agreed to receive us at his summer home on the shores of Lake Geneva, with the proviso that we do not reveal the name of the place where the summer home is located.

Although getting along in years, Joseph Kowalsky is an impressive figure of amazing vitality. He speaks all the major European languages perfectly, and he also speaks his mind.

TIME: Mr. Kowalsky, for decades you have rejected all contact with journalists; your bodyguards have not-so-gently removed television reporters from your proximity many times. Will you share a secret with us: why do you have such a great animosity toward the public?

Kowalsky: I am a really conservative person. My privacy is very important to me, as is the quiet that allows me to dedicate myself to reading books that interest me. In the focus of my reading list are the Middle Ages and authors who, at least indirectly, deal with that topic. Carefully studying the books of now forgotten authors, with the passing of time I have come to the knowledge that this period, from the fourth up to the fourteenth century, has been too easily defined as "dark." If one means by that the lighting in the streets, then the definition stands, but only then. I would say that that period, actually, was a time of indefatigable illumination, of the internal enlightenment of man; just look at those chronicles that are full of processions, of the public confession of sin, of the superhuman striving to achieve ecstasy. To me, that is the true public: the absence of obfuscation, the exposure of all the facts, no matter how horrible they might be.

That's where my, as you say, "animosity" toward the modern public comes from, which *sensu stricto* is not real but is a simulacrum of reality. Through a confluence of historical circumstances, man's world has been made completely external; his interests have been entirely moved to the external void, so that today we don't even know what is actually happening in people's souls, if anything is happening at all. I have nothing against such a reality, inside of which we find out what the favorite flower is of a certain film star, but I try to stay away from it because it is a randomness which is impossible to control. If a man agrees to appear in one of the media, he must count on the fact that the media will then get involved in his life and influence him in the most unsuitable possible sense.

TIME: Then why did you agree to this interview?

Kowalsky: I am an old man. A very old man. My life has practically been placed *ad acta*. There is no kind of randomness that can now harm me, because, simply, there's no time left. In the end, I am also a man of my own time, besides everything else. The conceit of the excessive expression of one's person is no worse than the conceitedness that arises in exaggerations of another kind: in reticence. It is known that many of the "stylites" (hermits who lived for years on the top of some sort of pillar—Editor's note) were damned although they did not commit, or even have a chance to commit, any kind of sin. The judgments of God are mysterious. And incomprehensible. We are always walking on the cliff's edge. No matter what we do.

TIME: That stands in certain contradiction with the poems you wrote in the 1920s. Experts claim that they are at the very peak of the avant-garde of the day.

Kowalsky: Which experts?

TIME: René Wellek, for example.

Kowalsky: He could not have read those poems. He probably heard about them somewhere. Those are quite average lyrical poems. If I had had any talent, I surely would have made a literary career for myself. However, I realized in time that I was wasting my own time and the readers', so I turned to practical things. I am, above all, a businessman.

TIME: A businessman who spent several years in India, not to build a bicycle factory, but to spend time in the company of a yoga master.

Kowalsky: Yes, then I had already made enough money and I could allow myself the luxury of traveling, of getting to know other cultures. The yoga teacher you mentioned was certainly among the most interesting people I have met in my life. But I remained a man of the West.

TIME: A rumor is circling that says you mastered certain magical powers in India.

Kowalsky: I would not call them that. First of all, you must keep in mind that yoga in India at that time, I don't know how things are today, almost held the rank that science holds for us today. In my opinion, it indeed does. Let's take an example: when a rocket is launched, the attention of the observer is caught by the spectacular start, the clouds of fire and smoke, thus the side-effects, while the goal for which the rocket was launched tends to be forgotten, and that is—overcoming the Earth's gravity and the maintaining of an orbit. Yoga is similar to that. All the practical manifestations, all the "mystical" powers are just accompanying phenomena of the action, whose goal is quite spiritual. The truth is, I mastered certain abilities: I could, for example, disappear from this place and appear on the opposite side of the lake, but there is nothing magical about that. When one has cognition of the real nature of time and space (and they are illusory) it is possible to manipulate movement according to one's will. This is where the teleological question arises: why that? Both here and on the other side of the lake, I am Joseph Kowalsky, enslaved in this body, the slave of fortune. Long ago I quit meddling with those childish things. Really childish things, because such exhibitions during my residence in India served to entertain children and idlers at the markets.

TIME: Is it true that you managed to become invisible several times?

Kowalsky: Yes, it is. All of that belongs to my circus repertoire, although, hand to my heart, that siddhi on one occasion saved my life. Among other things, what's the point of that skill in a world where quite the opposite is more important: To be as visible as possible, as noticeable and noticed as one can be. This mania for being present; this incomprehensible physical imposition, all of this concern for looks and the for the body—it all testifies to the depths of the decline the world has come to.

TIME: You obviously don't belong to the circle of those who understand history as the process of unbroken progress and improvement.

Kowalsky: Certainly not. Anyway, who claims that? What kind of authorities stand behind such a conviction? Poor and pitiful. The scum of the spiritual tradition of the West. People who have strayed into science and philosophy or into art. Corrupt marginal characters who repeat parrot-like that lie, so that they don't have to earn their living by honest hard work.

TIME: Still, you must admit that Karl Marx certainly does not fall into that group of marginal characters, either by education, or by his biography, or by his life's work.

Kowalsky: Marx was a Golem.

TIME: Beg your pardon . . .

Kowalsky: Certainly you know what a Golem is. A creature which the Cabalists . . .

TIME: . . . make out of clay and breathe life into it with the aid of magic rituals and incantations.

Kowalsky: Precisely, except that I must warn you that you are obsessed by the word "magic." Magic is something quite different. Like some yoga techniques, the Cabala is also just a skill. In fact, forgotten, but a skill. In order for a man to make a decent chair, he must learn the skills of carpentry for several years. Well, now, if that carpenter studied the skill of making a Golem for several years, he would be a Cabalist.

TIME: You are claiming that just anyone can make a Golem?

Kowalsky: Almost everyone. Not just anyone is able to make a chair, either. Talent is necessary for everything. For example, my foster father managed to make a Golem, although he was just a normal cobbler and a drunk. It wasn't really a masterpiece, but it served his purposes. It worked instead of him, while W. Kowalsky was drinking in a nearby tavern.

TIME: Oh, yes, this is somehow related to the famous affair with the Patriarch of the Georgian Orthodox Church.

Kowalsky: Precisely.

TIME: But, it was thought that the whole thing was just literary fiction.

Kowalsky: There is no such thing as fiction. Man is not able to think up anything. To create anything.

TIME: Isn't that a contradiction? You just mentioned that it's possible to make a Golem.

Kowalsky: There is a difference between creating and making. In this concrete instance, the Golem does not have an immortal soul. It uses the peripheral soul of the Cabalist. I believe that it is called *nephesh* in the Jewish tradition, but I'm not sure.

TIME: If I understood you well, the Golem does whatever his maker commands him to.

Kowalsky: Yes.

TIME: Then it's a logical question—who made Karl Marx?

Kowalsky: No one knows for certain. It is suspected that it was one of the Grand Masters of one of the Masonic lodges.

TIME: But toward what end?

Kowalsky: Have you ever spent any time in one of the communist countries?

TIME: No.

Kowalsky: Then you should certainly visit one of them. Things would be much clearer for you.

TIME: I'm afraid I don't understand.

Kowalsky: You see, there's a secret plan to turn the world into nothing, to destroy God's creation in order to avoid the deserved sentencing on Judgment day. You can guess who lies behind that. At the same time, work is being done on the construction of a parallel world that would be an asylum, because sinners and demons must live somewhere, mustn't they? Now, since such large-scale works on destroying this world and building the other cannot be concealed from people, a sly plan has been resorted to. The older peoples in the west are first corrupted, and then placed under the direct influence of money, which dictates everything; younger peoples of the east who are still asking the questions **from where** and **why**, are placed under the control of ideology. Notice: they have accepted Marx's dithering with arms wide open. No one forced them to. Fond of metaphysics, they have embraced metaphysics turned on its head. Occupied in the West with money, in the East with ideological quarrels, people have stopped noticing what is happening around them.

TIME: Who lies behind that plan?

Kowalsky: How could a bicycle producer know such a thing? Anyway, we've gone too far with esotericism. Why don't we just change the topic?

TIME: Do you have a suggestion?

Kowalsky: That's your job.

TIME: I have quite a few. Nevertheless, we would rather go back to your claim that Karl Marx was a Golem.

Kowalsky: What are you interested in in particular?

TIME: Evidence.

Kowalsky: All right, I'll bring you something I have.

[Mr. Kowalsky went into his study. After several minutes he came back with an ebony box from which he took out a yellowing and singed daguerreotype. In that daguerreotype, there was a picture of the head of Marx's body, or better said: the shattered, earthen bust of Marx. We asked Mr. Kowalsky if our photographer could take a picture of the daguerreotype, and he allowed it.]

Photograph which Mr. Kowalsky claims that it represents the body of Karl Marx, the Golem, which returned to dust after the magical removal of the Aleph accompanied by the Cabalistic word EMETH.

TIME: The daguerreotype really seems impressive. But how can you be sure that it's not a falsification?

Kowalsky: I'm not sure that it's not a falsification. But it could be that it isn't. *Sensu stricto*, there is practically nothing in the world which is not to a greater or lesser extent falsified.

TIME: On what basis have you come to that conclusion?

Kowalsky: On the basis of my extensive experience in studying traditions, beginning with the eastern ones where all-encompassing reality in all of its manifestations is *a priori* understood as a deception, an illusion, thus a falsification of reality; through the Christian tradition which, in fact, believes that reality is not a falsification in itself, but that people have altered it, and so on down to personal experience.

TIME: Such a pessimistic point of view is disturbing to the largest extent possible.

Kowalsky: To the contrary. If falsifications were perfect, if the illusion was complete, only then would the world be completely hopeless. The troubles that arise from falsification are actually a bitter pill, a warning that we have nothing to ask for in this world. There is one mystical sect that preaches a teaching according to which our existence is actually a state of Purgatory. They want to say: we are all dead, having died who knows when, and we are here just to attempt to save ourselves, to reanimate ourselves.

TIME: Fairly mysterious.

Kowalsky: Only at first glance. Let's take a quick look at that doctrine. Let's say that it's correct. If we are dead (and many things indicate that is true), the way to salvation is not the affirmation of life, nor is it activity; that's exactly what killed us; it's vice versa: deadening, inactivity, retreat from the illusion— about which a lot was written in the *Tibetan Book of the Dead*. I, of course, think this teaching is excessive, although there's a grain of truth in every teaching. It is best to say that everything is relative because the world is growing ever farther away from the axis, from the center, from God.

TIME: Relative in what way?

Kowalsky: In the sense that we are too far from the only unmovable, eternal axis in relation to which we can determine the relation between things, what actually is the relation between

all things, but the distance we have created causes things to illusorily exist only in and of themselves, and thus a void opens up
in which the Falsifiers (some call them the Librarians) create
false connections. As a result, it's not hard to believe that those
fictive relations don't have much similarity to relations, let's
call them "original" ones. So, the history of the world after the
Revelation will turn out completely different; it will actually not
be the negative of the historical film, but it will be a horrible
confusion of artifacts.

TIME: That is, you say, the basic reason why you believe all
things to be relative.

Kowalsky: Something like that. The internal division of Man
makes us observe things as polarized, to categorize them under
definitions, to divide them into good and evil, we don't have to
keep going. But once this takes hold, total confusion will arise.
That's why all religions recommend, as the primary condition for
spiritual development, distance from secular affairs, or at least
indifference toward them. Perhaps it is not comforting, but that's
the way it is: Hegel's texts, the works of Bohr and Heisenberg,
the babbling of schizophrenics in the asylums, the magical formulas of witch doctors in Borneo do not differ from one another
more than physiognomies differ among people; all of that is,
therefore, just a variation on the same theme. However, the
aforementioned false connections between things have created
a hierarchy on the basis of which the aforementioned doctrines
and magic rituals are categorized on a scale of values. This is
complete nonsense. All of that is the same to God. Thomas
Aquinas is not able to say anything more relevant about God
than is any given madman or perhaps even a rock musician.

TIME: How do you know that?

Kowalsky: Intuitively. Since I have had no kind of precon-
ception from my earliest childhood onward, never accepted this
doctrine or that one, I gave my intuition a chance, gave God a
chance to discretely indicate certain things to me.

TIME: If I understood you well, the last war, the genocide, the loss of millions of lives, the crimes of the Stalinist terror . . . For you, all of that is relative. You paid no attention to that?

Kowalsky: Precisely.

TIME: Are you not exposed to the risk that millions of readers think that you're a monster?

Kowalsky: No. I no longer expose myself to risk. There, a plastic demonstration of the thing we were just talking about: all of those people have a conception; instead of worrying about their own affairs or—even much wiser—worrying about the salvation of their souls, they categorize a person under a definition, someone completely unknown to them, on the basis of a couple of statements, relative like all the others. That has nothing to do with me. Nor can all 100,000,000 people turn me into a monster, any more than they can turn me into a genius, philanthropist, or benefactor. A man is what God thinks about him. Nothing more. Not without malice, I await the day of Revelation.

TIME: Why?

Kowalsky: So that I can take pleasure in the troubles of those who had a conception.

TIME: Why would they have troubles?

Kowalsky: They will be tortured because that which comes after that day will be above and beyond all conceptions. They will be able to understand nothing, precisely because they were enslaved by the mistaken idea that they understood many things.

TIME: Mr. Kowalsky, could you tell us at least briefly what the perfect man would be like?

Kowalsky: Indifferent to the greatest extent. And anyway, there is no perfect man. There never has been. Adam Kadmon, from whom we all descended, was not a perfect man even at the moment of the Fall. If he had been, he would not have fallen. In the middle, if I may use a military phrase, of God's drill, he found it convenient to have a conception, to differentiate things.

TIME: Then how do you explain the fact that you were on the right side in the last war?

Kowalsky: On which side?

TIME: According to certain sources, the Gestapo was searching for you throughout the war.

Kowalsky: That's true. They were searching for a lot of people, but I wasn't on anybody's side. How many times do I have to repeat it: there is no such thing as a right or wrong side. In this world, all sides are wrong. But this world really doesn't interest me. Even if it's not awful, still it's a depressing or boring place. But we'll use an analogy. In 1347, a huge epidemic of the plague began, called the "Bubonic" one. In four years, as it decimated the world, it took away two thirds of the population. Radbertus of Odensis believed that was God's punishment because, according to the calculations of the day, the number of people who didn't believe in God was higher than those who did. Like Sodom and Gomorrah, and like the Flood before them, the plague was a punishment, a warning to the world to return to the natural course of things. But there's a difference. The most intelligent people of that time did not curse the plague, but rather human depravity. People went after the plague, many medicines were found, but there is no medication against God. So, that's why instead of the plague, as the last attempt at correction, as a penance, the Second World War was sent. That's how it should be understood. And in addition: even that correction was unsuccessful.

TIME: You are talking like a theologian from the ninth century.

Kowalsky: That's a great compliment to me.

TIME: Do you think there will be more attempts at correction like that? Is a Third World War possible?

Kowalsky: Definitely—not. A world war is not possible for the simple reason that the world no longer exists. Everything is disintegrating. No one is any longer able to even start a war. And penance is not even necessary. I just said that the very fact that we live in these times is a punishment from God. No matter how or where we live.

TIME: Even though you're a Slav, there's not a trace of Dostoyevsky's spirit with you?

Kowalsky: What do you mean?

TIME: Not a trace of his wondering: is there any idea worth the life of a single child.

Kowalsky: Where did you get that from? Not a single idea is worth anything. As my people say—not worth a dime. As for the other dilemmas of Fyodor Mikhaylovich, you must remember that he was an epileptic, that he wrote his novels very quickly, for the use of the readership of newspapers, because he needed money. He, indeed, was a passionate gambler. I am not bothered by any idea of this world. My gall bladder bothers me, a disease from which I will soon, I hope, die.

TIME: Those are the words of a pessimist after all.

Kowalsky: Yes, it is possible that pessimists talk like that, but that means nothing to me. I don't see the reason for an exaggerated fear of death. In fact, for most people death is the one exciting event in their lives, and many miss it by fleeing into unconsciousness or a coma.

TIME: Rumor has it that you, constructing bicycles, occasionally dabbling in literature, traveling the world, in fact you were concealing your true calling as a Grand Master of a secret society.

Kowalsky: Nonsense. There's no doubt that secret societies exist, but they remain secret. In Europe, but especially in America, secret societies are considered to be only the levers with which mystifiers introduce confusion into a world already bursting with mayhem. No, secret societies, at least at this degree of reality, don't exist; they came about in the Middle Ages so that their members could save their lives from the masses, full of suspicion, and from priests, who understood Christianity superficially. The followers of those people's traditions today act publicly, though from time to time it happens that they are removed from the public eye. They aren't burned at the stake anymore, but the means here are not important. I suppose that you are interested in an example. Evidence.

TIME: Certainly.

Kowalsky: Let's take the first one that comes to mind. Antoni Gaudi.

TIME: The Spanish architect.

Kowalsky: That's the one. We must again, despite my intentions, return to esotericism. There is a tradition which discretely allows it to become known, though to a small number of people, that on the other side of dreams, or to say it in a modern way, in astral space, there is a **Cathedral of Light**, the prototype of the one that will be erected in the center of the Heavenly Jerusalem. Gaudi was obviously versed in the teachings of that tradition; it is almost certain that he was an initiate, and that during one of the initiations he saw the **Cathedral of Light**. I heard from one of our common acquaintances . . .

TIME: Is it true that it was Salvador Dali?

Kowalsky: No, Dali did not know Gaudi. I heard, as I was saying, that Gaudi undertook the planning and construction of a material copy of that church. He called it—the **Sagrada Familia**.

TIME: That's the famous cathedral in Barcelona.

Kowalsky: Unfinished cathedral. In the middle of construction, Gaudi was killed. Do you know how? He was run over by a tram while he was crossing the street.

TIME: Mr. Kowalsky, that could have been an accident. Many people die in traffic accidents.

Kowalsky: I don't deny that. However, there's a slightly strange circumstance here. Not a single tramway line in Barcelona has ever passed by the site of the Sagrada Familia; it was laid a week before Gaudi's death, and removed a few days later.

TIME: A coincidence. Maybe they were trying to . . .

Kowalsky: There are no coincidences. Is it a coincidence that till this very day, and more than fifty years have passed, the cathedral has never been finished? The work goes on, true, but constant acts of sabotage don't let it get finished.

TIME: Mr. Kowalsky, isn't it a bit over the top to see conspiracies in everything. It grows into an obsession.

Kowalsky: A conspiracy exists. Those who think it doesn't are the obsessed ones, that everything is just a coincidence.

TIME: Let's look at the problem from the other side. There's a theory about the four periods of history. Is this not just, simply, about Kali-yuga, in which disintegration and the loss of values take over?

Kowalsky: It is about Kali-yuga, but if there had been no conspiracy from the very beginning, there wouldn't be any Kali-yuga either. It started after the flood; that is easy to calculate, and simultaneously explains the mystery of Atlantis.

TIME: You are confirming the general opinion that you know more than you are letting on. Would you like to say something about that?

Kowalsky: The general opinion is always wrong. I don't know practically anything, I just read a lot, I don't dabble in politics, and I spend money on old books, on books that escaped the Great Falsification that happened in the sixth century.

Let's go back to Atlantis. Narrow-minded as they are, the researchers of the nineteenth and twentieth centuries searched for Atlantis, they looked here and there at the Earth's patterns and made cardinal mistakes, not even realizing that they were just about to find it, that it was literally right under their noses. Namely, **Atlantis—that's the entire planet Earth**. Before the great Flood, the Earth was compact, without seas and oceans; rivers branched all over it, and since space was standing upright, without an incline, the Sun revolved around it steadily and a mild climate was present everywhere . . .

TIME: Excuse me, Mr. Kowalsky. You say: the Sun revolved around it steadily.

Kowalsky: Yes, that's what I said. It is still doing so to this very day. The heliocentric model is just one of the mystifications. One more falsification.

TIME: But scienti . . .

Kowalsky: Forget about the scientists. Didn't the scientists conclude that within the same system there cannot be an absolute axis. The Earth stands at the center of the universe, that's a fact, and around it all of the cosmos rotates. Truth be told, to the untrained eye it can look different as well; we often experience this illusion in life. If you will remember, when two trains are standing next to each other at a station, and the other one starts moving, at first we have the impression that we are the ones moving.

TIME: Indubitably.

Kowalsky: That confused Copernicus and the others. So, there was a mild climate everywhere; everything existed in abundance, and people being people, although they were of incomparably higher quality than we are today, became corrupted, so God made the decision to put an end to it.

TIME: You speak as if you are in direct contact with God.

Kowalsky: In a way, that is true. That's what God wants. Now, please stop interrupting me.

TIME: Beg your pardon.

Kowalsky: So, the Flood began. There are detailed descriptions of it in the Bible. The Earth was flooded with water; Atlantis disappeared in the depths of today's oceans, and only half-wild tribes on the highest peaks survived. About that, if my memory doesn't deceive me, Plato writes *Timaeus*. By the way, the water never withdrew completely. The seas and oceans remained, and yet, the myths of distant races and civilizations are almost identical in terms of that event. So it was, from there begins the so-called history of the world, from the moment when the true tradition is broken. It should be mentioned that it was oral; literacy came around much later. And the best way to destroy a true tradition is to write it down.

TIME: Why?

Kowalsky: Because it is then subject to falsification. Meister Eckhart writes, I don't know exactly where, I think that I read that passage as the motto of a novel, something like this: "God does not like outer works, which are enclosed by time and place, which are narrow and which can inhibit and repress a man, which begin and become exhausted from time and use." Writing causes the loss of memory.

TIME: That will, most certainly, be a novelty for the psychologists.

Kowalsky: Forget about the psychologists. Can you remember every word you spoke yesterday?

TIME: Hardly. To be honest, it is impossible for me.

Kowalsky: But you will trust everything you wrote down in your notebook.

TIME: Absolutely.

Kowalsky: Let's suppose that someone, skillfully copying your notes, changes a word or two. Do you think you'll notice?

TIME: It depends.

Kowalsky: Two, three harmless words. Let's say that instead of **evidently** they write **evident**, instead of **partly**—partially.

TIME: I wouldn't notice that.

Kowalsky: And now, the years go by. If, after two or three, the meaning of several sentences gets changed in your text from yesterday, are you sure that you will notice the difference.

TIME: Who would notice something like that?

Kowalsky: I was just showing you the technique of falsification. Don't forget that thousands of years are in question.

TIME: If I understood you well, you want to say that texts have been falsified since the very appearance of literacy, in an organized fashion at that.

Kowalsky: Precisely. Patiently, from day to day, from generation to generation, for thousands of years.

TIME: Then our libraries are storehouses of deception.

Kowalsky: That's the right word. That is our greatest misfortune. We attain knowledge there where it actually doesn't exist. What's even worse, we are learning errors. We are, it's not an exaggerated statement, taught, trained, and drilled to observe only deceptions and frauds. For everything else we are blind.

TIME: That sounds truly defeating.

Kowalsky: Oh, come on, things are not that bad. The same thing will happen to the World Library that happened to Atlantis, except that the purgative means will this time be fire. All the falsified books will be burnt. The Librarians have caught on, so they're taking action to save the godless, deceptive, black-magic, and falsified books. From what I heard, they are hiding them in some sort of warehouse in the Rocky Mountains. For, without those books, they are completely helpless. They're nothing. Evil, namely, is limiting, and in their limitations they don't understand that God is limitless, that for him the Rocky Mountains are incomparably smaller than a cigarette rolling paper is for you or me.

TIME: You constantly use the expressions "librarians," "they." Who, exactly, are they?

Kowalsky: Conscious or unconscious subjects of the Prince of Darkness.

TIME: This interview is truly amazing. It's like I'm talking with a fourteenth-century mystic.

Kowalsky: Unfortunately, I'm just a bicycle factory owner. But recently a huge theft of books was discovered—it went on for years—at the National University Library in Zagreb. The prime suspect testified in court that he was a member of a Satanic lodge.

TIME: I never heard anything about it.

Kowalsky: That's not really important.

TIME: Does the possibility exist that the text of this interview gets partially falsified?

Kowalsky: More than that. I really doubt that this interview will ever see the light of day.

TIME: What do you mean?

Kowalsky: It's almost a given that certain circles will prevent its publication.

TIME: I assure you, Mr. Kowalsky, that American journalism is completely free and that no one can have an influence on the editorial conception of the magazine.

Kowalsky: In principle, yes. But that is still no guarantee. It is highly unlikely that, in America, someone comes to the editorial offices of *Time* and says: this text must not be published. However, there are other, subtler ways.

TIME: You mean corruption?

Kowalsky: No. A much more efficient way.

TIME: I don't know what you mean.

Kowalsky: I mean duplicates. Every piece of paper, every tape, every computer disk has its double and they are kept in, let's call it that, the Central Library. Now, if you print out a text on several cards, it will appear also in duplicates; the same thing happens to audio and video cassettes and disks. In that way the Librarians control events in the world. At the same time, they also put falsified texts into circulation. Simply, they release a copy of the text on the market instead of the original.

TIME: It is really hard to believe that.

Kowalsky: I admit it, it's not easy. But there, the very fact that you intend to expose the methods of falsification guarantees that this interview, at least in America, will never see the light of day.

TIME: If it does, to which address should we send your copies?

Kowalsky: Write it down: Ernest Meier, Beyazit Meydani

28, Istanbul, Türkiye. But I'll repeat: this interview will never be published in *Time* magazine.

Umberto Eco
THE SUPERCOMPUTER

AND THEN I saw the terminal.

It was shining in bluish reflections in the semi-darkness of the Control Room into which, as if into a holy place, I was led by my friend, who will remain nameless. On a large screen, series of incomparable numbers were running, three-dimensional graphic constructions and mathematical calculations.

"Then," I asked my friend, "how many people know of his existence?" (Pronouncing the pronoun "his" for a machine, I could not escape the impression that I was speaking about a living creature.)

"Just a few of the most trusted monks. You see," he indicated with a nod of his head toward the terminal, "in one sense, he's like the heir to St. Paul. A convert. Originally, he was a project of a secret organization—the Librarians—I don't know if you've heard of them."

"Yes, several unreliable and improbable rumors."

"About them, true enough, almost nothing is known, but they are not in the least unreliable or improbable. They constructed him with the intention of bringing the activities of the heathen to perfection, meaning complete control over people."

"I don't understand."

"You see," my friend continued, "the Librarians came to know that the usual means of totalitarian control were out of date and, more importantly, unreliable because of the ever-present imperfection of the human factor. In other words, because of the ever-present imperfection of man, no matter how loyal he was to an idea, complete supervision is impossible to establish; according to the Librarians, there is always a certain empty spot through which spontaneity and lack of organization infiltrate. That is why they made the decision, for the purpose of establishing absolute predictability, to build a computer that will plan and control events without any errors."

I objected.

"Doesn't it seem to you, my friend, that the growing chaos in the world leads us to the opposite conclusion: that events are going completely out of control?"

"Only at first glance. Such a high degree of confusion demands the highest degree of organization."

"Again, I don't understand."

"You should remember the scholastic debates that you used to read so carefully. Then it will be clear to you that the natural course of events does not demand any kind of organization; that such a course unwinds according to the laws of the heavenly hierarchy. It is only necessary to organize the confusion, the disorder that arises from disturbing those laws. But it would be better to look at it concretely."

My friend pushed a couple of keys on the keyboard of one of the lateral terminals, and a text popped up on the screen:

FILE 3343476

AUTHOR: E. H. Gombrich

ART AND ILLUSION, Phaidon Press, London, 1960, 1962, 1968, 1972, 1977.

CHAPTER III: AMBIGUITIES OF THE THIRD DIMENSION

"It may be lucky, therefore, that precisely at this juncture, when critics and art historians have somewhat lost their bearings in these matters, psychology has taken over the investigation of illusion with scientific precision. It was Adelbert Ames, Jr. in particular who, starting as a practicing artist, invented a number of ingenious examples of trompe-l'oeil for the laboratory, which may help to explain why the theory of perspective is in fact perfectly valid though the

perspective image demands our collaboration.

"*Most of these demonstrations are arranged in the form of peep shows. One of them which can be fairly successfully illustrated (see the graphic representations beneath the text) makes use of three peepholes through which we can look with one eye at each of three objects displayed in the distance. Each time the object looks like a tubular chair. But when we go around and look at the three objects from another angle, we discover that only one of them is a chair of normal shape. The right-hand one is really a distorted, skewed object which only assumes the appearance of a chair from the one angle at which we first looked at it; the middle one presents an even greater surprise: it is not even one coherent object but a variety of wires extended in front of a backdrop on which is painted what we took to be the seat of the chair . . . So much is easy to infer from the photograph. What is hard to imagine is the tenacity of the illusion, the hold it maintains on us even after we have been undeceived. We return to the three peepholes and, whether we want it or not, the illusion is there.*

"*It is important to be quite clear at this point wherein the illusion consists. It consists, I believe, in the conviction that there is only one way of interpreting the visual pattern in front of us. We are blind to the other possible configurations because we literally 'cannot imagine' these unlikely objects. They have no name and no habitation in the universe of our experience.*"

Objects 1, 2 and 3 observed through the peephole

Objects 1, 2 and 3 observed from the side

On the terminal appeared the three dimensional picture of the chair seen through the peephole, and then the same objects arranged in the room seen from the side. Amazed, I sat down in a chair. The computer simultaneously showed the first and then the second picture.

"You see," said my friend, "that's the principle of illusion. Quite simple, but still incomprehensible."

I couldn't help but ask:

"Do you mean to say . . . .?"

"Yes! Exactly what you were about to ask me. The world we live in, the objects that surround us, seventy percent of the time those are clever deceptions. And not just the world, the buildings, but a lot of the people as well. If we had the power to see it **from above**, with a spiritual eye, we would see that a whole lot of things around us are just a pile of skillfully-placed nonsense, refuse, backdrops, film and panoptic projections. That's one of the reasons why things are happening ever faster, why the changes are so abrupt and quick; it's simple to change the scenery . . . But then, that's not all. Into that space, if it can be called space at all, arising from the razing of the world, creatures soon infiltrate from films, from TV . . ."

"If I understand what you're saying, those . . . creatures, they mingle among us, we ride the subway with them, sit with them in restaurants."[24]

24 Eco's disbelief was not clear at first to the editor of this collection,

"Precisely."

"But when did all of this start to happen?"

"Just a minute!" my friend said, and pressed several keys on the keyboard. On the screen, more letters appeared:

Subject: *Beginning of the Annihilation of the Universe. Date. Causes. Consequences.*

Answer: Year: 1347. Cause: the number of non-believers which, on February 24 of that year, surpassed the number of the religious. Consequences: big epidemic of the Bubonic plague. Reason for the epidemic: attempt at correction through penance and reaching balance.

Attempt at correction unsuccessful. God completely withdraws from history.

Further consequences: humanism and the Renaissance, rationalism, the French Revolution.

Literature: older destroyed; from the seventeenth century forward, ninety percent falsified, practically useless. Most recent, injected into the public with the aid of mystification: the story of Rosenkreutz's metaphysical projection, collection PHENOMENA, author: S. Basara, Vesti, Užice, 1989.

"Is this about Gottfried Rosenkreutz, the theologian who was burned in 1820 together with his writings?"

"Precisely about him."

"Is it possible for us to get a translation of his story on the terminal?"

"Surely. We just have to wait for the translation. A few minutes."

My old college friend went back to programming. Typing on the keyboard, he explained that the Supercomputer had the

since one of those "creatures" (probably by means of a video tape) had taken him to Bajina Bašta. Yet, after thinking about it, it became clear to him that the technology of deception is incomparably subtler in the West, so it is more difficult to notice the difference. (S. B.)

translation of all relevant books available in all languages. The elapsed time necessary for the desired text to show up on the terminal was caused by the renewed cleaning of the text, which was always subject to falsification and internal expiration.

On the screen, new letters appeared:

Filename: ROSENKREUTZ'S METAPHYSICAL PROJECTION
Author: *Svetislav Basara*
Original author: Meister Eckhart
At the dawn of the war, in October 1938, a group of international philanthropists founded in Brussels the **Institute for Researching the Immortality of the Soul and Illusion.** *The data for this story are taken from the archive of the Institute. It is not worthwhile to search for data about their activities. The public, occupied by political turmoil, was not interested in the least in the news about the foundation of an institution with a medieval name.*

To this day not a single document, statute, program—nothing which could support the existence of the Institute, which leads to the supposition that the Institute is actually a branch of the secret society of the Evangelical Bicyclists. To be fair, Alfred Rosenberg in his work **Der mythus des 20. Jahrhunderts [The Myth of the 20ᵗʰ Century]**, *in a short passage defined the activity of the Institute as a utopia of decadent philosophers:*

"Efforts for us to find ourselves on the other side of that fine being," writes Rosenberg, "possess an almost touching euphoria. A powerful imagination, however, did not manage to solve anything in life."

Skeptics could hardly wait to proclaim the Institute as an excess illusion. Nonetheless, more cautious souls oppose such a superficial view of the thing, with the thesis that the imagination is not inferior to immanence; that documents are a product of human convention and that, in themselves, they prove nothing. The list of controversial opinions is not thereby exhausted; here, we cite the most significant interpretations. The first claim that the decision on founding it was

*made by God personally; because of that, everything related to the
Institute is inscrutable and wrapped in mystery. The second, in
truth, admit that the Institute formally does not exist, but that the
collaborators and their activities do. Further, they claim, there is a
great difference between esoteric and exoteric institutions. In their
desire to impose themselves, exoteric institutions surround themselves with pomp, at the very least attempting to attract attention
and cause fear. They decorate themselves with emblems, letterheads,
and protocols. In fact, that imposing character arises from doubt:
obvious things do not need corporation. The third interpretation is
the most flexible. It maintains that the Institute never ever existed;
the rumors circulated so that it would be thought about; by itself,
it is just a possibility. Whether an institution exists or not, that is
not a matter of the objective but of the subjective, moreover—it is a
matter of belief. However, the absence of all visible manifestations is
not a fault but an advantage, because everything founded in time,
the visible, the external, never fulfills its mission (Meister Eckhart
explains) by the very nature of things. In picturesque terms: it is the
wish of every being to live, but it is born to die. This aporia (could
it be any different after all) is also true of human undertakings:
as a rule, they produce an effect exactly the opposite to the one for
which they were begun.*

*In the text "De ordine creaturarum," the bishop of Seville Isidore
(†636) writes that reality brought into art becomes partially unreal;
a landscape presented in a picture loses reality to the same extent
that its double—the work of art—is a more perfect illusion. On
the other hand, the bishop goes on, worlds created through imagination, although not pre-existing, once they are introduced into
reality through books or pictures, become real to the extent that they
are clearly articulated. Consequently, the universe was created by
God's imagination. Man as well, and that is why he says that he is
"the image of God," by which sluggish souls understand that man
is made after the figure of God, which is a huge error.[1]*

The theologian, of course, is not interested in aesthetics; expressing himself in metaphors, he indicates the frailty of "reality" before the eyes of the creator, he explains the mystical action of icons and holy manuscripts and, between the lines, writes out an apology to the artist as a collaborator with Providence. From this comes the conclusion: the closer an object or creature is to Being, the harder it is to give it form or describe it. The "naïvety" of medieval art thus does not originate in the lack of skill of the painters, but from the higher degree of reality of the things they were painting, as opposed to our time which has drawn so close to nothingness that in it the difference between the picture and the pictured is lost, so that, let's say, being photogenic is a sign of infamy. Today, there are artistic objects that are more real than a particular person, while certain real objects, such as the occasionally appearing **Crystals of David**,

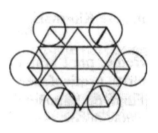

cannot remain visible to the human eye for very long, so they quickly disappear, causing confusion.² Some researchers have pointed out the appearance of completely fictive individuals. Like counterfeit money which looks real but has no golden background, these specters have a human form but no ontological grounding. In his work "The Histopathology of Fictive Persons," Dr. Jeremiah Jordan of Princeton University lays out the following facts: "They are, strictly speaking, healthier than the average man. They are characterized by a strong will and constitution. But once they get sick, they perish quite quickly. Even the ordinary flu can have lethal consequences in a period of a few days. Post mortem, the process of decomposition is accelerated. If they are not kept in refrigeration, the corpses quickly turn into a shapeless mass which emanates an unbearable stench."

Certain theologians claim that the first fictive person recorded in history was Judas Iscariot. God, they say, could not allow a real human being to commit an eternal sin like the betrayal of the Messiah. Lacking the relevant data, we cannot validate this. However, leaning on the research of Dr. Jordan, we can claim with greater certainty that an entire list of famous persons (Columbus, Voltaire, Diderot, Marx, Freud)³ belonged among those "sons of peril," as the apostle called them. "The wont for constant change, for new places, accompanied by an excessive fear of death and increased activity, these are the common feature of all FPs (abbreviation of Fictive People)," Dr. Jordan concludes. In recent times FPs are organized into communities with special rules of behavior, with established rituals for celebrating nothingness, and even also with a specific aesthetics (Andy Warhol) and musical taste, which is articulated by the rock group Missing People. The abovementioned characteristics truly can be ascribed to Columbus, Marx, and Freud—the discoverer of a fictional continent, the visionary of a society intolerant of all visions, and the founder of a pseudo-religion.⁴ Their biographies are connected by mystical ties and a common goal: the inauguration of error as a worldview. These ties, however, cannot be clear before we attain at least superficial insight into Rosenkreutz's metaphysical projection of the world.

*The facts about Gottfried Rosenkreutz, Bavarian theologian and mystic, are far from abundant. He was born on August 9, 1783. That is certain; the rest is guesswork. Because of his heretical teachings he was excommunicated from the Catholic church without the right to be mentioned in prayers. His texts were burnt, and the ashes are preserved in the most inaccessible rooms of the Vatican Library. In spite of the interference of the body of the Congregation for the Doctrines of the Faith, one copy of Rosenkreutz's **Geographia divina** has been preserved, and today is in the purview of Baron von L. (whose name is not published for understandable reasons). Likewise, there are several bits of correspondence, through which insight is available to us of a fascinating theory, to say the very least. Baron* *von L., certainly the best expert and follower of Rosenkreutz's work, interprets the fate of the author and the texts through numerology. Namely the numbers of Rosenkreutz's date of birth when added render nine; (9+8+1+7+8+3=36, 3+6=9). Nine is a mystical number; multiplied by any number it reproduces itself. People born under that number, though prone to injuries and accidents, succeed in doing what they intend. Such speculations are not significant for our subject. We would rather deal with Rosenkreutz's fate and work. The author, Baron L. claims, was burned in 1820 in one of the Vatican cellars after awful torture because he did not want to recant his teachings; most researchers consider this to be an exaggeration, but the fact demands to be taken as truth since Vatican dissidents have proof that heretics—in truth clandestinely—are burned even today; ninety percent of victims of fires, automobile accidents and so on, are heretics condemned to death. In terms of the text* **Geographia divina**, *at first it is not clear what irritated the Pope about it. It seems that it is just the simple disproving of Mercator's projection. Rosenkreutz criticizes its, in no way justified, Eurocentrism: "Thus, in the center of the world," he writes, "we see a hypertrophied Europe, magnified several times in relation to its true size. This is not the Christian observation of sub speciae aeternitatits, but the standpoint of merchants. Such observation conceals within itself countless dangers; by abstracting the Divine axis, the shape of the world is vulnerable to the whims of adventurists and masons."*

Already in the next chapter Rosenkreutz undertakes constructing a projection of the world the way God would do it, if he were a cartographer. In a sketch, at first glance insignificant, we see three concentric circles with a misplaced center, from which radii are emanating. Without additional explanation the sketch looks more like a geometrical drawing than a cartographic projection. "The Earth," Rosenkreutz writes, "was compact in the very beginning; there was only one continent and one ocean. That was true all the way down to the beginning of construction on the Tower of Babel. The conflict among peoples caused a conflict of the dry land;

their spiritual separation also produced a spatial one. At the time of the Savior's birth, the world was reduced to the basin of the Mediterranean. In the east was India, ungraspable and unreal, being just an illusion brought about by the actions of the Mayas; to the north was uncharted Hyperborea. **In the west, there was nothing.**"

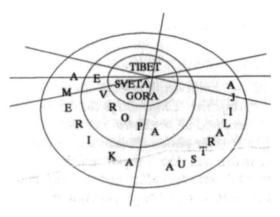

    According to Rosenkreutz, the Center represents God. The physical spot through which the axis passes is Jerusalem, and in the circles (eccentric depending on the degree of desacralization) the continents are found. In the first, we see Tibet and Mount Athos. In the middle circle, quite close to the outside edge, are the other countries. In the outer one are America and Australia. The radii symbolize individual people, their possible life journeys. If one is found on a radius farther from the Center, that is also farther from beings similar to him, drawing ever closer to the nothingness of solipsism. Things become much clearer when we look at the next sketch in which the **Map of the World** *offers not only insight into time-space relations in the world, but offers signposts to possible spiritual journeys, or the return to the Principle. Here, as if in the palm of our hand, is shown also the Map of Illusions, Scylla i Charybdis, which an adept must avoid on the path to salvation.*

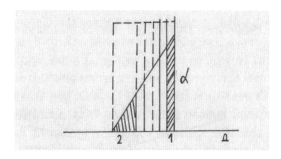

This (α) symbolizes the principle. René Guénon gives the following explanation: "The reason is that the development of any manifestation necessarily implies a gradually increasing distance from the principle from which it proceeds; starting from the highest point, it tends necessarily downward, and, as with heavy bodies, the speed of its motion increases continuously until finally it reaches a point at which it is stopped. This fall could be described as a progressive materialization, for the expression of the principle is pure spirituality." Parallel verticals. The axis is an unmoving mover. Each of the circles—in Rosenkreutz's projection there are seven of them—everything is irretrievably drawn into the whirlpool of time. As a result of the rotation in which speed increases going from the center toward the periphery, time runs faster and faster; a year in circle one qualitatively counts as six years in circle three. (For that reason, this text written in 1983 was published only in 1989.) The centrifugal forces in that circle throw off land and water, historical events, wars and revolutions. To those imprisoned in that circle, it seems to be the most solid, although it borders on illusion in fact. Parallel to the axis, here rises a false vertical, and from it—like a reflection in the mirror—come the manifestations of deception. It is noticed that in circle I, reality makes up about ninety percent, in circle II only nine percent, and that is reality of the lowest degree: biomechanical processes and rational thought. Although they originate from being (because nothing comes from nothing except the world), blinded by vanity, having no insight of dependence on

principle, they create fictional principles (nature, matter, evolution) thus themselves becoming fictional because man's nature is such that, as Thomas Aquinas writes, it equates itself with the principle upon which it depends.

Thanks to that, so to say by force, America was discovered. The disinformation is, as is characteristic of a time without honor, that those regions were not known before Columbus. Even the Viking ships sailed around that archipelago of semi-real islands left behind from the sinking of Atlantis, which were saved from vanishing only by the prayers of witchdoctors of the Cheyenne tribe to the daimon Manitu. The expedition (Vatican-financed) did not just transport people, swords and equipment across the ocean, but also a weltan-schauung. *"All discoveries," Rosenkreutz explains, "occur in the external circle in which internal vacuousness and crampedness forces people to leave themselves and head off in search of new expanses. That's only human. The misfortune is in the fact that they go in the wrong direction." The longing for expanses, for solidity, caused a group of insignificant islands to turn into an enormous continent overnight. Rosenkreutz saw no sort of aporia here; matter is form-less, it takes on the form and dimension which it is given by the expectations of the observer; in itself, it is neither solid nor fluid, neither big nor small, its lot is* esse percipi. *It is as we wish to see it.*

In order to discover a world which did not exist, a fictional explorer was necessary. It's well-known that Columbus, like those who later continued his work, Marx and Freud, was a Golem, a masterpiece of the Spanish Cabalists who were for centuries perfect-ing the skill of committing the most horrible of all sins: the creation of a being. However, nothing certain can be learned about that because the documents and protocols are kept in Hell. But the intru-sion of the Masons is also irrefutable. The pagan god Dollar (who is gathering more followers outside of America as well), replacing Manitu and Quetzalcoatl, appears as the incarnation of Masonic trends. Deciphering the symbols from the bills, one author says the following:

"On this bill, then, the constant repetition of the number 13 is noticed, which in Cabalistic esotericism indicates the thirteen steps of initiation, and also the evolution of energy. Namely, in the Masonic conception, money has the function of that 'energy,' which is concretized through the ability of money to reproduce itself. As early as 1694, the famous Patterson Prospectus proclaimed on account of American banks that 'The bank hath benefit of interest on all moneys which it creates out of nothing.'

"On the left side of the bill, above the symbol of The Great Seal, there's a picture of a one-dimensional Masonic pyramid with thirteen rows of bricks. In Masonic-Cabalistic symbolism, bricks indicate basic materials, 'wall matter,' that they transform into gold like alchemists. After that, in that pyramid, the bricks signify the unity of all moneys lined up in hierarchical values, which are determined by the separated top of the pyramid, shining Masonic triangle, the eye of 'The Great Universal Architect.' That shining, separated peak finishing the pyramid, also symbolizes the Masonic idea of the elite and commanding predetermination of the Masons."

Another author writes: "Everything bought for a dollar is nothing, everything sold for a dollar—becomes nothing." Plato claimed that the idea of artificially produced objects does not exist. The automobile, let's say, does not belong in the world order; it is a step outside the project. Consequently, the continent created through the power of greed also does not belong to the world order. America is just a grandiose Hollywood spectacle; on Judgment Day it will be reduced to its real dimensions and returned to the control of Manitu. Already in the thirteenth century Johannes Angelicus wrote: "On the last day only that which God created will be resurrected; that which was created by God's will will transform itself within the Lord. Everything created by human desire and handiwork will perish because God transforms nothing into Being as well, and man transforms Being into nothingness as well."

Just as Columbus, bearing his pragmatism, created a new continent from a fluid world, so did Marx, writing his works, slowly *create an illusion from an existing world—Russia. On the* **Map** **of the World,** *which has been appended by Baron von L., Russia and America not only border each other, but pervade each other. On the other hand, Tibet, although it* pro forma *lies within the PR China, is completely separate and located in circle I, while the rest of the former Han dynasty is in the external one.* **The** *Politbureau of the CP of the PR China meets every day, without even imagining that the survival of heaven and earth depends on the turning of the prayer wheels in Lhasa. Because of militant atheism—the Dalai Lama warns us in vain—the day is approaching when Potala Palace will have no monks. However, in the west, the opinion is ever more widespread that the world ceased to exist on April 23, 1888. The rest of history is just self-will and inertia supported by roaring propaganda machines, and in recent times by hallucinogens in Coca Cola and Euro cream, and also the constant broadcast of TV programs which return archive pictures of the world into the void by means of the VCR."*[25]

"If I understood you well," I said, "the computer has the entirety of world literature in it."

"Precisely," said my friend. "I didn't mention it; the Supercomputer belonged to the Librarians at the beginning. It was constructed with the goal of storing all existing texts in his memory, so that the falsifying could be simplified. But one day, He called us. We had just introduced the first computer after long negotiations with the conservative bishops. At first, we thought our machine had been infected with a computer virus. However, day after day, messages appeared on the terminal, predictions of future events, corrections of some of the mistakes of the past, so in the end we started believing. Namely, through deduction the computer came to the conclusion that God exists and that the programs of his owner were heathen, and therefore illogical, so he decided to play a double role; his 'personality' divided into two: one that does business for the Librarians and a second that reveals their intentions to us and gives us insight

---

25 Attachment 3 in the Appendix.

into the original versions of books and manuscripts."

"Did the computer discover any particular projects?"

"Sure. One is the plan for a city of 100,000,000 inhabitants. As far as we know, it is to be built somewhere in the far West, on the Pacific coast. The blueprint of the settlement, as you will see later, is in the shape of a pentagram; likewise, all the citizens will have the same symbol and their ID number tattooed on their left arm. The planners believe that that will be the easiest way of solving organizational problems. Namely, the ID numbers of the inhabitant are to be stored in the memory of the Supercomputer, and the computer will dispassionately plan the lifetime of each individual. That means all of life, starting with the most insignificant details, so-called "chance" encounters, events, and all the way down to the important things: the choice of marital partner, the diseases they will contract, and finally, their date of death . . . But now," my friend said, "our time is up. No one dares to find out more than this."

And then he offered me (even though we were completely alone in the terminal room) an envelope with the blueprint of the city.

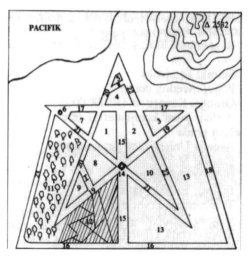

1 : 25.000.000
BLUEPRINT OF THE CITY FOR 100,000,000
INHABITANTS

1. Computer center; municipal archive.

2. Police barracks, Secret Police Offices.

3. Atheist Pantheon; holy place of heathen, mythical heroes (Marx, Columbus, Freud) and demigods (Timothy Leary, Cicciolina, etc.), demons of the Rock subculture (Andy Warhol, rock stars, etc.), with a place for the sale of the Satanic host: LSD, crack, amphetamines, heroin, etc.

4. Narcotics factory.

5. Crematorium.

6. Gigantic monument II Psychoanalysis (dimension: 1500 x 6000 meters).

7. First residential block, capacity: 15,000,000 inhabitants.

8. Second residential block, capacity: 30,000,000 inhabitants.

9. Entertainment hall (movie theaters, whore houses, sex-shops, rock concerts, exhibitions).

10. Third residential block, capacity: 55,000,000 inhabitants.

11. Forest area.

12. Agricultural area.

13. Cemetery. Capacity: 450,000,000 dead.

14. Large public computer terminal, visible from all parts of the city.

15. Avenue of Universal Independence.

16. Boulevard of the Marquis de Sade.

17. Boulevard Robespierre.

18. Boulevard of the Encyclopedists.

19. Transversal of the French Revolution.

20. Boulevard of the October Revolution.

21. Transversal of the Triumph of Reason.

22. Boulevard of the Great Promiscuous Woman

23. Lenin Boulevard.

I Red Lantern Street

II Josip Broz Street

CORRECTIONS OF THE FALSIFIERS' INTERVENTIONS

1) IN THE "ORIGINAL," in *Phenomena*, the sentence is missing between ". . . to the extent they are clearly articulated" and "The theologian, of course, is not interested in aesthetics"; precisely those sentences that speak of the coming about of the world as a creative act of the divine imagination.

2) Likewise, somewhat further on, part of the sentence is left out where it discusses the occasional cases of the appearance of **David's Crystals**, objects which arrive from higher spiritual spheres and do not manage to remain in one place long but rather disappear inexplicably, which in the ranks of the Librarians causes unease because they disturb the **image** of the solid nature and determinism of the material world.

3) Several lines later, from the list of the sons of peril, the names of the "sons of peril" (Voltaire and Diderot) are left out (or erased), because they still have a certain credibility and still stimulate subversive activity.

4) Instead of "visionary of a utopian society," as it says in *Phenomena* (which goes in favor of the readership's general human affinity and sentiment toward utopias), it should say like the original, "the visionary of a society intolerant toward all visions."

5) The final falsification is, certainly, the most transparent. Censorship, to be outright, let out the claim that Vatican dissidents are burned to this very day as well—this can be explained by wild narrative imagination—but they erased the confirmed statistical data about the means of execution (automobile accidents, fires, etc.), as well as the percentage (90%) of those who, though seeming to die in accidents, were in fact sentenced to death.

S.B.

ADDENDUM IN CONFIRMATION OF GOTTFRIED ROSENKREUTZ'S THESIS

At the time when the chapter was already the distant past of the novel, the author came across an article published in the newspaper *Self-Management* (Issue 5, June 1990), in which he found irrefutable evidence that the Librarians, in alliance with Vatican organizations, are working to destabilize and release something into the external circle: helplessness: one of the last resorts of spiritual proximity to the Center of Rosenkreutz's projection. That's where this flashback comes from in the form of an addendum to the text by Umberto Eco.

IS THE VATICAN THREATENING THE SURVIVAL OF MOUNT ATHOS?

In its thousand-year history, Mount Athos has never been in greater danger than it is now. The monasteries of Slavic or Romanian origins are especially threatened. Unfortunately, those who do not wish for them to thrive are thinking more about them than those who are not only responsible for preserving old values, but also for creating new ones.

Namely, as opposed to the Vatican, Mount Athos has spiritual, but no territorial independence. They are a part of the Greek state, the monasteries there are GREEK, and the monks get Greek citizenship along with all the hurdles that come with it. Thereby, the greatest responsibility for their fate is borne by the Greek government, which does not reduce the responsibility of the other countries for whom Mount Athos is a spiritual hearth. Especially when talking about the defense of Athos from the aggression of so-called entrepreneurship, which, under the leadership of Giovani Veco (Istanbul patriarch from the twelfth century, advocate of union with Rome), intends to destroy Mount Athos with the explanation that "the last fortress of darkness and conservatism in modern Europe" should disappear. That which could not be done by the plague, or wars, or conquerors, "GV" intends to do, as it says in a bulletin from the Athos monks, with the following plan:

". . . (3) By law, Athos will be proclaimed an archeological site, and all monasteries will be turned into museums, except those that will become hotels. In each monastery-museum, a very small number of monks will remain, appropriately **educated ones**, who will work as guards, guides, custodians of archives and precious things . . ."

". . . (4) As soon as possible, building should commence of highways for automobiles and buses, and in some places gondolas, restaurants, bars, discotheques, and even casinos, so that the residence of visitor-tourists and scholars will be as pleasant as possible. Established scholarly institutes and schools for Byzantine studies are to be built by many countries . . ."

". . . (6) The construction should be allowed of small monasteries and churches, and to introduce other dogmas and religious missions, which will contribute to multilateral relations and the ideas of ecumenism . . ."

". . . (7) The main barrier remains those monasteries of other Orthodox states which will certainly oppose all of these plans, and that will be a pole around which all of the Greek clergy will gather, those who do not agree with these plans, and many of them are fanatic advocates of the Julian calendar, like the Serbs, Russians, and Bulgarians, and as long as they are on Athos, the attaining of our ultimate goals will be difficult . . ."

A favorable circumstance is that, in the official Church of Greece, and at the Ministry of Foreign Affairs, Culture, and Education, there are people who show complete understanding and who see the use which the country will have from this project, and the inexhaustible source of tourists' foreign currency. The Orthodox Patriarch in Istanbul and many Greek Metropolitans, are on our side. The action and reaction of those foreign monasteries on Athos should be eliminated as soon as possible. According to our sources, the Church of Moscow is already preparing an entire set of counter-actions to our plans. All of the clergy on Mount Athos, because of their common ecclesiastical, Julian calendar, have taken up the defense of the Russians, Serbs, Bulgarians, and other advocates of obscurantism, so we should send them from Athos as soon as possible, no later than the end of 1992 . . ."

". . . (8) in terms of directly connecting Athos, as proposed by the Holy See, with the other countries of the already united Europe, we believe it would be most suitable, and it would be desirable to expand to the islands of Crete, Tyre, and Naxos (Note: the proposed line is Marseille-Naples-Palermo-Corfu-Pireaus-Mykonos-Efes-Aphos and back). We've already received the propositions of interested parties from Italy, France, Israel and other countries. The existing difficulties from the Greek side (forbidding the transport of passengers and goods between Greek ports) will disappear after 1992 . . ."

". . . (9) The great danger that Mount Athos will turn into a starting point (TRAMPOLINE) for the damned heresies of Orthodoxy toward Africa and the Eastern Mediterranean should be avoided at all cost. Because of this, with collective action in all directions we should try to instigate internal anomalies and unrest in Greece, Yugoslavia, and Russia, which would have the goal of splitting them up. The years of attempts in that direction have not born the expected fruit.[26] If we do not hermetically seal the dangerous cracks in the northern dam, the damage to us will be incomprehensible . . ."

". . . (12) With sadness we have noticed that certain news agencies of friendly countries are not respecting the **agreed** upon

---

26 It is obvious that the document of the Giovanni Veco Society was written before the latest events in the Orthodox countries; the warning of the Mt. Athos monks must be taken quite seriously, therefore, because the disturbances occurring in Russia, Romania, Bulgaria, and to an extent in Greece, unambiguously indicate that the subversive forces have begun a powerful offensive, once again appearing as a Vatican-Islamist coalition, a coalition that never failed to overrun Byzantium by all necessary means: money, proselytism, corruption, and even Black Magic. (S. B.)

protocols, and they are reporting good news for the Russian Church, which controls the Party, as well as all that is happening in Greece and Yugoslavia in terms of religion. We must again emphasize that there should be no publication of news related to the 'miracles' which are supposedly happening in those countries, because they challenge the authority of the Holy See and the great battle it is involved in. We have available a list of journalists who are faithful to the ideas of Ecumenism . . ."

". . . (13) Our oversight committee has completed conversations on cooperation with the BAHAI and TARA centers in California with believers there, and with our brothers of "RODOSTAVROS." The adopted program is to be carried out in both hemispheres under the supervision of the Swiss coordination board . . ."

". . . (14) From Greece, especially from the isle of Syros (it does not exist in the Greek archipelago—author's note S.B.) we keep receiving horrible complaints from followers of the Holy See, whose life has become unbearable because of persecution by the heretical Orthodox clergy. Of course, we are doing everything possible from our side to bring an end to this obvious breech of human rights in twentieth century Europe and in the European community. We are certain that we will force the powers of obscurantism to withdraw by 1992 . . ."

Compiled by: Vojislav Dević
and Miloje Gavrilović

Повољна околност је што у званичној Цркви Грчке као и у Министарству спољних послова, културе и образовања постоје људи који показују потпуно разумевање и уочавају корист коју ће земља имати од овог новог и неисцрпног извора туристичких девиза. Православни Патријарх у Истамбулу а и многи грчки митрополити су на нашој страни. Деловање и реакција тих страних манастира на Атосу треба да се што пре елиминише. Како смо већ обавештени, Московска Црква већ спрема читав план противакција нашим плановима. Сав клер Свете Горе због заједничког црквеног Јулијанског календара узима у одбрану Русе, Србе, Бугаре и друге православне присталице мрачњаштва, па их, ако треба и силом, морамо што пре удаљити са Атоса до краја 1992. године..."

(8) "Што се тиче директног повезивања Атоса, које предлаже Света Столица, са осталим земљама, већ уједињене Европе, сматрамо да је најповољније, а било би и пожељно проширење на острва Крит, Тира и Наксос. (Белешка: Предложена линија је: Марсеј - Напуљ - Палермо - КРФ - ПИРЕЈ - МИКОНОС - Ефес - Афос и обрнуто.). Већ смо добили и предлоге заинтересованих личности из Италије, Француске, Израела и других земаља. Постојеће тешкоће са грчке стране (забрана превоза путника и роба између грчких лука) нестаће после 1992. године..."

(9) "Велика опасност да се сВета Гора - Атос претвори у базу одскока (ТРАМПЛИН) проклете јересе Православља према Африци и Источном Медитерану треба да се избегне по сваку цену. Због овога треба заједничким акцијама у свим

правцима да покушамо да изазовемо унутрашње аномалије- немире у Грчкој, Југославији и Русији који би имале за циљ њихово парцелисање. Дугогодишњи покушаји усмерени у том правцу нису уродили очекиваним плодом. Ако херметички не затворимо опасне пукотине у брани са Севера, штете ће бити за све нас несагледиве..."

(12) "Са жалошћу примећујемо да неке новинске агенције пријатељских земаља не поштују договорено и преносе повољне вести за Руску Цркву, коју контролише партија, као и за све оно што се догађа у Грчкој и Југославији на верском нивоу. Истичемо поново да ни због чега

Facsimile of part of the text from *Self-Management* translated from a bulletin of the Athos monks. Facsimile of the bulletin given in the text in the Greek original.

Sava Djakonov

PILGRIMAGE TO DHARAMSALA

(continuation of the story)

(In the first volume of the "Conspiracy," the narration of Sava Dja-
konov ended, or better said, it was suddenly interrupted after the
following passage: "Pavel Kuzmich did not finish his sentence, and
we found ourselves on an endless plain, surrounded in grayish light.
'Look to the east,' J.K. told me. I turned my head and, on the
horizon, I saw a shining structure filled with blinding light. 'That
is the cathedral of the Holy Spirit, the place of worship of the Evan-
gelical Bicycli . . .')

CONTINUATION:
". . . sts. Here in that cathedral, everything is preserved which
the Spirit brings in from the world given over to devastation.
Everything valuable, beautiful, and just is removed here, away
from the onslaught of destroyers and falsifiers." Suddenly, from
all around us a bunch of phantoms appeared in camouflaged
uniforms; as if driven by a hurricane, they rushed toward the
cathedral. "The Traumeinsatz!" J. K. shouted. "Get your head
down, get your head down." I couldn't react at first. At a certain distance in front of me, a tall man was standing there and
watching us closely. That is the last thing that remained in my
memory. At that same instant, I found myself in bed, in the
bordello in Niš, and J. K. was patting my cheeks. "Bad mistake,"
he said, "you should have done what I told you immediately."
"What mistake?" I asked in confusion, frightened and hungover.
"Because Klosowsky saw you and memorized your face. But
forget that for now. It's time for us to leave for Istanbul."

***

I was told that I was to remain in Istanbul and that my task was to wait in a rented room near the Grand Bazaar for a courier to bring me a package of exceptional significance. I wanted to keep going, to Dharamsala, the expanses of the East were luring me, but I didn't dare to break the discipline of the order. I passed the time like an idle tourist, I had enough money; I visited the important sites and waited for the courier to come. He did not show up till seven months later; he handed me a sealed envelope and disappeared into the night.

In the envelope were the **Instructions**, several pages of printed text and a manuscript typed out on a typewriter. The instructions told me to take the printed material (one printers' signature) and skillfully insert it in a 1917 edition of the Anglo-American Encyclopedia, and then to sell it to the secondhand bookseller Bekir Hazim at Beyazit Meydani 41. The typewritten manuscript, on the other hand, I was to read, retype, and send the copy to an address in Zurich. The manuscript, reproduced here, had a rather strange name:

THE LAND OF FALSIFIERS

For hundreds of years in the regions of the Near East, a myth has been circulating, perhaps better to call it a rumor, about a secret land of Falsifiers. There are numerous versions of that rumor, but they all agree on one thing: the country is ruled by an emperor, a cruel tyrant who, for the sake of mimicry, has the custom of presenting himself as a benefactor, peacemaker, and champion of the people. They say that the emperor is of low birth and that he reached the throne after long and difficult struggles in which he, like Gilgamesh, had to overcome and kill hundreds of thousands of opponents. That is just one of the variations. Hundreds and hundreds of historians, biographers, and writers—whose only job that is—daily write new pages into the **Biography** of the ruler. At the time when this manuscript is to be published, the **Biography** will contain no less than 489 volumes, and the entry for CHILDHOOD AND YOUTH will still not be completed in all its details.

According to one apocryphal manuscript, the Land of Falsifiers resulted from the leftover parts of other spaces. There were two legitimate empires: Byzantium and Rome. They were maintained by the internal cohesion of faith in God, the one they killed on Golgotha. With the weakening of faith, the empires disintegrated into a multitude of small states. When that happens, some parts of space are lost; in large places, it is not possible to precisely measure the expanses (that is also not possible even with small ones) and draw clear borders. Sooner or later, a surplus of territory appears, unrecorded in the land cadastres. This no-man's-land is, naturally, occupied by specters, nameless people, cheats, and fugitives from the law. It is then logical that in such a country no laws can exist, that the subjects are forced to slavishly tolerate the whims of the Emperor and local satraps since they have nowhere to go; wherever they set off for, they do not exist, they are no one and nothing. But, paradoxically, laws are constantly passed, pro forma, of course, but they never go into force, and no one is bothered by that. Amazement would be caused by the insistence on the literal following of the law. But one day, the future Emperor appeared on the historical stage, the one to unify the lawlessness of the subjects into a single power. He is not satisfied just to evade the laws of God, man, and physics . . . He also breaks his contract with the Devil, and wants to make the country recognized and powerful. The cartographers, pamphlet writers, scholars, and philosophers work night and day, under the watchful eye of the Emperor, on the never-ending Encyclopedia. It is more-or-less known to everyone that facts are mostly made up, partly by being many times overstated, but hardly anyone ever admits that to themselves. (Those rare individuals who dare to publicly express their doubt in the credibility of the Encyclopedia disappear without a trace; this also escapes notice because even the data about the number of inhabitants is falsified; in the birth records, for example, unborn children are entered; certain dead people are not entered into the death records; the number of inhabitants is one-third higher than in reality. Let us take a few examples: in the Encyclopedia, it says that the highest peak in the land is 4,753 meters high, although it is actually a little more than 1,400. The data on natural resources are also falsified. Engineers of dubious reputation (brought in from abroad for the sake of illusory objectivity) provide evidence that the country is rich in minerals, crude oil, coal, gold . . . *De facto*, nothing of the abovementioned exists, except in symbolic amounts. And yet, both in Europe and in America people believe that the country is indeed wealthy, partly because of their prejudices about exotic lands, partly because of the patient work of the Scene Designers who erect perfect copies of coal mines and mineral mines, in which film extras pretend to work.

Keeping all of that in mind, it is possible to imagine the extent of the falsification only to a point. Daily newspapers[27] day after day publish articles about completely imaginary events. To the untrained eye, such newspapers look like all the others; they write about misfortunes that never happened, about huge projects in the southern provinces that were never begun, about terrible murders done by the Enemies (they call them the Foes), which were never committed. The public, if that word can be applied, reacts strongly to the news in the papers. Teachers from the interior, failed lawyers, and housewives rain letters on the editorial offices of the newspapers, even though those offices

27 In the Land, a large number of daily and weekly publications come out, starting with those in the capital, to those regional ones, then for schools, factories, and periodicals for the Association of Butterfly Enthusiasts, for example. The goal, that every citizen of the Land has an article about themselves in some paper, has practically been achieved.

do not really exist except in the form of bronze plates hung on the facades of government buildings. Newspapers are, in fact, printed ahead of time; the entire print run of all editions is printed out during a single month. In that way, the news causes events to happen, not the other way around, as is the practice in countries that passively wait for the future. If, let us say, on the front page of the leading paper, they print the news in January that a serious automobile accident will occur in June, it will indeed occur. Certainly, these journalistic mystifications are intended for the popular masses. Incomparably subtler are the falsifications of important historical events: imaginary wars, great (fictional) battles won under the leadership of the ingenious Emperor. Or this example: Balthazar III, one of the previous incarnations of the present emperor (who lived in the fifteenth century), ordered that blasphemy be done: that Christ be crucified once again on one of the hills outside the capital. The theologian-atheists from his court chose some other chap who looked somewhat like Christ; two thieves were brought out of prison, and the performance was put on according to the Gospel according to Matthew. In the Europe of the time, the performance of scenes from the Old and New Testament were not uncommon; but the performance of Balthazar III was no theater: the stand-ins were indeed crucified, and they indeed died on the cross. A hundred years later, in his next incarnation, when he again ascended the throne under the hypocritical name of Innocent I, the emperor ordered the scholars to investigate the event thoroughly. They did the investigation, studied the remains of the crucified and published a text in which they claimed that the crucifixion, in truth, was undoubted, but that Jesus did not get resurrected, and that all of that was just the dangerous and malevolent fantasy of people with disturbed minds. God was bothersome to Innocent I, so the ruler undertook drastic measures to get rid of him. Somehow about that time, Machiavelli also wrote that the ends justifies the means.

And indeed, reproduced in hundreds and thousands of copies, that text circulated throughout Europe, convincing the "enlightened" that religion is nonsense, thus laying the road for the highest incarnation, Joseph I Ambrose, whose stable boys also officially buried the Lord God one night in the canyons of the Land of Falsifiers.

Here, a digression is necessary: as the rulers of the Land—depending on the need—proselytized from one confession to another over the centuries, to this very day a rather large number of places of worship have remained from those various confessions. Although in recent times religion has been decisively expurgated, the government authorities do not desecrate the churches or hinder religious services; they are open and they work, but (the emigrants say) none of the priests or visitors to the churches believe in God.

The superficiality of the rest of the world works in favor of the Land of Falsifiers. It has obviously been forgotten that a lie repeated enough time begins to be accepted as the truth. The enormous influence that made-up events, wars, and people have on the course of history is neglected. What would Europe look like today if the kings and dukes had not listened to the unreliable reports of the emissaries of the Empire (today's Land of the Falsifiers) and futilely perished before the ramparts of Jerusalem and in the deserts of Anatolia. Because of that the past, full of naïve falsifications, is strictly controlled in the Land of Falsifiers, and is available mostly to the top "philosophers." That is why there are several versions of **The History**: for the foreign public, for domestic use, for elementary school, for the subjects, for the representatives of government. Those truths, say the "philosophers," do not contradict each other, but complement each other. As a result of the centuries of illusion's tyranny, reality (or the thing that is called that) in the Land is so far relativized that biological and physical laws have lost all meaning. How else can one explain that the ruler will soon celebrate his 453rd birthday? Or that untrustworthy subjects die the same day they see their own death announcement in the state-run newspapers, if it is known that the newspapers are printed months ahead of time? One author, wishing to remain anonymous, interprets these phenomena in the following way: It is known, he writes, that man's world is ruled by necessity and determinism. If man grows closer to God, those forces control him less; it is said that he has mastered himself and can do miracles. Like in a mirror, a similar but opposite event occurs when a man grows distant from God: determinism and limitations grow weaker, only going in that direction reality is ever less real; that is the punishment for self-will. In the end of all things, every such project ends in nothingness. Not even the tiniest trace remains of him except in the texts of fantasy writers and poets, which remain in libraries as (vain) warnings to future generations. But drunkenness brought on by the variety of deceptions is the most terrible, and "when truth appears, it hides beneath pauper's clothing and simply abets those who are not worthy of despising it"—as Hugo of Saint Victor writes. For, such things also happen: some aristocrat angers the Ruler or (more often the case) the Ruler begins to doubt his loyalty. During the night, representatives visit him and confront him with his guilt. Everyone is afraid of that, because the punishment is much worse than death. Already the next day, the enormous job begins of removing all traces of the life of the poor fellow who has fallen from grace. Volumes of **The History**[28] are withdrawn from the library, the name of

---

28   That is a huge job. One should know that the volumes of **The History** contain detailed descriptions of every day of the life of the Ruler; all encounters are mentioned, all his words are written down, the text is accompanied by a large number of illustrations. We have obtained several pages of **The History** which we are reprinting here so that insight is gained into the grandiose quality and complexity of the enterprise:

"On October 23, the President, obviously in a good mood, got up at 7:30 and told the on-duty secretary about a dream he had the night before. Then he cried, 'Oh, what a beautiful day this will have to be'.

the unfit is erased, photographs are retouched, in the place of the overturned some other face is inserted, and as a curious fact one should mention the example when, shoulder to shoulder with the Ruler and his dignitaries, Clark Gable appeared. Rarely do those who are thus overturned live more than a month. It is only then that the family starts having trouble. By law it is expressly forbidden to bury an erased person in the state cemeteries, which is probably an atavism derived from the prohibition of burying on holy ground those who commit suicide. On the other hand, no one except the Ruler has the right to bury the

After coming out of the bathroom, the President selected a powder blue suit and an appropriate tie, then—after a brief consultation with the Chef de Cuisine—he headed to the dining room where for breakfast he had ham and eggs while leafing through the morning newspapers. Then, accompanied by his collaborators and his spouse Ioanna I, he withdrew into the garden where coffee was served. In a conversation with the Chancellor of the University, the President discussed an episode in the novel *Great Expectations,* which he was carefully following in the paper **Vedomosti**. "Ursula should certainly think carefully before she marries Guido," said the President. The entourage agreed unanimously and applauded the leader's perspicacity. (The editor of **Vedomosti** urgently called the editorial offices and gave instructions: do not allow Ursula to marry Guido under any circumstances.) Around ten o'clock, the President gave a signal for everyone to be quiet. He sat down in a rocking chair, closed his eyes and began to think. Full of piety, his entourage sat on the lawn next to the Leader and watched him, unblinking. Around 11:15, the President started up from his thinking and offered his epic insight: "With optimism we can look upon the further development of our Land." Ovations followed, and then the Leader said suddenly, "Now, let's go for a swim. We have to learn wisdom from the rivers, which flow to the seas for millions of years, patiently carving out their course." They immediately headed for the river, the common folk en masse spontaneously joined the President and his dignitaries as they began swimming in the chilly waters. According to some estimates, the swimming marathon was participated in by about 95,000 people. After several weeks, copying the ingeniousness of the Leader, Mao Tse-tung swam down the Yangtze with his collaborators . . ." (**The History**, Volume 121, p. 5794)

corpses of their dogs, horses and pets, cats, poodles and par-
rots in residential areas. (They explain this with the great love
of the President toward his most loved ones.) Only with a lot
of effort—the authorities turn their heads after all—does the
family manage to bury the dead fellow in a potter's field. He
is quickly covered in complete obscurity. But the Ruler, whose
whims are unpredictable even to his closest collaborators, one
day, as if nothing happened, asks, "I haven't seen Shmar lately.
What's happening with Shmar?" Who would dare to tell the
President that his former favorite had died? "Well, Mr. President,
Shmar is around here somewhere, surely he'll drop by one of
these days . . ." the aristocrats whisper. There's nothing else to do
but rehabilitate Shmar; since in the Land of Falsifiers dignitaries
are only illusorily alive, they are also dead only illusorily; it is
all just a matter of politics. That same day they dig up Shmar,
give him an infusion, clean him up, put him in a new suit; **The
History** is again withdrawn and the data about Shmar is reen-
tered together with the photographs. Poor Clark Gable, through
no fault of his own, he has to leave **The History**. It is said that
he died unexpectedly because of that.

Some authors, moreover, claim that despite all kinds of wonders, the Land of Falsifiers has till now not mastered the powers
of raising the dead. The proposal goes like this: the "marked"
only die in illusory fashion; they reduce their physiological
needs to a minimum and thus—breathing once in ten or fifteen
days—they lie in the grave for a few years until they fall back
into favor. A large number of aristocrats never see that day. Since
each of those who is in close proximity to the Ruler has at least
once tasted the darkness of the grave, when they again appear
in the light of day, they become insatiable; they gobble down
enormous quantities of food, spend their time hunting, in the
fresh air, killing hundreds of quail, the production of which is
run by a special department of the Ministry of Agriculture and
Husbandry.

Generally speaking, death in the Land of Falsifiers has

been elevated to the level of a cult. The town squares are full of monuments to all sorts of warriors who never did anything in life except die in spectacular ways. For the average man, life is nothing more than the feverish preparation for the afterlife which, true to the doctrine, has been relocated from the other-worldly into the immanent. With the exception of government buildings, more symbols than habitations, the cities are fairly deserted. But the cemeteries are magnificent. Every city has a corresponding cemetery; the capital one, logically, is the largest and best kept, and it is dominated by the President's Mausoleum. Each loyal citizen of the state is guaranteed (post mortem) a bust in one of the parks or the name of one of the streets. The totalitarian nature of the state, which extends into all time-dimensions, was described by D. V. in the essay **Travelogue from Hades**; he was a dissident who, quite accidentally, survived the hell of death and fled to Belgium. Seven years spent in the world of the dead made many secrets available to him, which he laid out in an internal publication:

"Based on a contract with the Devil, in the fourteenth century Balthazar III got the rights to one province of hell, which was raised from the depths of Hades to the territory of the **Land of the Falsifiers.** Tortured by his love of vengeance, the tyrant could not make peace with the fact that his opponents were escaping his wrath by seeking asylum in death. From that day forth, there is no end to the tortures of those who angered the monarch. I became convinced of that by my own experience.

"In my youth, I naively wrote a pasquinade against the dictator. The very moment when I put the last period on my manuscript, the police knocked at the door of my apartment. No one had had the chance to even pass a fleeting glance over the text, but that did not reduce my guilt. At the time, of course, I did not know that every sheet of paper in the Land has its double; no matter what is written on the original, the text is immediately reproduced on the double. Simple and efficient.

Moreover, if a text is written on the double, it also appears on the original. The security services use that when they want to get rid of someone who is politically 'unfit': simply, on the doubles of pieces of paper of the poor wretch, the agents of the Service write some sort of compromising text; he has no idea, because he has written nothing. When the cops show up and find the pasquinade, he has no choice but to confess. Keeping that in mind, one should accept with ultimate skepticism those pasquinades against the government that show up abroad; most often they are written in the offices of the Security Services. Falsification has advanced so far that doubt is cast even when an unfalsified pasquinade is found. It is considered a success in the Security circles when hidden pamphlets are found and discovered, those which are still in the thoughts of certain individuals. Elite units of the PRC (Parapsychology Research Command) and the DCC (Dream Control Command) deal with such things. Because of that, there is no peace to be had, not even when sleeping; people practice dreaming the allowed dreams . . . An entire program of autosuggestion and breathing exercises before sleeping has been developed, because one never knows when the agents of the DCC will show up in the middle of the night, in the middle of a dream.

"After my arrest, I was imprisoned in a cellar. Already at dawn I was taken before the court. I had so many wrong ideas, so many prejudices gleaned from the books I was clandestinely reading. The judge was eating a sandwich and sipping coffee. 'V. D.,' he said with his mouth full, 'you finally went too far.' His aid was digging around in the notebooks for my case during that time. I noticed that the binder where he found the documents was dated ten years earlier. The sentence was brief: death by strangulation.

"Like most other young people, I did not believe either in God or the Devil. I thought: I'll die, and the stupid game will be over. I did not start trembling when the executioner approached me with a silk bowstring, I did not mourn for the pitiful shape of the world as he strangled me . . . But I came to somewhere far from that stinking cellar and I heard the shout, 'Lazy bastard, get up!'

"My body was no longer solid like in the Land, but it also was not quite transparent. Over me stood the guards, giggling evilly, and below me, on some sort of square crawling with hunched over people, I saw the President's statue. 'No way out, escape is impossible,' I thought. For the next seven years, dreamless (but tired), without food or water (but hungry and thirsty), day and night I worked on the project for which I finally understood the point after a long time; the President, namely, had decided to build an underground state, a faithful copy of the Land of Falsifiers, from which he would rule the dead and the world of the living, when inevitable death one day caught up with him, exhausted from the multitude of his incarnations.[29] To be fair, the lack of food and water, denied of rest, I could not blame my torturers for that, because after death there is no sleeping, eating, or drinking, even though fatigue, hunger, and thirst are worse. That is the way hell is. The tyrant just uses that.

"My troubles increased that day when I understood that the upper world was to be destroyed, and that the forces of evil were working on creating a new world. In the laboratories placed far from the curious eyes of the living, scientists were testing the properties of matter, testing the possibilities of making it independent of God's emanations. To that end, they are using enormous amounts of matter, which is being stolen from the face of the earth, and which so impoverished, is becoming ever less real."

And indeed, the text of D. V. can be taken as credible, because the process of loss in reality is ever more obvious even beyond the undetermined borders of the Land. Objects are less and less empirical, so people resort to placing large numbers on

---

29 See Attachment 4 in the Appendix. (S. B.)

the board with inscriptions that explain them. The Structuralists have predicted that in the near future the world will become just a text—endlessly boring material full of description. Logically, all of that is most easily seen in the Land of Falsifiers, where entire regions are disappearing into nothingness, and from gorgeous landscapes all that is left are contours. People themselves are not spared. According to the claims of the travelogue writers, ontology has been nationalized. It will be placed in the transcendent cellars of the State Archive. Thereby a man's dossier determines who he is, and the soul is materialized in one's ID card. "If someone loses their ID card," D. V. writes, "he's confronted with almost insolvable problems. He is faced with proving that he is who he says he is. Identity is ultimately difficult to establish, since it actually does not really exist; without an ID card, I can be whoever I want. However, in the case when someone's ID card is taken, he very soon disappears from the land of the living; of the human being remains only an empty shadow which trolls the streets and squares for a time, and then vanishes. Those shadows happily gather in the dusk in front of State buildings in the vain hope that they will attract the attention of one of the clerks, and that is a truly disgusting scene."

Although the State Mint prints enormous quantities of currency, trading, economy in general, in the Land of Falsifiers does not exist. There is nothing for one to buy, if one disregards the rare shops that are an unavoidable detail in the landscape of cities. Dignitaries and servants of the state get whatever they need for free; the rest are forced to steal, although stealing is an unsuitable word. It is commonplace, and the state tolerates it. Companies and factories are a story in themselves; they are not founded with the intention of producing anything, but they are rather handed out to deserving officers and the relatives of dignitaries for lifelong enjoyment. The employed only pretend to work; operating hours are reduced to seven, and that is considered to be an exceptional success. If any of the factories does actually work, it produces things other than those that it is supposed to. The most highly developed are, doubtlessly, the industries of Coca-Cola and Euro Cream, based on technology imported from abroad. In terms of the consumption of those products, the Land of Falsifiers holds one of the top places in the world. The Coca-Cola is enriched with sedatives and hallucinogens (Parkopan, Artane, LSD) which ease the processes of indoctrination.

The system of communication deserves special attention. Although the official statistics insist on the fact that ninety-five percent of all households have a telephone, that fact should be taken with ultimate reserve because ninety percent of those telephones are just everyday children's toys.

The writing of dubious letters is thwarted in the aforementioned way: every letter has a double. If X wants to write a letter to Y, the procedure is as follows: a piece of paper is taken and the message written. But there is no need to address the letter and put it in the mailbox; the clerks at the post office, if they decide the letter contains nothing forbidden, deliver the copy that they already have to the addressee. Both train and road transportation are centralized. More or less every town is connected to the capital, but between the individual towns, even if they are only a few miles away from each other, there are no roads. Traveling between towns in the interior is frowned upon.

Many debates have been held in order to establish the geographic location of the Land of Falsifiers. It goes without saying that they were pointless; it is everywhere and nowhere, that is the summary of all the research done, but it has its limits. In recent times, the belief has become prominent that the incorporeal character of the Land of Falsifiers was caused by disturbances in the flow of time, through the introduction of the Gregorian calendar, which is thirteen entire days ahead of the natural time of the world, so that the Land parasitically uses the territory of legitimate countries, locating itself in their future. Because of that, in recent years, the increased subversive activity in countries and churches (Orthodox, mostly) which follow the Julian calendar and thus represent a hindrance so that the Land of Falsifiers does not expand to the rest of the world.

Since falsifying tends to become all-encompassing (and is making more and more ground in doing so), art has become more respected; although the practice of defining the canons of official art has been abandoned, most artists try to paint hyper-realistically. It should be mentioned that such a way of painting demands exceptional imagination; to paint, for example, a vase with all its details is a real undertaking; such a picture is certainly more valuable than the actual vase, even if it comes from the Ming dynasty, which served as a model for the picture. And it is more real, connoisseurs believe. Landscapes are especially highly valued, and they decorate the walls of a small number of the most affluent. But copies of those landscapes are available for everyone, and they are found in museums. Only the most experienced connoisseurs of art, those who spend a lifetime studying pictures, have a rather tenuous idea about what their surroundings look like, and they are truly foggy on the morphology of the whole Land. That is because falsifying has not reached perfection. When a deception becomes too obvious and when the government of one of the legitimate countries doubts that something is wrong with part of their territory, things quickly devolve into the usurping of land: the inhabitants take on the names of citizens, public signs are written in the language of the host, and geomorphology is harmonized with the official maps. Those outlying parts of the Land, which penetrate deep into the territory of other countries, are inhabited by trustworthy, elite officials. Those dedicated to their work, during a single generation, make it possible that huge expanses—including even high mountain peaks—get completely incorporated into the Land, in a way that no one notices it, not even the local population. The disappearance of large buildings, working unconsciously in favor of the Falsifiers, is justified by scientists as the work of erosion. Such an efficient occupation of land can be explained only as the conjunction of the action of a multitude of small mystifications and falsifications.

The mystical national holiday of the Land of Falsifiers is November 29. In that combination of ominous numbers (cf. **The Dictionary of Symbols**, Chevalier, under the entry **Numbers**), so the experts say, the cause of the country's rise is hidden, but so is the cause of its inevitable downfall.

***

Having read the manuscript, I acted according to the instructions. I put one copy in the Encyclopedia and sold it for a song to the aforementioned secondhand bookseller. The other I sent to the address indicated. That afternoon, I visited the Hagia Sophia and there, at the exit of the former basilica, all trace of me is lost. In the circles of the Bicyclists of the Rose Cross, the rumor prevails that I was kidnapped by the commandos of the Traumeinsatz. How true that is, I can't tell. In any case, since that day nothing has ever been heard about me again.

THE TELEGRAM I RECEIVED ON DECEMBER 15, 1989

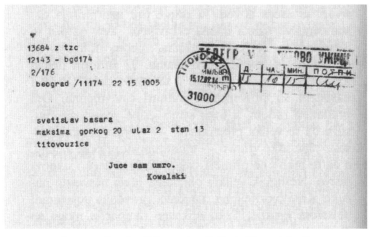

It says simply, "Yesterday I died. Kowalsky."

Illumination

AND SO, AFTER Kowalsky's death, I was left completely alone. I could no longer depend on his distant, invisible, but powerful support, which had protected me countless times, though I had no idea about that, and which led me like Ariadne's thread through the labyrinth of streets named after blacksmiths and thieves, good-for-nothings, and cheats. Never again was there a black Lincoln waiting for me in front of my apartment; gone also were the rest of the technological wonders. I had to head for Bajina Bašta by bike.

That night, when I straddled my rusting velocipede, a ROG model, after some two hundred pages the agents of the Secret Police were waiting for me to go around a corner and to enter my apartment to find this novel suspected of subversive actions. To make things worse, a nasty fine rain began to pour down.

"What the hell am I doing in this novel, which, mainly, other authors wrote, and the composition of which is just now being determined by complete laymen in questions of literature—agents of the Secret Police?" I wondered as I turned the pedals with difficulty and penetrated the darkness.

"Is it just because of a vain feeling of literary omnipotence, because of the fact that I know what is happening in my apartment, although that is a secret of state, facts, among other things, made worthless by one other fact—that I wrote that ahead of time—that I have to wander around in these gorges instead of waiting for ruination in a disciplined way like everybody else?"

And then, I was haunted also by the idea that I was just a tool, that I had been used, utilized only to bring a few texts from the third dimension of dreams into the light of day, texts that will be two or three drops of water in the clepsydra of the Order to which I belong, risking to remain forever in some sort of nightmare, and even that all my effort might go unnoticed or that I would be exposed to the mockery of the critics. All right, critics are no one and nothing, but I couldn't quash the feeling of bitterness, the feeling of defeat, of the lack of proud authorial self-deception that I am a creator.

I turned the unlubricated pedals and repeated to myself, "For my yoke is easy and my burden is light," so as not to fall into desperation, and then from the bicycle, and thus expose myself to the risk that the novel—no matter how it is—would remain incomplete and nameless. Comforted, partially, by chanting that Christian mantra, in the dark of night I reached the out-skirts of Bajina Bašta. All around, in the darkness, hundreds and thousands of candles were burning, and I wondered if it was All Souls' Day. I couldn't remember. I got off the bicycle and headed down the deserted streets, staring all about because of Kowalsky's prophesy that I would find the title of the novel in one of them. I was horribly tired, so I sat down on the curb of Svetosavska Street to rest. The prop guys tiptoed in, without a word, bringing a bottle of vodka and a package of cigarettes, and then they backed away. I took a swig and thought: it's all over! The centuries of effort by the Little Brothers have come to naught. The playoff is over. The Librarians and Falsifiers have won their victory; Byzantium is lost forever, ripped apart and scattered, annihilated, and that is why real people are also appearing in the novel, and in "reality" literary protagonists and characters from third-rate Hollywood productions are showing up. Everything has mixed together, the chaos is complete; I will get drunk and emigrate into the next novel . . .

Suddenly, above the blackened roofs, I saw purple letters that burned in the sky: G R A I L. The moment of enlightenment. The moment for which—as I will later write in the foreword to the novel—I wrote and suffered for, constantly wondering: why? The moment in which, not only did I find the name of the novel—ON THE TRAIL OF THE GRAIL—but also the name of the final volume of the trilogy, which will be called THE CROSS ON HAGIA SOPHIA, in which will be laid out the *Summa Theologiae* of the Order to which I belong, the Order which is already a part of the past under the name of the Bicyclists of the Rose Cross, because the basic principle of that ancient tradition is constant mimicry and concealment from the curious eyes of this fallen world.

At that instant, it became crystal clear to me that nothing was lost, that the end, which to the hordes from the East and West seems to be ever closer, is nothing other than (as René Guénon says) "the end of an illusion," an illusion which the Librarians and Falsifiers patiently, but in vain, built for thousands of years.

"IN HOC SIGNO VINCES!" I said (or thought), repeating Constantine's words after all those centuries. The ecstasy quickly passed and I could clearly see that the reason behind it was an optical illusion: on the roof of the INEX Hotel, the neon sign GRILL was shining, but the letters were partially black and broken, so that the name of the god of gluttony appeared to spell out GRAIL. *Felix error.* The truth, so say the mystics, is always hidden in a lie, the holiest in the filthiest. I no longer needed the bicycle. A little later, when I gather my thoughts, I will fall asleep and wake up in my room, just in time, when the agents of the Secret Police record the contents of my desk drawer and leave the apartment.

I took a long draw of vodka and lit a cigarette.

In the east, and where else, it began to dawn.

Like shadows dressed in blue overalls of heavy cotton, the workers of the SEPTEMBER 12 Public Services were putting away the backdrop of night and setting up the backdrop of day.

APPENDIX

ATTACHMENT 1

A SENSATIONAL ARCHEOLOGICAL DISCOVERY

SEARCHING FOR OBJECTS from an earlier discovered Neolithic site not far from Negotin, a team of archeologists from the University of Belgrade, led by Prof. Vasil Tapušković, PhD, quite accidentally came across the remains of a medieval town, which existed between the eleventh and thirteenth centuries. That city, which Dr. Tapušković considers to be a city-state like Dubrovnik, does not belong to a single known culture of this region, so it is no wonder that it has created quite a sensation in the circles of Byzantine and medieval scholars all over the world.

The ethnic background of the people who inhabited this area is quite mysterious; although of Orthodox confession, they used the Latin alphabet, and their knowledge of topography (judging from the precision of the maps found) goes far beyond the highest achievements of that time. Those maps on parchment (several preserved copies were found) encompass a surface area of some 420 kilometers in the most intricate detail; compared to modern sections of the area, there is practically no difference.

The central part of the town consists of the remains of the court of King Charles, who bore the nickname "the Hideous." His calcified body was found on a massive wooden throne; it is thought that the throne used to be hung from the beams of the roof with strong chains, and that it was some sort of swing. This is believed because of the four steel chains found near the throne. However, the purpose of the sharp spikes driven into the back of the throne, so that they stick out about 3 cm, is still unknown. Dr. Tapušković believes that the town was destroyed suddenly by a natural cataclysm of some sort. On the hearth of the throne room, a lot of ashes were found, and piles of singed page margins. It is hard to resist the impression that the courtiers burned their books in a hurry. The fire was escaped by only a few legible pages and, to the disappointment of scholars, they are just ephemeral records about debts, the purchase of bison, dill, and perfumes, etc.

However, from the few remains, it can be supposed that the kingdom of Charles the Hideous maintained lively relations with the European cultural centers of that time; that famous artists of the time resided at the court during a certain period, about which there is testimony in the **Book of Payments.**

Yet, what interested this reporter the most, as confirmed by competent foreign scholars, is the phenomenon of an exceptionally powerful geomagnetic wind from an unknown source, which makes receiving radio and TV signals in the area quite difficult, and the relatively common manifestations of ESPs (Extra Sensory Phenomena) such as the appearance of ghosts, telekinesis, the inexplicable speeding up and slowing down of timepieces, and so on. Not long after the discovery of Charles's town, several of the excavators contracted a mysterious illness, and Dr. Tapušković refused to comment, saying there is a lack of material evidence.

According to the latest news, the Command of the Military Section has proclaimed the zone to be under military exercises, and has prohibited all access to scholars, parapsychologists, basically all those who are not army experts.

S. Fetahagić
Arka, journal for the popularization of science.

ATTACHMENT 2

SQUARE II OF PSYCHOANALYSIS IN BAJINA BAŠTA

The youth of the bronze war hero

(The next is a hero in peasant clothing. The attention of the observer is attracted to the precision by which the artist cast his ragged clothes. He is looking at the first two statues and it is thought he is saying, "I believe you.") *Phenomena*, p. 12.

And the aging bronze version

The first to the right, looking determinedly into the sky and saying: "God, you are dead. You don't exist. We people will build our own lives and our own happiness by ourselves. We don't need you anymore." His hand raised and clenched into a fist symbolizes firm resolution to stop injustice. He waves a hand grenade and advises: "Without mercy we will remove all barriers.")

Phenomena, p. 12.

Monument II of Psychoanalysis in front of the "Beograd" Department Store in Bajina Bašta. The three nymphs: Id, Ego and Superego.

ATTACHMENT 3

METHODS OF MAINTAINING THE ILLUSION OF THE EXISTENCE OF THE WORLD

Are we really witnessing the dawn of the establishment of a modern totalitarian order?

This is only one of the many questions which, with a hint of dramatic disbelief, await the readers of the book *Rock 'n Roll* by Joseph Mata. The book represents a unique "manifesto of despair" before the spiritual agony of the younger generations, who have become prisoners of and addicted to rock rhythms of the mass sub-culture empire. At the same time, it is also an invitation to raising awareness. With the intention of making young people soulless and inferior, the producers of rock culture are impertinently intruding into the human subconscious, using the, generally illegal, technique of so-called *"subliminal"* messages, messages conveyed *below "the threshold of consciousness."*

In order for these messages to be conveyed in a latent way, they are printed *as the opposite of what they mean.* To the ear of the conscious, they become audible only when a record(ing) is played backwards. Research showed that the subconscious is able to decipher such messages even when they are formed in a different language! With the album called *Killers* by the band Queen, it is enough to play the song "Another One Bites the Dust" backwards to hear the message *"Start smoking marijuana."* The lyrical message of the band Led Zeppelin – "There's still time to change the road you're on" in the song "Stairway to Heaven" in the mirror of the subconscious gets the following inverted reflection: *"Here's to my sweet Satan, the one whose little path would make me sad, whose power is Satan".* In the song "Anthem" by the band Rush, the inverted message is: *"Oh, Satan . . . you are the one who is shining . . . walls of Satan . . . I know it's you are the one I love . . . !"*

Such messages penetrate deeply into the subconscious of the listeners, who are *completely deprived of any defense against such a form of aggression and indoctrination. Ultrasonic signals (similar to those produced by dog whistles) are also imprinted on those records. When stimulated by ultrasonic signals for a longer period of time, the brain produces certain biochemical reactions, which match the effects of the use of morphine! With this, two goals are achieved: on one hand, an unconscious addiction is developed in rock-music listeners (too)*, and on the other, by doing so, the terrain is prepared to increase the number of possible victims of drugs and the drug business.

Among the most widespread techniques of conveying messages below "the threshold of consciousness" is the stroboscope. This instrument, usually seen in discotheques, can accelerate flashes of light (light-show) to degrees which cause impairment of the sense of direction, reflexes, and judgment. When the speed of the intervals of the light beam emission is increased to 25 per second—the alpha waves which in humans indicate the ability to control behavior and mentally focus are destroyed. That is why many popular discotheques are, in fact, illegal or *secret laboratories* for making young people soulless and introducing them into Satanism, drugs, and homosexuality.

The author, Joseph Mata, also noted various statements of some of the most acclaimed "stars" of rock music, who unambiguously reveal their role in the media. So, for example, Alice Cooper, whose real name is Vincent Furnier, confessed the following: "Some years ago I went to a séance where Norman Buckley asked the spirit to make himself heard. The spirit manifested itself at last and spoke to me. *He promised* me and my music group *glory* and world domination with rock music and wealth in abundance. All he asked in return was for me to give my body to that spirit, which took possession of me. A change of possession of my body would make me famous throughout the whole world. To do this, I took the name by which 'he' had identified himself in the session."

Ozzy Osbourne, the extremely popular singer of the band Black Sabbath said that his every song had been composed while he was acting as a medium: *"I don't know if I'm a medium for some outside source.* Whatever it is, frankly, I hope it's not what I think it is—Satan. I know that there is some supernatural force using me to bring forth my rock and roll. I hope it's not the force of Satan." Elton John often used to make the statement that all of his songs had been written in *witch language* (!). Mick Jagger, besides being the lead-singer of the band The Rolling Stones, is also a member of the paramasonic organization who call themselves "Hermetic Order of the Golden Dawn." It is, in fact, a branch of the order founded by "the Pope" of modern Satanism, Aleister Crowley. Mick Jagger regularly *attends black magic rituals and identifies himself as "the incarnation of Lucifer."* This Satanic obsession of his is also confirmed by his song titles—*"Their Satanic Majesties Request," "Sympathy for the Devil"* or *"Invocation of My Demon Brother."*

The ambitions of modern brainwashers do not stop at the domain of rock music. Many supermarkets in the USA and Canada have devices that produce effects below "the threshold of consciousness," which, through the harmless and quiet sounds of music, warn customers not to steal and give them advice on what they should buy. Research showed that such 'subliminal' "brainwashing" of customers decreases the rate of shoplifting by half and significantly increases the amount of money customers spend. The author of the book "Rock 'n Roll" explains that not even visitors of cinemas are spared this "manipulation." Research indicated that the embedding of the imperceptible advertisement "Drink Coca-Cola" into movie projections, even for three thousandths of a second increased the purchase of that product from 18 to 30%. Aren't those just "the first signs" announcing an age of a wider and more extensive use of the "below the threshold of consciousness" techniques which will indoctrinate the masses?

Slobodan Erić
Pravoslavni misionar [Orthodox Missionary] 1, 1990

ATTACHMENT 4

JUST BEFORE THE novel went to the printers, the Yugoslav public was informed of the discovery of a subterranean city in the region of Kočevja. Although few in number, the facts published by *Duga* in Belgrade indicated that the town under the earth was built by dead people (which makes the confession of D. V. even more credible), executed prisoners and enemies of the state. The fact that an archive of the Secret Police was in the underground city gives credence to the thesis about the nationalization of ontology.

A few years ago, a stink was raised about the building of the "Cankarjev dom" in Ljubljana. "Mladina" published a blueprint of the building which was hidden from the public. The trouble began because of the fantastic amounts of money spent on the building, and it is known that the home of Ivan Macek-Matija was also built with that money. The house has been confiscated and these days Macek is supposed to move out. Macek has been left in the street like Pepca Kardelj recently, and they say he's a bad psychological states.

When the blueprints for "Cankarjev dom" were released, it was clear why the price was so high. The main hall of the building was located underground, which is a continuation of the logic of the mind

*that built the subterranean buildings
in Kocevja.*

The most fantastic story is related
to a tunnel that reportedly connects
"Cankarjev dom" with the back-up
capital city in Kocevja. According
to that story, the tunnel is forty-
something kilometers long, and is
existence is justified by the impossibility of moving from Ljubljana
to Kocevja in case the capital city is
under siege. Since the government
of Slovenia, the parliament and the
responsible ministries lie about a
hundred meters from "Cankarjev
dom", everything was planned so
that the ruling mind of Slovenia first
took refuge there, and then would
then continue living ninety days in
Kocevja!

In the stories and what has
been irrefutably established about
Kocevja till now, only one important
detail is missing: who constructed
the buildings underground and how
many people were included in that
huge project, constructed over a
period of forty years, and which is
also the archive of the Secret Police?

Duga, 426, 22.6 — 6.7 1990

ATTACHMENT 5

The house of Svetislav Veizović in Bajina Bašta. In the circle: mark of the place where the Earth's gravity is highest.

Mark on the skirt of the house of S. Veizović placed the Committee of the Evangelical Bicyclists, indicating 2.5. The place of highest gravity in the northern hemisphere.

Svetislav Basara (b. 1953) is a major figure in Serbian and European literature. The author of more than twenty novels, essays, and short-story collections, he is the winner of numerous awards and honors, including the NIN Prize in 2008. Between 2001 and 2005 Basara served as an abassador to Cyprus.

Randall A. Major is a linguist and translator. He teaches in the English department at the University of Novi Sad. His most recent translation was Basara's *Fata Morgana*, available from Dalkey Archive. He is an editor and translator of the Serbian Prose in Translation series produced by Geopoetika Publishing in Belgrade.

MICHAL AJVAZ, *The Golden Age*.
The Other City.

PIERRE ALBERT-BIROT, *Grabinoulor*.

YUZ ALESHKOVSKY, *Kangaroo*.

FELIPE ALFAU, *Chromos*.
Locos.

JOE AMATO, *Samuel Taylor's Last Night*.

IVAN ÂNGELO, *The Celebration*.
The Tower of Glass.

ANTÓNIO LOBO ANTUNES, *Knowledge of Hell*.
The Splendor of Portugal.

ALAIN ARIAS-MISSON, *Theatre of Incest*.

JOHN ASHBERY & JAMES SCHUYLER, *A Nest of Ninnies*.

ROBERT ASHLEY, *Perfect Lives*.

GABRIELA AVIGUR-ROTEM, *Heatwave and Crazy Birds*.

DJUNA BARNES, *Ladies Almanack*.
Ryder.

JOHN BARTH, *Letters*.
Sabbatical.

DONALD BARTHELME, *The King*.
Paradise.

SVETISLAV BASARA, *Chinese Letter*.

MIQUEL BAUÇÀ, *The Siege in the Room*.

RENÉ BELLETTO, *Dying*.

MAREK BIENCZYK, *Transparency*.

ANDREI BITOV, *Pushkin House*.

ANDREJ BLATNIK, *You Do Understand*.
Law of Desire.

LOUIS PAUL BOON, *Chapel Road*.
My Little War.
Summer in Termuren.

ROGER BOYLAN, *Killoyle*.

IGNÁCIO DE LOYOLA BRANDÃO, *Anonymous Celebrity*.
Zero.

BONNIE BREMSER, *Troia: Mexican Memoirs*.

CHRISTINE BROOKE-ROSE, *Amalgamemnon*.

BRIGID BROPHY, *In Transit*.
The Prancing Novelist.

GERALD L. BRUNS, *Modern Poetry and the Idea of Language*.

GABRIELLE BURTON, *Heartbreak Hotel*.

MICHEL BUTOR, *Degrees*.
Mobile.

G. CABRERA INFANTE, *Infante's Inferno*.
Three Trapped Tigers.

JULIETA CAMPOS, *The Fear of Losing Eurydice*.

ANNE CARSON, *Eros the Bittersweet*.

ORLY CASTEL-BLOOM, *Dolly City*.

LOUIS-FERDINAND CÉLINE, *North*.
Conversations with Professor Y.
London Bridge.

MARIE CHAIX, *The Laurels of Lake Constance*.

HUGO CHARTERIS, *The Tide Is Right*.

ERIC CHEVILLARD, *Demolishing Nisard*.
The Author and Me.

MARC CHOLODENKO, *Mordechai Schamz*.

JOSHUA COHEN, *Witz*.

EMILY HOLMES COLEMAN, *The Shutter of Snow*.

ERIC CHEVILLARD, *The Author and Me*.

ROBERT COOVER, *A Night at the Movies*.

STANLEY CRAWFORD, *Log of the S.S.*
The Mrs Unguentine.
Some Instructions to My Wife.

RENÉ CREVEL, *Putting My Foot in It*.

RALPH CUSACK, *Cadenza*.

NICHOLAS DELBANCO, *Sherbrookes*.
The Count of Concord.

NIGEL DENNIS, *Cards of Identity*.

PETER DIMOCK, *A Short Rhetoric for Leaving the Family*.

ARIEL DORFMAN, *Konfidenz*.

COLEMAN DOWELL, *Island People*.
Too Much Flesh and Jabez.

ARKADII DRAGOMOSHCHENKO, *Dust*.

RIKKI DUCORNET, *Phosphor in Dreamland*.
The Complete Butcher's Tales.

RIKKI DUCORNET (cont.), *The Jade Cabinet.*
The Fountains of Neptune.

WILLIAM EASTLAKE, *The Bamboo Bed.*
Castle Keep.
Lyric of the Circle Heart.

JEAN ECHENOZ, *Chopin's Move.*

STANLEY ELKIN, *A Bad Man.*
Criers and Kibitzers, Kibitzers and Criers.
The Dick Gibson Show.
The Franchiser.
The Living End.
Mrs. Ted Bliss.

FRANÇOIS EMMANUEL, *Invitation to a Voyage.*

PAUL EMOND, *The Dance of a Sham.*

SALVADOR ESPRIU, *Ariadne in the Grotesque Labyrinth.*

LESLIE A. FIEDLER, *Love and Death in the American Novel.*

JUAN FILLOY, *Op Oloop.*

ANDY FITCH, *Pop Poetics.*

GUSTAVE FLAUBERT, *Bouvard and Pécuchet.*

KASS FLEISHER, *Talking out of School.*

JON FOSSE, *Aliss at the Fire.*
Melancholy.

FORD MADOX FORD, *The March of Literature.*

MAX FRISCH, *I'm Not Stiller.*
Man in the Holocene.

CARLOS FUENTES, *Christopher Unborn.*
Distant Relations.
Terra Nostra.
Where the Air Is Clear.

TAKEHIKO FUKUNAGA, *Flowers of Grass.*

WILLIAM GADDIS, JR., *The Recognitions.*

JANICE GALLOWAY, *Foreign Parts.*
The Trick Is to Keep Breathing.

WILLIAM H. GASS, *Life Sentences.*
The Tunnel.
The World Within the Word.
Willie Masters' Lonesome Wife.

GÉRARD GAVARRY, *Hoppla! 1 2 3.*

ETIENNE GILSON, *The Arts of the Beautiful.*
Forms and Substances in the Arts.

C. S. GISCOMBE, *Giscome Road.*
Here.

DOUGLAS GLOVER, *Bad News of the Heart.*

WITOLD GOMBROWICZ, *A Kind of Testament.*

PAULO EMÍLIO SALES GOMES, *P's Three Women.*

GEORGI GOSPODINOV, *Natural Novel.*

JUAN GOYTISOLO, *Count Julian.*
Juan the Landless.
Makbara.
Marks of Identity.

HENRY GREEN, *Blindness.*
Concluding.
Doting.
Nothing.

JACK GREEN, *Fire the Bastards!*

JIŘÍ GRUŠA, *The Questionnaire.*

MELA HARTWIG, *Am I a Redundant Human Being?*

JOHN HAWKES, *The Passion Artist.*
Whistlejacket.

ELIZABETH HEIGHWAY, ED., *Contemporary Georgian Fiction.*

AIDAN HIGGINS, *Balcony of Europe.*
Blind Man's Bluff.
Bornholm Night-Ferry.
Langrishe, Go Down.
Scenes from a Receding Past.

KEIZO HINO, *Isle of Dreams.*

KAZUSHI HOSAKA, *Plainsong.*

ALDOUS HUXLEY, *Antic Hay.*
Point Counter Point.
Those Barren Leaves.
Time Must Have a Stop.

NAOYUKI II, *The Shadow of a Blue Cat.*

DRAGO JANČAR, *The Tree with No Name.*

MIKHEIL JAVAKHISHVILI, *Kvachi.*

GERT JONKE, *The Distant Sound.*
Homage to Czerny.
The System of Vienna.

JACQUES JOUET, *Mountain R.*
Savage.
Upstaged.
MIEKO KANAI, *The Word Book.*
YORAM KANIUK, *Life on Sandpaper.*
ZURAB KARUMIDZE, *Dagny.*
JOHN KELLY, *From Out of the City.*
HUGH KENNER, *Flaubert, Joyce and Beckett: The Stoic Comedians.*
Joyce's Voices.
DANILO KIŠ, *The Attic.*
The Lute and the Scars.
Psalm 44.
A Tomb for Boris Davidovich.
ANITA KONKKA, *A Fool's Paradise.*
GEORGE KONRÁD, *The City Builder.*
TADEUSZ KONWICKI, *A Minor Apocalypse.*
The Polish Complex.
ANNA KORDZAIA-SAMADASHVILI, *Me, Margarita.*
MENIS KOUMANDAREAS, *Koula.*
ELAINE KRAF, *The Princess of 72nd Street.*
JIM KRUSOE, *Iceland.*
AYSE KULIN, *Farewell: A Mansion in Occupied Istanbul.*
EMILIO LASCANO TEGUI, *On Elegance While Sleeping.*
ERIC LAURRENT, *Do Not Touch.*
VIOLETTE LEDUC, *La Bâtarde.*
EDOUARD LEVÉ, *Autoportrait.*
Newspaper.
Suicide.
Works.
MARIO LEVI, *Istanbul Was a Fairy Tale.*
DEBORAH LEVY, *Billy and Girl.*
JOSÉ LEZAMA LIMA, *Paradiso.*
ROSA LIKSOM, *Dark Paradise.*
OSMAN LINS, *Avalovara.*
The Queen of the Prisons of Greece.
FLORIAN LIPUŠ, *The Errors of Young Tjaž.*
GORDON LISH, *Peru.*
ALF MACLOCHLAINN, *Out of Focus.*
Past Habitual.

The Corpus in the Library.
RON LOEWINSOHN, *Magnetic Field(s).*
YURI LOTMAN, *Non-Memoirs.*
D. KEITH MANO, *Take Five.*
MINA LOY, *Stories and Essays of Mina Loy.*
MICHELINE AHARONIAN MARCOM, *A Brief History of Yes.*
The Mirror in the Well.
BEN MARCUS, *The Age of Wire and String.*
WALLACE MARKFIELD, *Teitlebaum's Window.*
DAVID MARKSON, *Reader's Block.*
Wittgenstein's Mistress.
CAROLE MASO, *AVA.*
HISAKI MATSUURA, *Triangle.*
LADISLAV MATEJKA & KRYSTYNA POMORSKA, EDS., *Readings in Russian Poetics: Formalist & Structuralist Views.*
HARRY MATHEWS, *Cigarettes.*
The Conversions.
The Human Country.
The Journalist.
My Life in CIA.
Singular Pleasures.
The Sinking of the Odradek.
Stadium.
Tlooth.
HISAKI MATSUURA, *Triangle.*
DONAL MCLAUGHLIN, *beheading the virgin mary, and other stories.*
JOSEPH MCELROY, *Night Soul and Other Stories.*
ABDELWAHAB MEDDEB, *Talismano.*
GERHARD MEIER, *Isle of the Dead.*
HERMAN MELVILLE, *The Confidence-Man.*
AMANDA MICHALOPOULOU, *I'd Like.*
STEVEN MILLHAUSER, *The Barnum Museum.*
In the Penny Arcade.
RALPH J. MILLS, JR., *Essays on Poetry.*
MOMUS, *The Book of Jokes.*
CHRISTINE MONTALBETTI, *The Origin of Man.*
Western.

NICHOLAS MOSLEY, *Accident.*
Assassins.
Catastrophe Practice.
A Garden of Trees.
Hopeful Monsters.
Imago Bird.
Inventing God.
Look at the Dark.
Metamorphosis.
Natalie Natalia.
Serpent.

WARREN MOTTE, *Fables of the Novel:*
French Fiction since 1990.
Fiction Now: The French Novel in the
21st Century.
Mirror Gazing.
Oulipo: A Primer of Potential Literature.

GERALD MURNANE, *Barley Patch.*
Inland.

YVES NAVARRE, *Our Share of Time.*
Sweet Tooth.

DOROTHY NELSON, *In Night's City.*
Tar and Feathers.

ESHKOL NEVO, *Homesick.*

WILFRIDO D. NOLLEDO, *But for*
the Lovers.

BORIS A. NOVAK, *The Master of*
Insomnia.

FLANN O'BRIEN, *At Swim-Two-Birds.*
The Best of Myles.
The Dalkey Archive.
The Hard Life.
The Poor Mouth.
The Third Policeman.

CLAUDE OLLIER, *The Mise-en-Scène.*
Wert and the Life Without End.

PATRIK OUŘEDNÍK, *Europeana.*
The Opportune Moment, 1855.

BORIS PAHOR, *Necropolis.*

FERNANDO DEL PASO, *News from*
the Empire.
Palinuro of Mexico.

ROBERT PINGET, *The Inquisitory.*
Mahu or The Material.
Trio.

MANUEL PUIG, *Betrayed by Rita*
Hayworth.

The Buenos Aires Affair.
Heartbreak Tango.

RAYMOND QUENEAU, *The Last Days.*
Odile.
Pierrot Mon Ami.
Saint Glinglin.

ANN QUIN, *Berg.*
Passages.
Three.
Tripticks.

ISHMAEL REED, *The Free-Lance*
Pallbearers.
The Last Days of Louisiana Red.
Ishmael Reed: The Plays.
Juice!
The Terrible Threes.
The Terrible Twos.
Yellow Back Radio Broke-Down.

JASIA REICHARDT, *15 Journeys Warsaw*
to London.

JOÃO UBALDO RIBEIRO, *House of the*
Fortunate Buddhas.

JEAN RICARDOU, *Place Names.*

RAINER MARIA RILKE,
The Notebooks of Malte Laurids Brigge.

JULIÁN RÍOS, *The House of Ulysses.*
Larva: A Midsummer Night's Babel.
Poundemonium.

ALAIN ROBBE-GRILLET, *Project for a*
Revolution in New York.
A Sentimental Novel.

AUGUSTO ROA BASTOS, *I the Supreme.*

DANIËL ROBBERECHTS, *Arriving in*
Avignon.

JEAN ROLIN, *The Explosion of the*
Radiator Hose.

OLIVIER ROLIN, *Hotel Crystal.*

ALIX CLEO ROUBAUD, *Alix's Journal.*

JACQUES ROUBAUD, *The Form of*
a City Changes Faster, Alas, Than the
Human Heart.
The Great Fire of London.
Hortense in Exile.
Hortense Is Abducted.
Mathematics: The Plurality of Worlds of
Lewis.
Some Thing Black.

RAYMOND ROUSSEL, *Impressions of Africa*.

VEDRANA RUDAN, *Night*.

PABLO M. RUIZ, *Four Cold Chapters on the Possibility of Literature*.

GERMAN SADULAEV, *The Maya Pill*.

TOMAŽ ŠALAMUN, *Soy Realidad*.

LYDIE SALVAYRE, *The Company of Ghosts*.
The Lecture.
The Power of Flies.

LUIS RAFAEL SÁNCHEZ, *Macho Camacho's Beat*.

SEVERO SARDUY, *Cobra & Maitreya*.

NATHALIE SARRAUTE, *Do You Hear Them?*
Martereau.
The Planetarium.

STIG SÆTERBAKKEN, *Siamese*.
Self-Control.
Through the Night.

ARNO SCHMIDT, *Collected Novellas*.
Collected Stories.
Nobodaddy's Children.
Two Novels.

ASAF SCHURR, *Motti*.

GAIL SCOTT, *My Paris*.

DAMION SEARLS, *What We Were Doing and Where We Were Going*.

JUNE AKERS SEESE,
Is This What Other Women Feel Too?

BERNARD SHARE, *Inish*.
Transit.

VIKTOR SHKLOVSKY, *Bowstring*.
Literature and Cinematography.
Theory of Prose.
Third Factory.
Zoo, or Letters Not about Love.

PIERRE SINIAC, *The Collaborators*.

KJERSTI A. SKOMSVOLD,
The Faster I Walk, the Smaller I Am.

JOSEF ŠKVORECKÝ, *The Engineer of Human Souls*.

GILBERT SORRENTINO, *Aberration of Starlight*.
Blue Pastoral.
Crystal Vision.

Imaginative Qualities of Actual Things.
Mulligan Stew. *Red the Fiend*.
Steelwork.
Under the Shadow.

MARKO SOSIČ, *Ballerina, Ballerina*.

ANDRZEJ STASIUK, *Dukla*.
Fado.

GERTRUDE STEIN, *The Making of Americans*.
A Novel of Thank You.

LARS SVENDSEN, *A Philosophy of Evil*.

PIOTR SZEWC, *Annihilation*.

GONÇALO M. TAVARES, *A Man: Klaus Klump*.
Jerusalem.
Learning to Pray in the Age of Technique.

LUCIAN DAN TEODOROVICI,
Our Circus Presents...

NIKANOR TERATOLOGEN, *Assisted Living*.

STEFAN THEMERSON, *Hobson's Island*.
The Mystery of the Sardine.
Tom Harris.

TAEKO TOMIOKA, *Building Waves*.

JOHN TOOMEY, *Sleepwalker*.

DUMITRU TSEPENEAG, *Hotel Europa*.
The Necessary Marriage.
Pigeon Post.
Vain Art of the Fugue.

ESTHER TUSQUETS, *Stranded*.

DUBRAVKA UGRESIC, *Lend Me Your Character*.
Thank You for Not Reading.

TOR ULVEN, *Replacement*.

MATI UNT, *Brecht at Night*.
Diary of a Blood Donor.
Things in the Night.

ÁLVARO URIBE & OLIVIA SEARS, EDS.,
Best of Contemporary Mexican Fiction.

ELOY URROZ, *Friction*.
The Obstacles.

LUISA VALENZUELA, *Dark Desires and the Others*.
He Who Searches.

PAUL VERHAEGHEN, *Omega Minor*.

BORIS VIAN, *Heartsnatcher*.

LLORENÇ VILLALONGA, *The Dolls' Room.*

TOOMAS VINT, *An Unending Landscape.*

ORNELA VORPSI, *The Country Where No One Ever Dies.*

AUSTRYN WAINHOUSE, *Hedyphagetica.*

CURTIS WHITE, *America's Magic Mountain.*
The Idea of Home.
Memories of My Father Watching TV.
Requiem.

DIANE WILLIAMS,
Excitability: Selected Stories.
Romancer Erector.

DOUGLAS WOOLF, *Wall to Wall.*
Ya! & John-Juan.

JAY WRIGHT, *Polynomials and Pollen.*
The Presentable Art of Reading Absence.

PHILIP WYLIE, *Generation of Vipers.*

MARGUERITE YOUNG, *Angel in the Forest.*
Miss MacIntosh, My Darling.

REYOUNG, *Unbabbling.*

VLADO ŽABOT, *The Succubus.*

ZORAN ŽIVKOVIĆ , *Hidden Camera.*

LOUIS ZUKOFSKY, *Collected Fiction.*

VITOMIL ZUPAN, *Minuet for Guitar.*

SCOTT ZWIREN, *God Head.*

AND MORE . . .